THE MAN WHO
KILLED FORTESCUE

THE MAN WHO
KILLED FORTESCUE

John Stephen Strange

COACHWHIP PUBLICATIONS
GREENVILLE, OHIO

The Man Who Killed Fortescue, by John Stephen Strange
© 2025 Coachwhip Publications edition

Cover: *New York, Early 20s,* by Thomas Hart Benton

First published 1929
Dorothy Stockbridge Tillett (pseud. John Stephen Strange),
    1896-1983
CoachwhipBooks.com

ISBN 1-61646-615-4
ISBN-13 978-1-61646-615-2

I

Despite the oppressive sultriness of the night, the bus that rattled down through the curtained Thirties about half-past nine was almost empty. A shower, sweeping the city early in the evening, had discouraged the crowd, and although the moon had since come out again, white and sharp against the roof tops, only an occasional passenger, hurrying home after the storm, remained to look at it. When the bus, slithering on the rain-soaked asphalt, passed the sightless windows of the shopping district, only two upstairs passengers were left.

In the comparative dimness of the upper Twenties, the conductor, lounging half asleep against the rail of the little rear platform, was startled awake by the sudden sharp ringing of the bell. A man descended hastily from above, brushed past him, and sprang down before the lumbering vehicle had come to a stop. The conductor had a hasty impression of a well-tailored back, a well-set-up figure in evening clothes. Even as he raised his hand and touched the starting bell, the man rounded the corner and disappeared.

The silence of the deserted lower Avenue echoed with the passage of the bus; Washington Arch seemed to approach, ghostly in the moonlight, and fall away behind. As they drew to a stop the conductor mounted for a final survey of the upper seats. The last man sat up front, slouched forward, his head pillowed on the rail. The conductor remembered now that he had recognised him as a dweller in one of the old houses on the north side of the Square. He had often seen him riding down on a late bus, crossing the Square with impatient strides, and letting himself in at the old-fashioned white doorway.

The conductor scratched his head doubtfully. Then he went forward and tapped the man on the shoulder

"End of the run, sir," he said. There was no response. He bent nearer. Beginning at his toes and shivering up his spine, a tremor shook him. He shook the lax shoulder nearest him.

"Wake up, sir; wake up!" He broke off, for at his touch the man fell heavily sidewise against him, his head dangling, his white shirt front showing a widening crimson stain.

At sound of the conductor's horrified cry, a policeman, passing on the sidewalk, looked up. One glimpse of the man's white, twitching face and wildly gesticulating hands sent him dashing up the steps to the roof.

"He's dead," moaned the conductor, apparently dazed with horror. "I came up and found him sitting there, dead."

An instant's examination proved the truth of the man's surmise. The policeman leaned over the rail and whistled to another bluecoat across the Square. Then he reached into the dead man's pocket and began to look for identifying papers.

"I know who he is," volunteered the conductor. "At least I know where he lives. It's that house next but one to the corner—next door to the apartment house. I've seen him go in there lots of times."

The policeman ruffled through the letters in his hand.

"Anstruther—that'll be him: G. M. C. Anstruther— what's the number? Oh, I get it. Yup, you're right. It'll be that house north side the Square." He leaned over the rail and spoke tersely to the officer below. Then he turned again to the conductor. "Better come along," he said. "You may be wanted." He spoke to the starter who, by this time, had joined them. "Shunt this bus off somewhere and rope her off till our man gets here to look her over. Get off, now, and don't touch a thing. There'll be some one right along to take charge.

An hour later Van Dusen Ormsberry, immaculate in the evening attire in which he had escorted to dinner, and afterward to her theatre, New York's most recent musical comedy star, stood on the steps of the house on Washington Square North. His annoyance at being summoned away from a thoroughly good show had subsided, as always, in the excitement of the chase. The message from headquarters had been brief and peremptory. The powers that be seldom wasted words on the polite indirectnesses that pleased the fastidious soul of Van Dusen Ormsberry.

"You know Anstruther, the popular novelist, don't you?" had asked the crisp voice at the other end of the line. And, not waiting for an affirmation, it had proceeded: "Get on down to his place on the Square. He's been murdered—top of a bus—about twenty minutes ago. The bus is roped off in the Square. Take a look at it and at his place, and come on here. Want to see you."

And Ormsberry had sent a regretful note backstage to the musical comedy star and obeyed.

Sitting on the step of the bus, Hennessey, his aide, had been awaiting him. Together they had made a brief but thorough examination which had disclosed absolutely nothing beyond the fact that the man's throat had been deftly, expertly cut. There was no weapon. Ormsberry had turned him over to the police surgeon, summoned Hennessey, and proceeded to the novelist's apartment.

Now he stood on the step and rang the bell. He rang it several times.

"His man must be out. Let's get on in." He pushed another button at random and entered unhesitatingly as the lock clicked. "Parlour floor, as I remember. Yes, to be sure, it is the parlour floor." He raised his hand to knock on the inner door and then paused. "Well, that's funny!"

The hall within was dimly lighted. The stair rail threw the rear part of it into heavy shadow. The back door of Anstruther's apartment, which, as Mr. Ormsberry recalled, opened into his study, stood blankly closed to their eyes, but under the edge a narrow line of light showed in the darkness.

"Must have left his lamp burning," muttered Ormsberry. And then suddenly the light went out. Stung into action, the detective stepped down the hall and knocked on the door. No answer. He knocked again firmly and loudly. Still no response came from the soundless interior. Or—yes; one faint, sharp sound: the click of a raised shade.

"Can we smash the door?" whispered Ormsberry. His voice was as sharp as the snapping shade. He thrust his hand into his pocket and found the comfortable, cool touch of his automatic.

"Just stand aside a bit, sorr," muttered Hennessey. The next instant his ponderous shoulder struck the door with a force that would have staggered an ordinary man. The ancient wood cracked smartly, but it held. Again Hennessey charged. "Once more will do it!" he said cheerfully, and charged again. The lock split with a rending of rotten wood and the two men catapulted into the room.

"The window!" cried Ormsberry, recalling the snapping shade.

He hurled himself across the room and leaned far out. The window overlooked a backyard that had, of recent years, been made over into a charming little garden surrounded by a high brick wall and flanked on either side by other gardens. But Mr. Ormsberry was not interested in the horticultural improvements of this most exclusive corner of the Village. As he thrust his head out of the window he caught a fleeting glimpse of a dim figure crouched for an instant on the top of the righthand wall—a figure that hurled itself out of sight into the garden beyond. He sent a spurt of flame after this vanishing figure, only to see it emerge again into his line of vision, dart with incredible swiftness across the tiled terrace that adorned the rear of the apartment house next door, and plunge out of sight in the street beyond.

Hennessey had already swung himself down on to the top of the wall in pursuit. Ormsberry followed and gripped him by the arm.

"No use," he said crisply. "It's a clean get-away. We hardly got a real look at the fellow. I couldn't even swear to his clothes."

"Evening dress," stated Hennessey.

"Well, that's that!" He paused, startled, for out of the shadow of a bush in the next garden, almost directly under his feet, darted the slender figure of a girl in a silver gown, a pale, blonde girl, who ran across the terrace and joined on the sidewalk a young man accompanied by a brass-buttoned officer of the law.

Mr. Ormsberry's well-regulated heart gave a sudden knock in his breast, and he stood, for a moment, like a man paralysed. For he had recognised the girl in the silver dress, and the sight of her worked on him now, as always, with a sense of shock. It was Joan Archer, protagonist of the dramatic Fortescue murder mystery of the year before, the most disastrously unsuccessful, the most humiliating case of Mr. Ormsberry's professional career.

"Well, by Jove!" he drawled softly. Superstition had no place in his well-ordered and neatly pigeonholed intelligence, and yet it is quite true that he felt a faint twinge, the veriest ghost of a cold premonition, as this trace of an old failure crossed the scent of his new quarry.

2

Every one remembered the Fortescue murder trial, the *cause célèbre* of the year before. It had stirred New York society to its depths. Not only the social eminence of the murdered man and his wealth, which made him a prominent figure in every money market in the world, but the peculiar circumstances of the affair that threw the burden of presumable guilt upon his stepdaughter, Joan Archer, and especially the character of the accused, lifted the case out of the rut of the usual. The accounts of the trial and editorial wranglings over the justice of the verdict flooded for several weeks the newspapers of the world.

John Fortescue, whose mother had been a Miss Van Zandt and whose father inherited from a long line of shrewd men of affairs one of the biggest and most solid fortunes in the country, was a widower of many years' standing. He had lived in the old Fortescue house on upper Fifth Avenue, with his sister, Estelle Fortescue, many years his junior, and his stepdaughter, Joan Archer. Many people had forgotten that Joan was not Fortescue's own daughter, so warm was the affection between them, until the fact was raked up in court and made to assume dire proportions—afterward.

A year and a half before the night on which Anstruther was killed—on February 7, 1926, to be exact—Jarvis, the Fortescue butler, going into the library to draw the shades one fine morning, had found Mr. Fortescue slumped forward on the blotter of his desk, which was stained, as was the rug, with an ominous, brownish stain. The rug had not yet dried and came off red on his trembling fingers. The windows of all the ground-floor rooms were locked, as he had left them the night before, and the front door, with its elaborate double lock, had not been tampered with.

The doctors, hastily summoned, found a small, expert incision in John Fortescue's throat, made by the sharp little desk knife that was discovered on the floor just under the dangling hand.

This seemed so evident that both the doctors and the police were seriously annoyed when Mr. Ormsberry, detailed to the case on the insistence of Charles Edward Speck, Fortescue's lawyer, demanded a more careful examination. Mr. Ormsberry was urged to this step by his usual insatiable curiosity, roused to fever pitch by the absence of any finger-prints whatever on the knife handle. The examination revealed, to the considerable chagrin of the authorities, that the wound in Mr. Fortescue's throat was far deeper than could possibly have been made by any blade of the pearl-handled trinket supposed to have been the means of death.

For a few days the word *murder* screamed across the headlines of the papers, and then, to the unspeakable horror of Mr. Ormsberry and his friend Mr. Speck, Joan Archer was arrested and tried for the crime.

So young she was, so exquisite, so ineffably appealing, that sympathy ran high in her favour among many people, despite the damning nature of the evidence against her. The papers took violent sides for and against the accused. Editorials were written about her. Her simple life, the commonplaces, the innocent reticences of a young girl's existence were dragged into the light and held up to the cruel prominence of a worldwide publicity.

Her little coquetries, the naive, tentative, unsubstantial flirtations of extreme youth were aired and made to assume the proportions of sophisticated affairs.

She was, it seemed—and on this delicate tissue the state's evidence rested as on a rock—in love with, and secretly engaged to, Brian Channing, a young painter of good family but exceedingly modest means, a guest in many exclusive drawing rooms. This love affair, as yet so new and sweet as to be scarcely confessed between themselves, was publicly discussed as a probable motive for her supposed impatience to inherit her stepfather's fortune. Brian's letters to her—tied together, incredibly, with narrow blue ribbon, as her mother might have cherished her father's love letters—were produced in court. And her letters to him—prim, half-articulate little letters, written in a round, precise, schoolgirl hand—were read into the evidence and printed in sensational newspapers here and abroad.

The evidence on which she was held was entirely circumstantial and rested chiefly on the testimony of Jarvis, the butler. The events of that tragic afternoon and evening were briefly as follows:

It seems that Estelle Fortescue, sister of the murdered man, had returned from Europe on the morning of the day of the crime, and directly on landing had gone to her brother's home. Their meeting, apparently, had not been friendly. They had quarreled, according to Estelle, about Joan, concerning whom they were continually at odds. Estelle—so the defence brought out—was fiercely jealous of the girl. At two o'clock, scarcely an hour after she entered the house, she left it, bag and baggage, and went off to Philadelphia to stay with a friend. She arrived there in time for dinner and returned to New York only after she had been notified of her brother's death.

Meanwhile—so Jarvis testified—at dinner that evening John Fortescue told Joan that he had had a difference with his sister, and had that afternoon altered his will, leaving his entire fortune, except for a few gifts to charitable institutions and a small annuity to Estelle, to her, Joan.

That evening, about ten o'clock, Joan, who had heard through her maid about a party to which the entire staff of servants wanted to go, summoned Jarvis to the library, where she was sitting with Mr. Fortescue, and told him that she had gained her father's permission to give them all the night off. Half an hour later there was no one in the house but Joan and her stepfather. Not more than an hour after that, according to the medical authorities, John Fortescue was killed.

Joan's own story was that she had gone to bed immediately after Jarvis had left the library and had heard nothing further until morning. That was all. There were several witnesses to testify to the character of the accused. There was Brian Channing to testify that, so far as he knew, John Fortescue had never objected to his attentions to Joan; that the only reason their engagement had been kept secret from him was the pleasure they took in keeping it, for a week or two, their own private affair; that they had intended to tell him about it within a few days, in full expectation of his approval; that, while Brian's own fortune was insignificant in comparison with the Fortescue millions, nevertheless there was no reason why he could not have married Joan without a penny of her own.

The jury had deliberated for ten agonising hours and had brought in a verdict of "Not guilty."

Mr. Ormsberry was not likely ever to forget those ten hours. Convinced as he was of Joan Archer's innocence, confounded by his own failure to find the actual murderer, baffled at every hand by blank walls, which, when scaled, revealed no promising clues to the mystery, those ten hours had been hours of sheer torment to him, when, for once in his successful, orderly life, his self-confidence was shaken to the depths and his natural reticence gave way to an outburst of self-reproach, of bitter self-condemnation. He had been thankful afterward that his monologue had fallen exclusively on the sympathetic ears of Charles Edward Speck, who had had the delicacy never afterward to refer to it.

Those ten hours had, however, brought forth one very definite, positive result. Mr. Ormsberry's chagrin had crystalised into a determination to find and bring to justice the true murderer of John Fortescue, if it took him the ten best years of his life to do it. He made no public protestations, but he swore to himself by a curious and secret oath to his private gods, which were Justice and the Sanctity of the Law, that he would accomplish this thing.

Others besides Mr. Ormsberry were moved by the verdict. Despite a minority sentiment in favour of the accused, it was a case where public opinion tried and condemned without reference to juries. The press frankly talked of the pernicious power of wealth even in the administration of so-called justice. Joan Archer's life was as effectually ruined as though it had been cut short by a capital sentence. Eyes followed her wherever she went. It was a brave hostess indeed who received her. Of all the friends who had made much of her when she dispensed the hospitality of her stepfather's house, only two or three remained faithful. Even Brian Channing—or so the avidly interested public supposed—had deserted her. But the facts of this episode never got into the newspapers. What actually happened was this:

Brian saw Joan just once after the verdict. Then he took passage for Italy. On his way to his ship he dropped into Mr. Speck's office. Mr. Ormsberry was present at that interview. That again was something he would not soon forget.

He had acquired a decided liking for this quiet, up-standing young man, who had borne himself with considerable courage and dignity through the horrible ordeal of his fiancée's trial. And he experienced no diminution of his respect and liking when he heard the young man's reasons for his abrupt and ignominious flight.

"You see, it's this way," he explained to Mr. Speck, his white, drawn face showing plainly the strain of what he had gone through and what he was still suffering. "As soon as she was acquitted Joan wrote me a little note breaking off our engagement. She thanked me"—he stumbled and then went on determinedly—"for the comfort she said I'd been to her through the trial and said she couldn't possibly think of burdening me with a notorious wife. Those were her very words, sir.

"Well, of course I went to her and told her that was all rot, and that we'd be married quietly and slip off to Europe and forget about it. I'll never forget—" The young man broke off and blew his nose violently, while Mr. Speck walked to the window and looked out, presumably at the view—an admirable view, over the harbour, by the way, but it is to be doubted if Mr. Speck saw it very distinctly. When he returned to his desk Channing was quite composed again.

"I think, sir, that this thing has broken her—I mean for the time being, of course. I used every argument and every plea I could think of, but she never wavered an instant. She told me it wasn't only for my sake; that she herself couldn't contemplate the idea of marriage—now or ever. That there was no longer any possibility of happiness for her. And when I refused to accept her decision, and said I'd wait until she'd changed her mind, she said that she would not see me again, and that, if I persisted in attempting to reach her, she would go away. I—well, I—" The tears were frankly in his eyes now, but he was past noticing them.

"Of course, I told her I'd go, sir. I promised her I wouldn't bother her until she sent for me. I begged her to promise, in turn, that, if the situation altered, if her mind changed, she would write me to come home, but she wouldn't promise anything—just stood there like a little white statue, waiting for me to go. I've never seen anything so—so heartbreaking. So I'm going, sir. I'm going clean away—to give her time."

"Just so," said Mr. Speck thoughtfully. "Quite right."

"Of course, I don't need to ask you to look after her, sir."

"My dear boy, if she were my own daughter—"

They said nothing more along that line.

"But I want you to promise me," young Channing went on, "that you'll cable me if she needs me, or if you think she may need me, or if you think it is time for me to come home."

Mr. Speck gave him the required assurances and they discussed the best arrangements for Joan's immediate future. Then Channing rose to depart. He got as far as the door and then came back, his face twitching in spite of his efforts at self-control.

"She—she's morbidly sensitive, of course, about having the case reopened, and I know it may be impossible to do so, but if it should ever be possible—if you should ever happen on some clue that has been overlooked, some chance of tracking the beast who is hiding behind her skirts—well, if you ever do, cable me. I'll come from the end of the earth for the joy of exterminating him with my own hands."

With that he shook hands with them again, hastily, and went off without waiting for their protestations.

Since then more than a year had passed, with no further development in the Fortescue case except Joan's quixotic gift to Estelle Fortescue of the sum originally left to her in

John Fortescue's first will. Mr. Speck combated Joan's intention, foreseeing, as actually happened, that many people would believe it a confession of guilt; but, on coming of age and coming into her inheritance, Joan overrode his protests. She did not wish, she said, to profit by a momentary irritation on the part of her stepfather, which, had he lived, would doubtless have passed away. The affair was a nine days' wonder in the press and was then forgotten.

Meanwhile, Estelle had gone abroad to avoid the painful publicity that had followed her at home, and had only recently returned.

Joan had lived in absolute seclusion in the old Fortescue house with a companion. She had gone nowhere, seen no one. Mr. Ormsberry was, therefore, the more astonished to encounter her, at this time in the evening, elaborately gowned, and clearly—as he surmised, taking a moment for observation—a guest at a party which, judge by the now audible sound of vigorous jazz and the flare of lights, was being held in the little brick house at the other side of the terrace.

That, he recollected swiftly, was where Mrs. Mortimer lived. He remembered her as a good-natured looking, middle-aged woman of the optimistic type who attempts to control age with a rouge compact, avoirdupois with a corset, and a faint lack of genuine good breeding with a lorgnette. She had been among those called at Joan Archer's trial to testify to the character of the accused. He had gathered from stray gossip that she was something of a social climber and had used Joan as a useful step upward. What on earth was Joan doing at her house?

He dismissed the futile query with a shrug, pigeon-holed it for future reference, for Joan and her young man and the policeman were coming back across the terrace.

3

We must go back, for a moment, to the beginning of Sally Mortimer's party and explain, among other things Joan's presence in that slightly dubious gathering and the curious events that led up to her appearance on the terrace when the mysterious intruder escaped from Anstruther's apartment.

In the days before John Fortescue's death, when Joan was the petted and courted heiress, mistress of a great house, and dispenser of lavish hospitality, she had met Mrs. Mortimer and had been attracted by something sound and sweet underlying that ambitious lady's somewhat laughable exterior. That had been shortly after the death of Mrs. Mortimer's husband, the E. P. Mortimer who had made a fortune in shipbuilding during the war and lost much of it in law suits afterward. Mrs. Mortimer, disembarrassed of the social encumbrance of a husband who had only a bowing acquaintance with grammar, had sprung up like a lioness refreshed, rented the newly renovated little house at the lower end of Fifth Avenue, just before it wanders through Washington Arch into the Square, and plunged into what she fondly believed to be the *haut monde* of artistic society in New York.

Her good nature, which led her into all sort of indiscretions, no less than her uncertain origin, had prevented her from gaining a very firm foothold in the society she craved. She had, therefore, been the more grateful to Joan Archer, who had made much of her in the happy days before the weight of tragedy fell on her young shoulders and made her acquaintance no longer an asset but rather a liability to her friends.

This debt of gratitude Mrs. Mortimer was now paying—not, to be sure, without some misgivings. About ten o'clock, the evening well under way, she looked about her drawing-room and thanked her lucky stars that there was so little constraint apparent among her guests. They were not, she realised, a particularly distinguished crowd, but at least they were gay and friendly; and gaiety and friendliness were, she reflected, the two things that Joan Archer at that time most needed. Certainly the child would go mad if she were left alone in that huge, lonely house, companioned by one elderly woman, deprived of all the legitimate outlets for youthful enthusiasm and spirits. It didn't bear thinking of. Mrs. Mortimer's kind heart ached with pity under her elaborate French gown. She hoped—she did so hope—that Joan was enjoying herself.

In the farther room perhaps a dozen people were dancing, and here she saw Joan with Jerry Howard. With what an extraordinary quality of contrast the girl stood out against that background of the vaguely *déclassés!* It was not only the exquisite simplicity of her silver gown, or the almost childlike and entirely perfect severity of her silver-blonde hair; more particularly it was the fine-drawn line of her figure, the thoroughbred poise of head and shoulders, the delicacy of hands and slender ankles. Most particularly, it was the haunting, heartbreaking, wistful loveliness of her face. This drew the eyes. No child of such youth and fragility had a right to that look of tortured resignation. Yet to-night it was quite unconscious, for she was smiling.

Only her eyes held it, like a forgotten experience retained below the level of consciousness.

She was dancing with her head thrown back, her body surrendered to the rhythm of the music. Mrs. Mortimer saw what the girl did not—the look in Jerry Howard's face as he held her. Suppose Joan should turn in her loneliness to the dangerous sympathy of a Jerry Howard, fortune hunter, amateur of women? Howard had a wicked charm when he chose. He was tall, well set up, good-looking in a conventional sort of way, and some satiric devil had endowed him with handsome eyes fringed with long, curling lashes, eyes of an almost feminine, disarming beauty. Yes, he was unquestionably dangerous for any inexperienced girl to play with. Mrs. Mortimer had had bitter knowledge of men of that type and she had heard gossip— nasty gossip—about Jerry Howard and Yvonne Lorimer.

She looked uneasily over her shoulder into the other room where Mrs. Lorimer was holding court. It had not been, she supposed, in the best of taste to invite all three on the same evening, but what was one to do? In the present state of society, if one paid attention to every bit of stray gossip one heard, one would never be able to get a party together. And certainly Yvonne was ornamental!

She was lounging in a corner designed for tête-à-têtes, a magnificent red-haired creature in a jade-green gown, a very Brunhild with handsome, massive shoulders, her eyes raised in a curious, slanted look to the man beside her. She looked what she was: something of a "super-woman" surrounded by the aura of her colourful adventures, which she rescued by a superb aplomb from the name of scandal. She had been twice divorced, and was, besides, the heroine of innumerable whispered affairs. She had been on the stage for a brief and meteoric career. She had gambled in a small way on the Street—or men had gambled for her—

and made what was reputed to be a considerable fortune. And yet she had contrived to give to even the most sordid and questionable aspects of her life a sort of fairy-tale glamour that made her half a legend, even to her friends. A curious rival for pale little Joan!

At the moment Mrs. Lorimer was talking to Reggington Johns, a blond man of indeterminate age whose pale lashes accentuated the red rim of his eyelids. Johns, who bore the doubtful distinction of being the sole intimate of the eccentric president of Heron Oil, was one of the financiers whose names had been mentioned in connection with Mrs. Lorimer's Wall Street manoeuvres, but just what the relation between them might be nobody knew, although everybody was quite prepared to hazard a guess.

To-night she was at her best. This party quite fitted in with her plans, she reflected with satisfaction. So much better to meet Johns in this way, casually, than to arrange a meeting, and so put him on his guard. For she wanted to come to him unexpectedly, subtly; the bit of information that she badly needed, and that he alone could give her, could never, she was confident, be had by a direct attack. Once, yes; but not now. She was too shrewd a woman not to know when the period of her power had waned. So she treated him to the coolness of her banter; she had a power given to few women—the power of interesting a man who had once been, and was no longer, in love with her. She studied him carefully in that slantwise gaze: the dissipated face; the close-set eyes; the mouth with its vast potentialities for evil—a dangerous face, although, at first glance, he was merely a sufficiently presentable young man. Yvonne Lorimer had no illusions about him. She knew men. But he could be useful to her, and she was not in the habit of being afraid of man or ghost. She broke suddenly through her nonsense. She leaned toward him.

"My dear Red, I see you're about to make a killing." He looked at her, not understanding.

"I wish I could flatter myself—" he began, but she cut in, smiling:

"I've been your victim for a long time. I didn't mean that."

He looked at her with a glow at the back of his eyes. He was still able to appreciate her extraordinary allure. She saw the look and went on with a contralto warmth in her tone that she had often used to great advantage in the making of both love and money. What she said was:

"I meant, of course, the Heron Oil merger."

She never knew what it was that had betrayed her. Perhaps some involuntary tightening of pose, some expectancy in her look. At any rate, he drew back.

"So that's what all this has been leading up to!" he murmured, and grinned at her unpleasantly.

She had no time to recover her lost ground, for at this moment a pallid man with black lacquered hair detached himself from a group in another corner and strolled across the room toward her. It was Robinson Tyler, whom she had once known very well, as a sort of partner of Reddington Johns. His wife, Miriam Tyler, was perhaps the nearest thing to a woman intimate that Yvonne Lorimer had ever had. So she greeted him, perforce, with at least surface cordiality. She had very little use for him—of any sort—so the cordiality was not very deep.

"Where's Miriam?" she asked with idle malice. "I thought Mr. Anstruther was bringing her."

"They haven't come yet," said Tyler coolly, but she saw the faint ugly flush that rose above his immaculate collar. It was common gossip that Mrs. Tyler was solacing herself for conspicuous neglect on the part of her husband by a platonic affair with the novelist. Mrs. Lorimer knew better than Mr. Tyler the truth of this rumour, and she revenged herself for his interruption by rubbing it in. Johns, understanding perfectly, turned away to hide his amusement from his friend. Mrs. Lorimer went on, still with that idle, deliberate utterance:

"Perhaps they have found—something better to do." She caught her hostess's eye and called across the room: "Where's your lion, my dear? I thought Mr. Anstruther was going to roar for you to-night." She glanced again at Tyler with that odd, oblique look, and noted with malicious pleasure the white rage in his face. She was cold with anger at the failure of her trick and was making him pay for it. She added a soft private thrust: "Too bad of Miriam to keep him away."

Mrs. Mortimer's reply cut off Tyler's retort, if, indeed, he had been about to make one.

"I dare say he's been delayed. He said he might be late—finishing a new story or something." She turned away. She had not missed that little by-play in the corner. What a rotten set they were, she reflected, with unaccustomed clarity of vision. It was like throwing a child to the wolves to introduce Joan to such a crowd, and yet they were the best she could do for her. Poor child! The good-natured soul sighed deeply. Even she could perceive the danger of being tied to a broken reputation and the Fortescue millions. She gave thanks privately that Brian Channing had come back and would be there soon. And high time, too.

Should she tell Joan he was coming or should she not? She debated again the question that had been running through her mind since he had called her up from his hotel early in the evening, announced that he had just landed, asked if it was true that Joan was to be with her during the evening—as he had been told when he called at the Fortescue house—and if he might come in. No, she wouldn't tell Joan. Better wait and see what happened.

Mrs. Mortimer knew nothing of the situation between the two or the reasons for Brian's sudden departure the year before. She felt, indeed, considerable disgust for what appeared to be his cowardly flight from a difficult situation. But anyway he was a gentleman, and perhaps this return, even if somewhat tardy, betokened a change of heart. She would, in any case, let the affair take its own course without any meddling interference on her part. She wished, however, that he would come. She would be restless and uneasy until he did.

As though in answer to her thought, a servant crossed the little entrance hall and opened the door. She followed him quickly and met Brian Channing on the threshold.

She saw at a glance that the year of his absence had changed him. His tall, spare outline was the same, but he carried himself with more assurance. His look was graver. And when he came forward to meet her she perceived that he was entirely poised and that, except when he smiled, all trace of boyishness had left him. He was more good-looking than ever. Decidedly, she approved of this new Brian Channing.

"Well," she cried banteringly, "I am relieved that you have actually come. I was afraid you had grown too good for us."

He grinned at her.

"By George, I'm glad to see you! Now I feel as though I'd really come home. I haven't seen a familiar face for so long—"

"That's very sweet and complimentary of you," she laughed, "but I know another familiar face you'd much rather look at than mine, so I won't keep you."

His glance left hers to sweep the room swiftly. A shadow fell across his eyes, a look she could not read. She went on hastily:

"I haven't told Joan you were coming. I thought perhaps you'd rather I didn't. I don't know what the trouble was between you, my dear, and I'm not prying, but if you still feel as you once did—and I fancy you do—I advise you to lose no time. You'll have to forgive me for meddling, Brian. I'll apologise if you like. But I'm worried about her. I want your help."

He sighed briefly and frowned.

"It's yours to command," he said gently. "But I'm afraid it won't be of much use to you." He went on hastily, as though in explanation: "You see, I may not be in town for more than a few days. I'm expecting some news that may send me away again very soon."

Mrs. Mortimer studied him shrewdly.

"Then you'll have to change your plans. Unless, of course, you'll stand by and see Joan married to Jerry Howard."

That shook him.

"Not that bounder!"

"She's lonely, Brian—horribly, unnaturally lonely. And, for all she's been through enough for a woman of fifty, she's only twenty-one. And she's been so abominably treated after you went off to Italy and left her to face the music"—he winced at that, but said nothing—"that she's ready to be unnecessarily grateful for the slightest kindness and sympathy. And for the benefit of pretty heiresses Jerry simply drips kindness and sympathy. It rains like the gentle dew from heaven—only that kind of kindness doesn't fall from heaven; it rises from the other place. I've met them together three times this week, teaing or dancing."

"And so," suggested Brian dryly, "you asked them both here to-night."

"Yes, they're both here. What difference does that make? And it's difficult enough to get any one to meet her, poor dear."

That did get through his guard. He paled perceptibly.

"Oh, poor child!"

"Then you'll help me?"

He gave her a straight look.

"I haven't even a ghost of a right to interfere in Miss Archer's affairs."

"This isn't the time for a lawyer," murmured Mrs. Mortimer rebelliously. "It's the psychological moment for a cave man."

At that instant Joan Archer came through the door.

For a breath she stood quite still and the colour drained away from her face. Then she came forward with outstretched hand. Not for nothing had she served her hard apprenticeship in the art of concealing her feelings.

"How do you do?" she said in her cool, soft little voice. "I didn't know you had come back from Italy."

"You didn't precisely encourage me to write." His voice was deliberately light, but beyond his controlling it was threaded through and through with pain.

"No, of course—I didn't mean that. I mean, it's very nice to see you again." Her lip quivered. For an instant longer she strove to control herself. Then her eyes overflowed and she put her hands up to her face line a child. Neither noticed that Mrs. Mortimer had left them alone in the little entry and was standing guard on the other side of the curtained door. "It's just that I was so surprised—to see you—and it's so hard to bear—a friendly face."

He put a gentle arm around her, steadying her trembling with the exquisite torture of holding her so. He had been a fool to leave her. In spite of her protests her threats, he should have stayed near her. He deserved to lose her. The yielding of her body against his arm smote him to the heart. How they must have tortured her to break her fine, gallant spirit! He had a vivid memory of a boy at school who had been sent to Coventry, and of how he had broken under the strain of it.

"Joan!" he whispered. He was holding her as a lover would now, his lips against her hair. "Joan, darling, don't you love me a little—still?" He fancied that she yielded to him. He turned her head back and sought her lips.

After a moment she spoke in a cool, emotionless little voice:

"Let me go, Brian. I'm engaged to marry Jerry Howard."

4

After Channing had left the house, Joan stood for a long time leaning against the wall of the entry, breathing rather fast. Then she smoothed her hair with a steady hand, opened the outer door, and went into the garden. The moon shone white and round above the arch. The terrace with its fragile trees and silver net of fountain lay magically cupped between the bulking masses of houses on either side. The sweet scent of earth after the rain hung in the air. She walked down the bricked path, heedless of the wet underfoot, her slippers making little crunching sounds. Here Jerry Howard overtook her.

"Where on earth have you been?" he demanded with something less than his usual urbanity.

"I wasn't feeling very well. The heat, I think. It's so pleasantly cool here, isn't it?" She accepted a cigarette from his proffered case, and, seeing that her hand shook still, she hurried on to cover her perturbation: "I wonder where Mr. Anstruther is? Wasn't he supposed to be here to-night?"

Jerry grinned as he lighted his cigarette.

"I expect," he said between puffs, "that Mr. Anstruther is—wherever Miriam Tyler happens to be."

Joan looked her distaste.

"Aren't you ashamed of yourself to quote rank gossip like that? He's probably detained finishing a story or something. Yes; look!" She nodded toward a lighted rear window of the house next door to the corner apartment. "Isn't that where he lives? I'm sure that's his study window. I went there once—a year or so ago." She did not add "with Brian," but she thought it, and a pang shot through her. "You see," she said lightly, "I was right. He's still working."

Howard smiled down at her.

"I accept the correction," he said. "Of course Anstruther is—still working." His gaze lingered until hers fluttered and fell. He eyed appreciatively her delicate loveliness. Not unfastidious was Jerry Howard. His taste was unimpeachable. And he felt that here again he had not erred. Moreover, he was suddenly impressed with the need of haste, if his plans were not to fall through. He was by no means blind to Joan's agitation, not far from guessing the cause of it. So he went on quickly: "What do you say we make it soon, Joan? There's nothing to wait for, and I'd like to get you away from all this. We could be married on the Q.T. and get off for Europe before those buzzing reporters got after us. What say?"

Joan traced an invisible pattern on the path with the toe of her slipper.

"Yes," she whispered brokenly; "I do want to get away from—from everything!"

"Good girl!" he approved cordially, but he glanced at her with some shrewdness.

Suddenly she looked up and laid one slender hand on his arm.

"You've been terribly good to me, Jerry. If it weren't, as you say, that you could use some of my money—"

"Me dear girl!"

"Why, I don't mind, Jerry! I'm glad. Glad I've something to offer you that makes me not too ashamed of accepting your protection—your companionship. As it is—would the first week in September be too soon?

"Fine! I'll look up sailings to-morrow and see about reservations."

Her hand tightened in grateful pressure on his arm, and she smiled.

It happened that at this time they were standing at the inner side of the garden, within a few feet of the wall that separated it from the backyard beyond. It was very quiet. Except for the hum of busses in the Avenue there was not a sound. Then suddenly the silence was broken by that most prosaic of noises, the strident note of a door bell, which sounded, apparently, almost directly over their heads. They moved apart, startled, and looked about for the source of the sound. The rear windows of Anstruther's apartment, over the wall, still glowed dimly through drawn shades that flapped lazily in the faint stirring of air.

"Oh!" gasped Joan. "That startled me." And then she paused, smitten dumb by the sudden little thrill of excitement that shot through her.

The shade over the nearest window, caught by some sudden draught within the house, blew out into the darkness, leaving a triangular frame of light in which was photographed for an instant a scene of confusion: drawers of papers emptied and scattered on chairs, on the desk, on the couch; a filing cabinet with drawers standing open and empty, crazily dropping scattered papers. Over the confusion crouched the tall, spare figure of a man. His face was turned away toward the door, and the light fell only dimly on him, yet Joan fancied it was Brian Channing. If it had not been so crazily impossible, she would have been sure it was Brian Channing. And yet, with her mind so full of him, it might easily be that she imagined the likeness to him in this poised, expectant figure. And then, before she could make up her mind one way or the other, the blowing shade blotted out the picture. She turned to Jerry excitedly.

"Jerry, did you see—"

And then suddenly she paused. Some instinct of caution silenced her. Better wait. Better be sure what it was all about before mentioning Brian. She looked searchingly at Jerry, wondering whether he, too, had recognised the man in the disordered room, but his lace told her nothing.

Again the strident ring punctuated the noises of the street.

"That's funny," muttered Jerry. "Why doesn't he open the door?"

Again the bell rang. A moment later the light in the room went out. There was a sharp banging within, as though some one were knocking on the inner door. In the short pause that followed, they could distinctly hear the crisp, sharp snap of a raised shade.

"It's a burglar," whispered Jerry. "Get on back into the house. I'm going for a cop." He ran off across the garden toward the Avenue.

But Joan did not go into the house. She stood where he had left her in the shadow of a bush, and waited. She had an undefined feeling that she must warn Brian—if it was Brian—that Jerry had gone for a policeman. She saw the man swing himself from the window to the top of the wall above her. Of course he must come this way. The other side was barred by a high, blank wall. Above her, in the dark apartment, the knocking had given place to a dull thudding sound, as of heavy bodies being hurled against a door.

The man on the wall heard it, too. Standing in heavy shadow as he was, she could see him turn his head and look back, listening. Across the street Jerry was standing under the light, talking to a bluecoat and gesticulating toward the garden. This, too, the man on the wall appeared to see, for she heard his sharp breath, and then, before she could call out either in summons or warning, he had leaped to the path and darted past her and across the garden.

As Jerry and the policeman entered at one gate, the refugee darted out the other. In the distance she saw him hurl himself under the wheels of the swiftly moving traffic, jump into a taxi, northward bound, lean out to speak briefly to the driver. The taxi took on speed and disappeared beyond her line of vision. Running forward, she found Jerry and the bluecoat standing disgustedly on the curb.

"Got his number, anyhow," the officer was saying. "Just my luck to lose him. Which apartment was it he came from?"

They took him into the garden and showed him. He whistled softly.

"Gee, ain't that my luck, though? That's where that guy lives—Anstruther, his name was—that was croaked this evening—top of a bus; throat cut, just as neat—"

Joan put out a vague hand toward Jerry and a curious sound came from her parted lips. Before he could reach her she had slipped to the path and lay quiet, a little silver pool under the moon.

The policeman, however, hardly saw her. He had noticed something moving in the shadow of a jutting angle of the wall, A sharp, authoritative voice followed the movement.

"It's all right, officer," said Mr. Ormsberry, and dropped quietly to the path. He turned and spoke to Hennessey, still perched on the wall. "Go back into the apartment and wait till you're relieved," he ordered crisply. He had a way of dropping his suave circumlocutions under the press of action. Then he turned to the policeman. "'Phone that cab number to headquarters and have them trace it at once and get a description of the passenger, if they can. And ask them to send some one round to relieve Hennessey."

Only after the man had gone did he turn to Joan. She was conscious, but, he saw at once, almost hysterical. She looked up at him with astonishment and something like terror in her face.

"Why, Mr. Ormsberry!"

"Sorry you had such a fright, Miss Archer," he said gently. "The man must have jumped almost over you in getting away."

"Yes—yes, he did," she admitted hastily. "Of course— of course I didn't know then about Mr. Anstruther."

"Of course not." Mr. Ormsberry took her hand and patted it reassuringly. "Now just sit here for a moment." He drew her toward a stone bench and forced her gently down upon it. "And now, Mr.—" He turned to Jerry and hesitated; the man's face was familiar, but he could not place him.

"Mr. Howard," supplied Joan faintly.

"Ah, yes, Mr. Howard. Now, if you could just tell me what happened, exactly what you saw . . ."

Briefly Jerry recounted their side of the adventure.

"I suppose you would not be able to identify the man if you saw him again?" asked Mr. Ormsberry when he had finished. The detective fancied, although he could not afterward be quite sure of it, that Jerry Howard glanced swiftly at Joan before replying.

"I hardly think so. When I saw him in the room his head was turned away, and it was, of course, only the merest glimpse. And afterward I was too busy giving chase to notice his appearance. All I could swear to was that he was in evening dress."

"And you?" Mr. Ormsberry turned to Joan. "He passed quite near you. Perhaps you saw him more distinctly."

"No," said Joan nervously. "No, I didn't indeed. It was quite dark, you see, and he moved so quickly. I really didn't see his face at all." This was strictly true. If Mr. Ormsberry noticed the wording of her denial, he made no comment.

"That's unfortunate," he said. "Well, perhaps we shall have better luck with the chauffeur of the cab he got away in. Meanwhile, Mr. Howard, if I may suggest I think it would be an excellent thing to get Miss Archer home as soon as possible. She's had a severe shock."

The girl looked at him with frightened eyes, wondering if there was any double meaning in his words.

When they had gone Mr. Ormsberry made a mental note of two facts: Joan Archer had recognised the burglar, and Jerry Howard knew that she had.

It was a very white and silent Joan who leaned back in a corner of the cab on the way back to the Fortescue house; she looked like a stricken child, staring straight ahead with terrified, unseeing eyes. But her inward vision was acute. She saw hovering before her mind's eye a picture of Brian—Brian crouched in an attitude of terror over a rifled desk—Brian running for his life across a dark terrace. Brian whom she loved—loved so deeply that she had sent him away rather than absorb his life in the ruin of her own.

Of course it had not been Brian—it couldn't have been. Her eyes had played her tricks. Rather than believe him entangled in this grisly affair, she would disbelieve her own eyes, disbelieve truth itself. After all, her mind had been so full of him that it was only natural that she should see him where he was not, imagine him in every man who had anything approaching his figure and bearing. All this last year she had seen him so—had fancied him approaching down the street, had seen him passing in cars, standing, a little turned away from her, in shops—only to know again the heart breaking stab of disappointment when the stranger turned toward her, and was not Brian. And yet— The horrid round began all over again.

Meanwhile Jerry watched her covertly. He was quite sure she had recognised the man in the room, and quite sure she could put a name to her surmise, but he must be certain. He gave her a little time—as he put it—to agonise a bit, and then he said suddenly:

"Jolly plucky of you not to give him away."

She turned startled eyes on him—a look that would have melted any heart not hardened to self-interest. It had no effect on Jerry.

"Oh, Jerry!" she wailed. "Did you see him, too? It couldn't really have been Brian, could it? After all we only got a glimpse into that room."

Jerry took her hand and patted it tenderly.

"Poor little girl," he murmured. "I'm afraid there's no mistake. You see," he said glibly, "I got a pretty good look at him when he ran into the street."

There was a moment's silence, while her hand clung frantically to his. Then she turned to him with a little cry.

"Oh, Jerry, Jerry, be generous! Help him! Don't give him away. You see,"—she fumbled for some adequate explanation—"for the sake of our old—our old friendship, I couldn't bear to have anything happen to him. Please, Jerry, please! I'll be grateful—so very grateful."

Her lovely eyes implored him. Jerry responded with admirable alacrity.

"My dear, you needn't get so excited about it. I'm not going to give him away. Poor devil, why should I? Besides, if you wish me to keep still about it, that's enough. At the same time, it's a risk, you know, concealing anything from the police. However, for your sake—" he murmured astutely, watching her.

He had the satisfaction of seeing her lovely eyes fill, of hearing her grateful whisper. Not so bad, he reflected, and profit on both sides of the ledger.

5

At half-past nine the next morning, in the same spacious office, perched high, in a towering building on lower Broadway, where Brian Channing had said good-bye on his way to Europe the year before, Mr. Speck was closeted with Van Dusen Ormsberry. Charles Edward Speck had been John Fortescue's lawyer and was now trustee of his vast estate. He had been, moreover, a close personal friend of the murdered man and his friendship had been extended to include Joan Archer, whom he had known from her childhood. His interest in discovering Fortescue's murderer and in clearing Joan was, therefore, twofold, and more personal than professional. The prospects of success, however, had appeared increasingly slim during the past year, and while he had prosecuted every possible line of inquiry with unflagging energy, he had, in his secret heart, nearly abandoned any hope of ultimate triumph.

He was shaken from his usual professional calm by Mr. Ormsberry's communication. When the latter had completed his account of the events of the previous evening, Mr. Speck exclaimed:

"Well, by George!" He leaned back in his mahogany desk chair, put the tips of his fingers carefully together, and looked down with narrowed eyes on the craft-dotted waters of the lower bay, spread maplike below his office windows. Charles Edward Speck, while a very big man indeed wherever two or three lawyers were gathered together, was, physically speaking, diminutive. He made one think of a bright little chicken. His small head was almost entirely bald, and his round, bright eyes were naively inquisitive. People said that, as he couldn't possibly have room in his head for all his brains, he kept them in the neat mahogany shelves that lined his office. But it is certain that he always had his wits on hand when he needed them.

"But I don't see," he said at last, after a thoughtful pause during which Mr. Ormsberry waited with some impatience, "I don't see how Anstruther could be shot down in such a place without the conductor or some one hearing."

"Shot?" repeated the detective. "Who said he was shot? His throat was cut with a very thin sharp knife, like—" He broke off abruptly. A look of startled

speculation dawned in his eyes. He took a quick turn up and down the room and came back to stand before his friend. "Good Lord," he groaned, "I don't like this. You know, there's no doubt in the world but what Joan Archer recognised the man that escaped over the wall while we were breaking into Anstruther's apartment."

"I don't," confessed Mr. Speck, "see the connection."

"You would see it," said Ormsberry grimly, "if you had seen the wound in Anstruther's throat. Ask any criminal expert, and he'll tell you that a man's way of killing is as characteristic as his manner of signing a cheque. Some do it with an axe; some strangle; some use picture wire and window weights. This man uses a very thin, sharp knife, and cuts the vein in his victim's neck just above the collar."

Speck said nothing but paled somewhat. For a moment the two men looked at each other. Presently Ormsberry said:

"If you remember, that was the way Fortescue was killed. It was a very neat job."

Mr. Speck took out his handkerchief and mopped his forehead.

"And you say Joan recognised the fellow?"

"Not a doubt of it," asserted his friend. "If I could think of any conceivable motive that might connect the two crimes, I'd say there was no shadow of doubt that the same man perpetrated both. In fact, I say so now. Just consider what happened. Anstruther, who was an acquaintance, if not a friend, of John Fortescue—"

"Coincidence," murmured Mr. Speck.

Ormsberry went on without honouring this remark with more than an annoyed glance.

"Anstruther is mysteriously killed in precisely the same manner—probably even with the same weapon—with which Fortescue was murdered. Half an hour later some one, whom we must presume to be either the murderer or an accomplice, rifles Anstruther's apartment for reasons as yet unknown, and, on being surprised there, escapes over the wall. In doing so, he is, beyond any doubt, recognised by Joan Archer. Is that another coincidence?"

Mr. Speck said nothing.

"Anstruther and Fortescue," murmured Ormsberry thoughtfully. "What possible connection? And what does Joan Archer know about it?"

"Nothing!" snapped Mr. Speck. "I won't have you bothering her. She is not to be tormented any more about this matter."

Ormsberry looked coldly at his friend.

"What do you think I am?" he demanded. "An unmitigated brute? Of course I'm not going to bother her. But there is a connection, all the same, as sure as I stand here saying it. I don't know why I didn't know it last night, as soon as I laid eyes on Anstruther's body. If the same hand didn't make those two wounds, I'll retire to the country and breed guinea pigs."

"But the motive?" murmured Speck.

"That's still to be found. I haven't the remotest idea what it could be," Ormsberry admitted. "There was something behind the murder of John Fortescue that we never understood, some fact we never knew and to which we held no slightest clue, some situation that was solved last year by Fortescue's death and was solved again yesterday by the murder of Anstruther."

"Come down to brass tacks," urged Mr. Speck. "My legal imagination cannot follow your subtleties. What sort of situation do you mean? Are you suggesting some vast organisation of crime of which these two men were members or dupes? I'm afraid, my dear fellow you are being a little romantic."

"I don't know what I mean," said Ormsberry crossly. "If I did, I'd go right out and arrest the murderer. But I will know—before I get through," he added grimly. "That wound, I tell you, is something that can't be gotten round. And when you add three coincidences all pointing in the same direction— Well, I certainly mean to take a look-see down that alley." He began pacing excitedly the length of the office.

"Take my word for it, the fellow's put his tail out of the hole, and we'll beat him this time. I'll bet you the best dinner Louis ever cooked to a five-cent cigar, that when I land the murderer of Anstruther behind the bars his other name will be—the Man Who Killed Fortescue."

"Nothing will give me more pleasure," said Mr. Speck grimly, "than to forfeit that dinner. Tell you what I'll do. If you catch the fellow I'll make that five-center a whole box, and you can name your own brand."

"You know I never smoke," retorted Mr. Ormsberry aggrievedly.

At this moment the Admiral, Mr. Speck's three-foot-six of office boy, knocked and entered. He was an arrestingly bright-looking little chap, with shining, green-gray eyes and a blond thatch slicked back until it shone. His boots shone, too; the very freckles on his nose were radiant.

"Gentleman to see you, sir. Mr. Howard."

Mr. Ormsberry's brows went up and he nodded abruptly behind the Admiral's back.

"H'm, yes!" murmured Mr. Speck. "Don't know him. Is he a nice man, skipper?" He had a way of gravely consulting the Admiral about his clients.

"No, sir," returned the boy, without hesitation, his bright, straight glance on Mr. Speck. "Not a bit nice. Kinda—kinda crawly."

"H'm! Well, we'd better see him right away, then, and get it over with. Ask him to step this way, Admiral."

"Yes, sir." The boy wheeled abruptly and vanished.

"Smart little shaver," murmured Ormsberry. "Who the dickens is he, anyway? Looks like somebody—I can't think who."

Mr. Speck glanced at him with surprise.

"Didn't you know? That's Mona Adams's boy. She's been in bad straits since Adams's death. Wouldn't let me do a thing for her, except take Bill—and Heaven knows, that's no sacrifice. Bright boy. Make a fine lawyer some day."

Mr. Ormsberry nodded sympathetically but made no other comment, respecting his friend's reticence, knew that it was because of Mona Adams that Speck had retained his estate of bachelorhood and lived a comfortable but somewhat cheerless existence between office and club.

The lawyer went on evenly:

"This Howard—he the man who was with Joan last night?"

The detective nodded.

"What the deuce can he want?"

But before Ormsberry could answer, the man himself entered composedly, even, it may be, with the air of a conquering hero.

"Mr. Speck, I believe? Ah, Mr. Ormsberry, good-morning." He bowed to the great detective with a faint air of mockery. "I am in luck. I have been trying to reach you at your home—on a matter of importance. I wonder if I may have a word with you—presently?"

Mr. Ormsberry took the hint.

"I have some business with—er—the Admiral," he told Mr. Speck. Then he added to Howard: "I'll see you in the reception room on your way out." He withdrew and softly closed the door.

When Howard joined him in the reception room ten minutes later, the young man's face was dully flushed and his handsome eyes were opaque with—the detective guessed—a smouldering rage. Glancing round, as though to reassure himself that they were beyond the reach of eavesdroppers, he plunged at once to the point.

"I understand from the newspapers that you have been put in charge of the investigation into Mr. Anstruther's death."

Mr. Ormsberry nodded, wondering what would come next. For a moment Howard toyed with the light gloves he held in his hand. Then he looked shrewdly at the detective.

"I fancy," he said, "you were not deceived by that little by-play last night in Mrs. Mortimer's garden."

Ormsberry permitted himself a surprised lift of the brows.

"I'm afraid I don't understand you."

"You understand me right enough." Howard's tone was silky soft. "But before I go any further, I want to make it clear that I won't be involved in this case. I'm tipping you off because"—he smiled crookedly—"I don't want to stand by and see a miscarriage of justice. But, if you quote me,

I shall deny, under oath, that I ever said what I am about
to say to you."

"Yes?" murmured the detective.

"Perhaps," Howard went on imperturbably, "I had better begin at the beginning. I'd been dancing with Joan at
Mrs. Mortimer's party, and some one cut in on me. It was
frightfully hot in the room where we were dancing, so I
went into the garden for a breath of air. Just as I did so, I
saw a man come through the gate and up to the front door.
It was Brian Channing."

"Brian Channing?" For an instant Mr. Ormsberry
betrayed genuine surprise. "I thought he was in Italy."

"I learned afterward that he got back only yesterday.
Well, he was admitted to the house. He stayed about ten
minutes. When he left he was obviously very much disturbed about something, for he almost collided with me
in the path and never saw me. He brushed past without
speaking, like a sleep-walker, went out at the gate, and
turned down the Avenue to the Square.

"I could make a fair guess at what it was all about, for
some minutes later Joan came out at the same door and
began walking blindly round the garden. She was plainly
as disturbed as he had been. Of course, remembering the
rumours of their engagement at the time of the trial, I was
able to put two and two together."

"I see. Well?"

"I joined Joan and we talked for ten minutes or so before the shade in Anstruther's library blew out and showed
us the burglar at work." He paused and glanced shrewdly
at Mr. Ormsberry, "You asked me last night if I recognised
the man, and I said I did not. That was a lie, I did."

"And just why," murmured the detective, "didn't you
tell me that you did?"

"For a very good reason. I want to marry Joan Archer—
and the man in the room was Brian Channing."

There was a brief and somewhat breathless little pause.

"I happen to know," Howard added then, "that Joan, also recognised Channing. As a matter of fact, she told me so on the way home in the cab. I fancy if you question her you'll know how to get her to admit it. It won't be necessary for you to mention—me."

Ormsberry studied him with growing distaste, which did not, however, appear on his well-schooled countenance.

"Do I understand," he said at length, "that you are to marry Miss Archer?"

The dull flush crept back into Mr. Howard's face.

"Yes," he said shortly. "The first week in September."

"It's all settled, then? I don't wish to appear to doubt your word, but ladies are sometimes—indefinite about such things."

"It is quite settled."

"And I may assume"—the detective glanced at closed door of Mr. Speck's private office—"that her guardian approves?"

A vindictive look tightened the lines of Howard's mouth.

"As a matter of fact, he does not, but, fortunately, Mr. Fortescue's will gives him no authority to refuse consent to Joan's marriage to any one she might choose. I looked it up."

"I see," said Ormsberry thoughtfully. "Then you want me to proceed against Channing—why?"

"Why?" Howard looked at him with well-affected amazement. "Why, because he's guilty, of course."

"And besides that?"

"Well, I'm not jealous, of course"—he grinned—"oh, dear no! But I don't want Channing to stand between Joan and me, now or at any future time."

"You're frank."

Jerry Howard smiled a surprising, secret smile, very disquieting.

"I can afford to be."

"Suppose I were to tell Miss Archer you came to me?"

"I should deny it."

"Ah!" murmured Ormsberry.

"Sorry!" said Howard. "Thanks so much. Good-morning." He picked up his hat and sauntered out.

Directly he had gone Mr. Ormsberry rejoined his friend and repeated word for word his astonishing conversation with Mr. Howard, and then the two sat together for a moment in dismal silence.

"I have a horrible feeling," said Mr. Speck softly, "that we are getting into the same old morass: Joan and Brian—Brian and Joan, everywhere you look. If I didn't know that it simply wasn't credible that a man like Brian Channing could be concerned in this beastly mess—"

"But we do know just that," struck in the detective.

Speck looked weary and old as he glanced across at his friend.

"I've seen too much of human nature," he said, "not to have some measure of doubt always at the back of my mind—"

"That's just the trouble with us," interrupted Ormsberry. "We *have* seen too much of human nature in its less creditable aspects. We incline to forget that there are decent folk—like Joan and young Channing."

Mr. Speck's face cleared.

"Quite so!" he said with a faint smile. "Well, the fellow did get under my guard, didn't he—with his talk about marrying Joan! There's this about it, though, my dear fellow, and don't forget it. The only possible reason for Howard's talking in that foolhardy way is that he's so sure it was Brian Channing in that room, and so sure that the affair can be tacked on to him, that he felt quite safe in coming out openly and showing his whole hand."

"Howard's a gambler," opined Mr. Ormsberry decisively. "I don't believe he ever showed his hand in the whole course of his existence. There's something extremely subtle behind all this, to my way of thinking. At the same time," he concluded, laughing, "I've not the smallest doubt that Howard counted on your reasoning about it precisely as you did." And with that he went away, chuckling at the confusion in his friend's face.

6

When he left Mr. Speck, Mr. Ormsberry went directly to Anstruther's apartment, where he found Hennessey waiting for him. Although he had made light of the matter to his friend, Ormsberry was more than a little disturbed at the course affairs were taking. Howard's accusation of Brian Channing tallied all too well with Joan's fainting fit of the night before. The detective was obliged to admit that, but for his strong predisposition in Channing's favour, he would have had no hesitation in fixing the burglary, if not the murder on his shoulders. But Ormsberry had considerable faith in his own ability to read character—a faith, it is only fair to say, which had been often justified. And he believed Howard to be a liar and Channing to be an honest man. There was, however, this modicum of doubt in his mind, and it made him exceedingly uneasy: he knew that sometimes liars tell the truth, and that sometimes honest men are cornered and driven into situations that they would never seek of their own free will.

He brushed the thought from him, but it returned again and again to plague him. Action was the immediate need of the situation, he decided. A few more facts to go on and less theorising. He began with a rapid-fire questioning of Hennessey.

"Did you trace that taxi?"

"Yes, sor. Harrigan got the number. The taxi man says his fare told him he was trying to make a train at Grand Central, and promised him a fiver if he made it in fifteen minutes. He did, got his fiver, and saw his man disappear into the station."

"Could he identify the man?"

"Well, he's afraid not, sor. Says he never got a really good look at him."

"H'm! Were you able to get Anstruther's club?"

"The Fontenoy Club, sor. Just been up there. The doorman says Mr. Anstruther arrived there about six-thirty and asked for Mr. Reddington Johns. Then I talked to the waiter, sor, and he told me that Johns and Anstruther had dinner together at a quarter to seven. So I thought I'd best have a little chat with that gentleman. It seems he lives at the club, so I sent me name up to him and he came down in a pretty temper at being got up so early.

"'What is it you want, me man?' says he, middling ugly. So I told him, and begorra I thought he was going to pass out on me. He's white and pasty-faced anyway, but he got whiter yet and shook like a leaf. 'I'll be wanting a drink after that,' he said. 'Well, well; so Anstruther's dead, and me dining with him last night! Come along,' he says to me; 'I guess you can wink at a bit of a bracer, what?' Well, sor, I told him I never touched a drop when I was on duty. 'We'll make it coffee, then,' says he, and we went along to the dining-room.

"'Now,' he says, when we'd had a cup, and his colour had begun to come back, 'tell me what it is you want.' So I told him we knew he was almost the last to see Anstruther alive and we'd be glad to know anything he could tell us that might throw any light on the business. He thought a while and then he shook his head.

"'You've got me,' he says, 'I can't think of a thing. He was very cheerful—quite on the crest of the wave. He was talking about some investments he intended to make with some money he expected to get in.'

"'Money?' I says. 'How was that?'

"'I don't know,' he says. 'He didn't tell me. But I got the impression it was for a story he'd just written.'

"'And was that all you talked about?' I asked him.

"'Yes,' he says. 'We talked about the market all through dinner. Wait, though. He did say something about hoping that Brian Channing would run in before he had to leave the club. He wanted to see him. I was surprised,' says Mr. Johns, 'because I though Channing was still abroad. But Anstruther told me he thought his ship had just about got in.'

"Then I asked him what he'd done after dinner, and he said he'd left Anstruther at the door of the dining-room, saying he'd see him later at Mrs. Mortimer's party, and had left the club right away. And that he'd got to Mrs. Mortimer's at nine o'clock."

"What was he doing between seven-thirty and nine?" asked Ormsberry.

"That's what I asked him, sor, and he refused to tell me. 'I can and I will supply that information,' says he, 'if I have to—later, but I'm hanged if I'll tell you now. I can prove I left the club at seven-thirty,' he says, 'and I can prove I got to Mrs. Mortimer's at nine, and, by your own say-so, Anstruther was killed about nine-fifteen. It's none of your business where I was in between.'

"'Suppose you start proving then,' says I. 'It'll look black for you, being unwilling to tell where you were.'

"'He gave me an ugly look. 'The doorman will know when I left the club,' says he. But when we got hold of him, he couldn't remember seeing Mr. Johns leave the club at all the night before. The best he could do was to admit that he'd been away from the door for a few minutes around seven-thirty, so that Mr. Johns might have gone out without his noticing.

"Well, that stumped Johns for a moment, and then he had another idea. 'By Jove,' says he, 'I'd forgotten Sommers.'

"'And who may he be?' I asks. Well, it seems his name is Gregory, and he's a young Englishman who came over with letters to a member of the club, who put him up for a sort of guest membership. From what Johns said, I made out that he's one of these here fortune hunters who's been buzzing around Miss Estelle Fortescue ever since Miss Archer turned all that money over to her. 'What's he got to do with it?' I asks Johns.

"Well, it seems that it was raining hard at seven-thirty, and Johns stood on the steps of the club trying to hail a taxi, but they were all full, as they always are when you really need them. Just then this fellow Sommers drives up in a cab and gets out. Johns calls to him to keep the cab, and as soon as Sommers had paid off the driver he dashes out and gets in, and Sommers goes into the club. So we send upstairs for Sommers, and after a few minutes he comes down. A nice-looking young fellow he turned out to be—not the sort Johns described. And he backs up Johns's alibi. Says he noticed it was just twenty of eight when he gets into the hall, and that he's willing to take his oath on it."

"Did you check up what time Johns arrived at Mrs. Mortimer's?" asked Ormsberry. "That's the main point, of course."

"Of course, sor. I called up Mrs. Mortimer and she and her maid both set the time at nine o'clock, sor."

"H'm!" murmured the detective thoughtfully. "That would seem to let him out. Well, anything else?"

"Not very much, sor," said Hennessey doubtfully. "I did find out a little about Mr. Anstruther's doings after

Johns left the club. It was early and, as far as I can make out, Anstruther went up to the library and sat around smoking for some time. One of the club waiters saw him there about eight o'clock. Around nine o'clock another man who lives at the club—Peter Jepson—you know, the lawyer, sor—found him there, and that's the only living soul I could find who spoke to him after Johns left him before seven-thirty, except—"

"Well?"

"Well, sor, I don't know whether this has anything to do with the case or not. Jepson told me that the instant he stepped through the door into the library Anstruther came toward him, as though he had by looking for him, and began to ask his advice about some legal point in a story he was writing. But—and this is a funny thing, sor—Jepson says that Anstruther was standing on the hearth at the other end of the room facing the door, and it's Jepson's belief that some man was sitting in one of the big chairs before the fireplace. He couldn't see any one, but that wouldn't be surprising, because the chair is one of them big, upholstered affairs that would hide any man sitting in it if you looked at it from the back. Jepson thinks that Anstruther leaned toward one of these chairs and said something in a low voice before he came toward the door. The room's so big he couldn't be sure."

"What sort of fellow is Jepson? Imaginative chap?"

"No, sor. I should say hard-headed, noticing sort. Don't believe you'd get much change out of him in cross-examination."

"I'll bear the thing in mind. What happened next?"

"Jepson and Anstruther stood talking for a few minutes. Then they walked together to the corner. By that time it had stopped raining, and Anstruther said he'd ride down on a bus. Jepson was going uptown, so he waited on the near side of the street for a taxi. He saw Anstruther cross, get his bus, and climb up top. No one else got on at that corner, and, so far as Jepson remembers, the top of the bus was empty. Just then another man from the club rolled up behind him and offered him a lift. He got in and they drove uptown. They were together for nearly an hour, and that lets Jepson out."

"And on the way downtown," pursued Ormsberry, "between Fifty-fourth Street and the Square, on the top of an unroofed bus, at the early hour of nine-thirty on a summer evening, within fifteen feet of a husky conductor and in full sight of the city of New York, a prominent novelist was killed and his murderer escaped without leaving a trace or a soul who could swear to his identity. Extraordinary! It's either, as you might say, beginner's luck, or the work of a remarkably cool and practised hand. And when you add to that the fact—as we must assume it to be—that the murderer had the nerve to go direct from the scene of his crime to the apartment of the man he had murdered, ransack it, and make a second clean get-away under the very noses of the police—well, it really is unique."

"The burglar might have been a confederate," suggested Hennessey.

"Possible, but hardly probable," said Ormsberry thoughtfully. "The time dovetails too well. I lean to the opinion that it was the same man. He would just about have time to jump a taxi after he left the bus at Twenty-eighth Street, come down to this neighbourhood, get into the flat with the key he took from Anstruther's pocket—if you remember, his keys were missing—and do this much damage"— he waved his hand about the disordered room—"before we got here about ten-thirty. Furthermore, although the conductor's description was vague enough, and our own impression still vaguer, such details as we have of the man— height, evening clothes, general build—tally closely. No, I think it is safe to assume that it was the same man.

"We have to do, then, with a man of singular resolution and ability, such as it is, actuated by a motive of more than common strength, or he would hardly have taken such risks to achieve his ends. It was, I think we may safely say, a premeditated crime, committed, so far as we can guess from the circumstances, with the definite purpose of securing some paper in Anstruther's possession. I say paper," he repeated slowly, with the air of a man thinking aloud, "because it seems to be Anstruther's files that the burglar was interested in. The safe has not been touched, nor was the wallet in his pocket disturbed.

"Well, we'll have a look at that presently. Have you found out anything about Anstruther's domestic arrangements? Who looks after this place?"

"Hatu, a Jap servant, who seems to have been a sort of man of all work. He served as Anstruther's valet took care of these rooms, got his breakfast and lunch—he almost invariably dined out—and looked after him generally. He's downstairs now in the kitchen. I told him to wait, in case you wanted to talk to him."

"We'll have him up presently. Who else?"

"No one."

"Secretary?" suggested Ormsberry laconically.

"No, sor."

"But he must have had a secretary," objected the detective with considerable surprise. "No writer of Anstruther's prominence, who wrote as much as he did, could possibly get along without a secretary."

"Well, don't blame me," grinned Hennessey, who was on excellent terms with his chief. "It's a fact that he didn't have one. He usually did, as you say, but Hatu tells me he quarreled with the last one about two weeks ago and hadn't got a new one up to last night."

"Quarreled with him, eh?" asked Ormsberry quickly.

"Yes, sor. When I heard that, I put a wire through to Newark where Roberts—that's the ex-secretary lives, and asked them to find out where he was last night. They've to 'phone here as soon as they get anything definite." And Hennessey grinned again. He saw by Ormsberry's quick nod that his efficient work was appreciated, and was quite content to wait for more substantial and outspoken recognition.

For a moment Ormsberry meditated while Hennessey waited with eager attention. He had a respect that almost amounted to adoration for his chief, and with the ardour of the pupil for the master, he included not only his methods of work, but his mannerisms and foibles, in a blanket admiration. He admired the exquisite fit of Mr. Ormsberry's summer tweeds, worn with a distinguished negligence that he could never hope to copy; he was filled with ungrudging but hopeless envy of the manner with which this Beau Brummel of Broadway carried off the cornflower languishing brightly in his buttonhole.

"Well," said Ormsberry, getting suddenly to his feet, "let's have a look around and see if the burglar has left his visiting card."

He went into the front room and Hennessey followed him. The apartment consisted of drawing-room, study, bedroom, and bath, with a kitchen downstairs and a small room where Hatu performed his mysterious offices. The drawing-room, which had been the parlour of the old house before it was converted into apartments, of course overlooked the street. Here the most meticulous search revealed no trace of any intruder. Everything was in place, undisturbed. There was no sign that any one had crossed the threshold. It was clearly a room seldom used, admirably furnished, and entirely conventional.

The bedroom, which opened from the study at the rear, was also undisturbed. The bed was turned down, as

Hatu had left it for his master the night before, and Anstruther's sleeping things were laid out. The shade had not
been raised. There was something uncanny about the dark,
silent little room. Ormsberry came out quickly and closed
the door.

"Nothing there," he said shortly. "I doubt very much
if the burglar did more than glance into either of those
rooms. He was in a hurry, and there was clearly nothing to
interest him either in the bedroom or the drawing-room.
I fancy he confined his attention—as we must—to the
study."

He stood for a moment taking in his surroundings. The
study was evidently the room in which Anstruther really
lived. It had an air of ease, a comfortable, much-used look.
The walls were lined with book-cases, except where a row
of tall filing cabinets broke the uniformity. A small typewriter desk stood in one corner and indicated where the
secretary ordinarily sat. In the window, facing the room,
stood a huge old desk, evidently Anstruther's work bench,
on which stood another typewriter. Several comfortable,
pleasantly used-looking chairs stood about with ash-trays
and book-stands conveniently at hand. It was a typically
masculine room, workmanlike yet comfortable, and, under the surface disorder, well kept. At the moment it was
strewn from end to end with papers taken, apparently,
from the files. After the momentary pause for inspection,
both men set expertly to work. Foot by foot they went
over the room, searching the floor, delving into the recess-
es of upholstery, studying, sorting, classifying papers. An
hour's work left them, so far as a clue to the mystery was
concerned, precisely where they started.

Hennessey cast a despairing glance at the disorderly
piles of manuscript.

"You'd have a swell chance of finding a paper in this
room—even if you knew what you were looking for," he

grumbled. "You don't mean to tell me that one guy wrote all this stuff?"

"And a lot more!" Ormsberry nodded toward a neat row of Anstruther's published novels on a shelf across the room surmounting two shelves of current magazines, also neatly stacked.

"What you want is a college professor," muttered Hennessey.

"Do not despair, my dear fellow, do not despair." Ormsberry smoothed the ruffled perfection of his hair with one backward thrust of a languid hand. "Since blind action does not enlighten us, let us, if only for a moment, exert our intelligence."

"What beats me, sor," objected Hennessey, "is how you're going to find a paper that probably isn't here."

"Your view, then, is that the burglar found what he was looking for and took it with him?"

"It's possible," said Hennessey doggedly.

"It's highly probable," said Ormsberry softly. "We may, however, by a process known as reasoning, arrive at some conclusion about the nature of that paper. We can, at any rate, deduce this much: not a book out of place. We may assume, therefore, that it was not an irresistible thirst for culture that moved our marauder." He shot a humorous glance at his subordinate. Hennessey grinned. He suspected his chief of getting himself out of a blind alley with a jest. But Ormsberry went on briskly: "What's in that row of closed file cases over there—the ones that have not been touched?"

Hennessey investigated.

"Personal correspondence, sor. Letters in one drawer—answers in another; personal papers, bills, and so on in the bottom one."

A spark of excitement woke in the cool Ormsberry eye.

"It's dashed funny the burglar wasn't interested in his personal papers. Why was that, Hennessey? Why was that?"

"Probably hadn't got round to those files when we came along."

"Think so? But we've got a man of extraordinary intelligence to deal with—and extraordinary nerve."

"I don't get you, sor," said Hennessey.

"He wouldn't start looking blindly, if you get what I mean. There'd be a system in his way of doing it. He'd look first—in the place where he'd be most likely to find what he was looking for." He shook his head impatiently, as though to shake cobwebs out of his eyes. "There's something there I don't understand," he complained.

Hennessey grinned. His look seemed to say: "You don't mean it!"

At this moment the telephone rang.

"That'll be Newark calling," suggested Hennessey.

Ormsberry grabbed the 'phone as though it had been a life preserver.

"Yes? . . . Ormsberry speaking. . . . Yes . . . Oh! . . . No, that's all. . . . Thank you very much." He replaced the receiver and sat back dejectedly. "Too damned many alibis," he groaned. "Our secretary was at the movies with a friend from eight o'clock until ten-thirty last night."

"Exit Roberts," commented Hennessey.

7

"Well," sighed Mr. Ormsberry, "that's that! Not much light in that direction, although, of course, we'll have to question the fellow. Now let's have Hatu up and see what he can tell us."

Hennessey lumbered off and returned in a moment followed by a diminutive Jap with a round, good-natured face, divided from ear to ear, as he entered, by a conciliating grin.

Ormsberry nodded briefly and motioned him to a chair. Hatu chose one at a respectful distance, perched himself on the extreme edge, folded his hands, and waited with beaming expectancy.

"I understand you are Mr. Anstruther's valet," said the detective, studying the Jap with the helpless feeling of the Occidental seeking to penetrate the Oriental mask.

"Yes, sir," answered Hatu promptly; "I am Mr. Anstruther's valet and also house-man for five years." He spoke English with a curious foreign precision.

"Did you have entire charge of Mr. Anstruther's apartment? By that I mean did you do all the work yourself, or did you have assistance—a cleaning woman, perhaps?"

The Japanese spread his hands with an expressive shrug.

"Only once, five years ago, we have one cleaning woman, sir. Never again. I like clean house, sir."

"Then Mr. Anstruther had no other servants?"

"No, sir."

"A secretary, however?"

"Yes, sir; all time one gentleman—Mr. Roberts. Two weeks ago they have quarrel. Mr. Roberts go away; Mr. Anstruther use writing machine himself, and swear very much."

"They quarreled, eh? Can you tell us the cause of this quarrel?"

"No, sir."

"You didn't, by any chance, overhear a few words that might give us a hint of the nature of their disagreement?"

Hatu looked shocked.

"No, sir."

"H'm!" Mr. Ormsberry stroked his chin thoughtfully. "Well, leaving that for the moment, can you tell us, in your own words, just what Mr. Anstruther did yesterday, as far as you know; whether he had any visitors—anything that occurs to you that might be of help to us in finding the man who killed him? For instance, did Mr. Anstruther go out during the day, before he went up to the Fontenoy Club for dinner?"

"No, sir. All time Mr. Anstruther work, work on writing machine. I come half-past seven as usual. I go in through downstairs door and I hear click-click of writing machine. I get breakfast and take it up at eight o'clock. Mr. Anstruther he is sitting at desk there"—pointing to the big desk in the window—"working. He tell me to put tray on desk beside him and say that all the morning he will see nobody. I must answer telephone—of which there is extensive attachment downstairs—and must say he is out."

"Did any one come or call up?"

"Nobody came, sir; but some one he call on the telephone. Mr. Matheson, the editor who print Mr. Anstruther's stories, call up on the telephone and say tell Mr.

Anstruther he is in very bad hurry for story which Mr. Anstruther promise him for that day. I say Mr. Anstruther is out, and Mr. Matheson swear very bad."

"No one else called?"

"No, sir. At one o'clock I take up lunch to Mr. Anstruther. He very mad by then and say go to"—Hatu looked apologetically at his two inquisitors—"he say go to hell and let him alone. So I go," he concluded, smiling brightly.

"Was he alone all afternoon?" asked Ormsberry, covering the involuntary twitching of his lips with a thoughtful hand.

"Yes, sir. Mr. Anstruther was what in America you call bear for work, but not until on the day when a story was due. Other times he play very much."

"I see. Well, what happened then?"

"About five o'clock he ring and say whisky and soda. He all smile, all grin then. He say, 'Well, Hatu, it is all finish now. Now we take a long breath.' Then he say he go dress and go to club for dinner, and afterward he would go to party at Mrs. Mortimer's house, sir. And I could go home when he go out because he not need me any more and not be home until very early."

"So you left as soon as Mr. Anstruther had gone?"

"No, sir. Many things I have to do, so I work downstairs in my room until nine o'clock."

"And that's all? Nobody came—nobody telephoned before you left?"

"Yes, sir," said Hatu amiably. "Somebody came and somebody telephone."

Mr. Ormsberry sat forward with a jerk. "When was that? Tell us just what happened."

Hatu glanced from one to the other with a deepening smile.

"Mr. Anstruther go out round six o'clock. About half-past six lady call up; say she want to see Mr. Anstruther.

She not give name, so I say Mr. Anstruther out and I do not know when he come in. That is what he always tell me to say."

"Yes? What then? Did you recognise the lady's voice?"

"No, sir. Then I work some more and at eight o'clock telephone ring again. This time gentleman call up. He, too, want to see Mr. Anstruther pretty damn quick."

"Did he give his name?"

"Yes, sir; so I told him Mr. Anstruther was at the Fontenoy Club and that he would go to Mrs. Mortimer's party afterward. That was what Mr. Anstruther told me to say."

"Who was the man?"

"Mr. Channing, sir."

For a long moment Mr. Ormsberry sat quite silent. Channing again! He drew a long breath.

"Then Mr. Anstruther expected Mr. Channing to call up?"

"I do not know, sir. He say if he do call, tell him that."

"That all?"

"No, sir. At nine o'clock I make ready to go and door bell rings."

"Yes?" Darn the fellow, thought Ormsberry. Why the deuce can't he tell his story and get it over?

"I open door and there is lady. She say she want to see Mr. Anstruther and is he home yet. It was, I think, sir, the lady who call up on the telephone."

"Know who she is?" Ormsberry shot at him eagerly.

"No, sir. I mean, sir, I do not know her name."

"You had seen her before?"

"Yes, sir. Once before she had come to see Mr. Anstruther."

"The deuce you say! When was that?"

"One month, two month ago."

"What did she look like? Describe her."

"Tall lady, very black hair like Japanese lady; thin; not very young: about thirty years of age, maybe so. Got on black cloak and big black hat with lace around—so!" He demonstrated with a gesture. "I not see her face very plain."

Hennessey noted down the description. Ormsberry proceeded impatiently:

"What happened when you told her Mr. Anstruther was out?"

"She say she come in and wait. I tell her Mr. Anstruther not come home long time yet, but she say she wait anyhow." Hatu shrugged. "I do not argue with ladies, so I ask her sit down. Then I go home."

"You went home and left a strange woman in your master's apartment?" exclaimed Ormsberry.

To his amazement, Hatu winked once, definitely and unmistakably.

"It was all right, sir. I know. First time lady come Mr. Anstruther say: 'Hatu, you did not see lady, you do not know lady, you do not know she ever come here,' and he give me twenty-dollar bill. I know." The little Jap turned the full bloom of his cherubic countenance on Ormsberry with the bland innocence of a child.

"H'm! And that's all you know about the affair? You did not return to the apartment?"

"No, sir. I go away and come back this morning seven-thirty o'clock, and find here a policeman, and he tell me sad news about my excellent and honour-worthy employer, the great writer Mr. Anstruther." And Hatu smiled more broadly than ever.

Mr. Ormsberry gave him up.

"Well, that will do. You can take your things and clear out, but leave us your address in case anything else turns up. We might want some more information."

"Yes, sir; certainly, sir." Hatu bobbed and smiled and sidled himself out of the room.

"Well, what do you make of that?" demanded Ormsberry. *"Cherchez la femme,* as usual."

Hennessey whistled softly.

"The plot thickens, sor."

"It's too darn' thick already," complained Ormsberry. "The lady might at least have left us a scented handkerchief or a card case to trace her by. Darn it all, there isn't even a cuff link or a monogrammed hairpin in the whole flat. The lack of consideration among the criminal classes is—well, it's criminal!" His spirits were rising. He felt like embracing Hatu for introducing this mysterious female and opening up a line of inquiry that could have no possible connection with Brian Channing.

At this point Hennessey spoke up. He was still poking about the room, being of that persistent nature that declines to give up even a hopeless task. Now he came forward with the waste-paper basket.

"Just cast yer eye into this, sor."

Ormsberry bent to look. In the bottom of the basket were two crumpled pieces of carbon paper, one worn ragged, the other scarcely used.

"It's clear he wasn't used to being his own secretary, or he wouldn't have thrown that away," ruminated Mr. Ormsberry, even as his hand reached for the sheet of notepaper which lay beside these articles. The scrawled signature caught his eye as it had caught Hennessey's. Deliberately he spread it out before him. It was addressed to Anstruther and it was signed "Brian Channing." The date was some weeks old and it was written from the Hotel St. James et Albany, Paris.

> "I am sailing next week on the *Belgravia*. Needless to say, your letter interested me exceedingly. I'll call you up as soon as I get in and arrange to talk it over with you."

Ormsberry pondered for a moment.

"It is a fact that, before he went abroad, Channing and Anstruther used to be rather intimate," he said at last. Then he burst out with: "I don't like this—I don't like it at all." The presentiment that had dogged him since the evening before closed down on him with an icy chill. Just so had he felt when he saw the toils closing round Joan Archer. "See if you can find a carbon of Anstruther's letter in those files." His voice was sharp as the voice of an officer on parade. Hennessey sprang to obey.

When the carbon was found and placed before him, when he had read it and the purport had sunk into his benumbed intelligence, he sat for a long minute over the desk, feeling rather sick. One paragraph before his eyes:

"I have definitely and positively solved the mystery of Fortescue's murder. It has always seemed to me that the tangle was capable of solution by clear logic, and I have proved my point. When all other things are proved impossible, the remaining improbability must be true. It would be to your advantage to come back and hear what I have to say about the affair. I'm writing it up in fiction form—and, by George, what a story it makes!—but I'd be glad to talk it over with you before I publish it, if you can come soon."

It sounded like blackmail. Any jury could be made to believe it was blackmail. Only Brian Channing could say whether it was or not. It all fitted together so well: the story finished on the preceding day; the murder; the stolen keys; the rifled apartment, with only the manuscript files disturbed—and all following hard on Brian's return in answer to such a letter as this. And, according to Hatu, Brian knew where Anstruther was dining, so that it would have been quite possible for him to follow the novelist from his club.

It must be confessed that Mr. Ormsberry's hands shook as he gathered up the two letters and put them into his pocket.

8

Meanwhile Jerry Howard, having left Mr. Speck with a pleasing glow of triumph, had himself driven uptown to the Fortescue house. He was well satisfied with the turn affairs had taken. Joan had, without knowing it, given him the whip hand of the situation and he meant to use it. No more waiting upon her whims! She should jump to his bidding now. At her door he asked for her, and was shown up to her sitting-room where he found her with Mrs. Mortimer. The damp handkerchief in the girl's hand and the faint redness at the tip of her nose seemed to indicate that she had been crying, but he chose to ignore these symptoms. He entered with a fine air of the fortunate lover and bent with *empressement* over Joan's hand. Then he turned with a smile to the older woman.

"Have you heard our good news?" he asked. A man far less astute than Jerry Howard must have caught the horrified amazement in the look of inquiry she bent on Joan, but he went on imperturbably: "You haven't told her, then, my dear?"

"No," faltered Joan; "I thought—I don't see any reason—"

"But, my dear!" Howard corrected her with gentle raillery. "After all, it's hardly worth while to keep our engagement a secret when we are to be married so soon."

"Your engagement?" gasped Mrs. Mortimer. "Why, I—I hadn't an idea that—" She floundered desperately. "Joan, dear, is this really true?"

"Yes," said Joan uneasily. She knew that there was more to be said—more that she should say—but the words would not come.

"Well," said Mrs. Mortimer cordially, but her voice lacked conviction, "I hope—I hope you'll be very happy."

"Thank you," said Joan. She felt as though her heart were encased in ice, so painfully and slowly did it beat. This was, somehow, more than she expected—more than she had bargained for. She was not ready; she had not meant to go so fast. Jerry must, somehow, be stopped. But she was powerless to stop him, for there was Brian. She dared not offend Jerry now for Brian's sake.

He saw her hesitation and guessed pretty accurately at the cause of it. And he used his advantage ruthlessly.

"Poor child," he said gently. "You're terribly upset over that adventure last night, aren't you?"

Mrs. Mortimer, watching them, had a curious impression of a snake and a fascinated bird. Jerry went on softly:

"It would do you a world of good to get out and about a bit, wouldn't it, Mrs. Mortimer? Help me to persuade her to come to lunch with me. Come on, dear; we'll lunch—say on Henri's roof—and then we'll drive on out into the country and spend a long, lazy afternoon."

Alarm woke in Joan's eyes.

"No, no; I couldn't. Everybody'll be at Henri's—and I've an engagement at four."

"Well, come to lunch anyway. Suppose everybody is there? We can tell them our news. Personally I want to shout it from the housetops." He smiled at her unpleasantly. "I'm sure," he said softly, "that it would be very good for you—to do as I suggest."

Mrs. Mortimer cackled suddenly with nervous shrill-
ness. "Isn't that just like a man? Always telling women folk
what to do. Just like my poor dear Ephraim. Well, dearie,
I'll run along now."

The girl turned to her desperately.

"Won't you lunch with us? Please do!"

Mrs. Mortimer glanced nervously at Howard.

"Well, I don't think I'd better, Joan."

"Mrs. Mortimer has too much delicacy, Joan, to want
to make a third on such an occasion."

Mrs. Mortimer went. On the stairs a frantic, frightened
girl ran after her.

"You'll see he gets the note without fail, won't you?
Without fail?" Joan whispered, and, without waiting for
further assurance, she ran back into the sitting room.

As Joan had anticipated, the cool, breezy roof restaurant
was crowded, and she recognised several groups of acquaintances as she passed between the long rows to a table at the
coping which Jerry had evidently reserved in certainty of
her acceptance of his invitation.

That was Reddington Johns lunching alone at a nearby table, and farther along a young man whom she knew
slightly, a boyish-looking, very much bronzed young man,
was lunching with a lady.

"That's Gregory Sommers, isn't it?" she asked Howard
as they seated themselves.

He nodded and his eyes turned to the young man's vis-
a-vis. He glanced then at Joan and said in a low voice:

"By George! Look who he's got with him!"

Joan looked and the colour drained from her face.

"Oh, Jerry, I've got to go. I can't—really I can't!"

For the woman sitting with her back half turned to
them was Estelle Fortescue, whom Joan had not seen

since the last day of her trial, when, after the reading of
the verdict, the older woman had turned on the girl just
acquitted and said bitterly: "I don't care what they say.
You and I both know that you killed my brother."

Now, in this crowded dining-room, filled with the
subdued sound of voices, shot across with light, redolent
of the smell of sweet summer breezes, Joan heard again
that bitter voice and shrank from any meeting with those
implacable eyes.

Meanwhile, gossip was flying round the room. Many
people there recognised the two women whose names had
been connected with the murder trial of the year before—
divided by a hundred differences of temperament and
character, yet held together by that tragic thread. Surely
no two women could have formed a more marked contrast:
Joan so young and lovely and pathetically harassed; Estelle
Fortescue plain and middle-aged, for all her attempt at
youthful smartness, a bitter woman, clinging to the last
illusion her wealth had left her—Gregory Sommers.

The room was a-tingle with excitement. What chance
had brought these two, whose mutual hatred was well
known, together? Would they recognise each other? Would
they not? Like eager spectators at a play, they waited, and
they got their thrill; for as Joan, after choking down an
inadequate lunch, came face to face with Miss Fortescue
on her passage to the door, the older woman looked her up
and down, through and through, and deliberately turned
her shoulder. With a lift of the head the girl walked quietly past and out of the room. In the taxi she said faintly:

"Don't stop to argue with me, Jerry. Take me home at once."

And this time Jerry Howard thought it wise to obey her.

As Joan and Howard disappeared through the restaurant
doorway, Gregory Sommers looked at Estelle Fortescue
with a faint smile.

"By Jove, you did give it to her!" he murmured.

Miss Fortescue's face under the brim of her wide, co-quettish hat, darkened suddenly.

"Nothing will ever convince me that she wasn't guilty of my brother's death—nothing!" she declared fiercely. A blight seemed to have been laid upon her, shriveling and ageing her. She looked every one of her forty years. Sommers looked at her solicitously.

"You're distressed," he said. "I'm terribly sorry."

As suddenly as it had fallen the blight lifted. Her eyes softened as she looked into the ingenuous, boyish face opposite; the harsh line of her mouth curved into gentleness. One saw for a moment the girl she might have been.

"It's nothing," she said softly. "You're a dear, Greg, to care."

He made no secret of his infatuation. He leaned forward and touched her hand for an instant with light fingers.

"Very soon, now, I hope to be able to take you away—from all this," he said.

Their glances met and clung.

At this moment Reddington Johns, who had finished his lunch, strolled over from his table across the room.

"Jolly good of you to help me out of that hole this morning," he said to Sommers. "If any one thinks it's a lark to have the police suspect him of being connected with a murder mystery—well, it isn't. You know about it?" he asked Estelle.

She nodded.

"Gregory told me. You know, I've been wondering— I used to know Mr. Anstruther; he was a friend of my brother, you remember, and I've been wondering—he always seemed to be hobnobbing with curious people—criminals and so on. He told me once he picked them up deliberately and used them and their experiences in his stories. I wonder if one of them might have done it."

"Cold-blooded fish," said Sommers thoughtfully. "Always picking people's brains—anything for material for his books. He boasted about his heterogeneous acquaintances. But, of course," he added slowly, and with a certain significance, "there were other things about him that were—not cold-blooded."

Reddington Johns looked across at him quickly, with an interest that was very apparent. Sommers, idly drawing rings on the cloth with his fork, did not look up as he said:

"There's one person who will not unduly mourn Anstruther's—er—passing, and that's Robinson Tyler."

For an instant there was absolute silence between them. They knew what Sommers meant. The novelist's flirtation with Miriam Tyler was a subject of common gossip in their set. Reddington Johns gave voice to their unspoken thought.

"But Tyler isn't that sort of man."

"You put words in my mouth," said Sommers sharply. "Of course, I meant nothing of the sort."

"Of course, you did," contradicted the other dryly, and he smiled with offensive politeness.

For a moment Sommers seemed on the point of losing his temper. His brow clouded threateningly. Then he smiled and shrugged.

"Well, suppose I did!" he said. "The same thought is in your mind. We know that Tyler may have had good reason for wishing Anstruther out of the way. And one can never tell what a man will do—under provocation of that sort."

Johns's face flushed with a dull, angry tide. He rose abruptly.

"It would be well—for you—if you allowed your speculations to go no further," he said.

Sommers laughed, but the look that accompanied the laughter was piercing as a blade.

"And just what, if one may ask, is your interest in this matter? You must remember, after all, Mr. Johns, that I have, in a sense, involved myself in this by going sponsor for you this morning. I warn you, if anything suspicious comes to my attention, I shall consider it my duty to pass my knowledge on to the police."

Johns seemed about to say something further; he hesitated, shrugged, and capitulated.

"Well, well," he said. "Let's not quarrel about it. I know Tyler well, and—your supposition is absurd, that's all." He bowed abruptly to Estelle, nodded carelessly at Sommers, and left them.

"Do you really think Mr. Tyler had anything to do with it, Greg?" asked Estelle, when he had gone.

He frowned thoughtfully at the door through which Johns had disappeared.

"At least, he had a motive. I've a great mind," he went on slowly, "to drop in on this detective fellow—what's his name?—Ormsberry—that's been put in charge of the case, and tip him off. He may not know about that phase of the situation. And then there's something else— Oh, well, we'll see." And he signaled the waiter to bring him his check.

9

Miss Fortescue, it appeared, had an appointment with her dressmaker after lunch, and at half-past two Gregory Sommers escorted her to a discreet gray-stone doorway on a fashionable side street just east of the Avenue Here he made his regretful farewells and, when the door had closed upon her, stood for a moment thoughtfully on the curb, debating what he should do next. After a moment's hesitation, he got back into the taxi that had brought them there, and gave an address to the driver.

His little flurry with Reddington Johns on Henri's roof had disturbed him. When he had spoken as he did of Anstruther's whispered affair with Mrs. Tyler, it had been a sudden impulse, with no very clear idea of how real and vital a bearing this affair might have on the solution of the murder mystery. Johns's obvious irritation, however, had brought it suddenly home to him that this might be a clue of genuine importance to the police.

Much as he detested the thought of involving himself in any way in a business of this sort, he decided to pass this hint along to those interested in tracking Anstruther's murderer. A little reflection showed him that, in going sponsor for Reddington Johns that morning, in assisting to establish his alibi, he had already accepted a certain responsibility in the case. It could do no harm to pass on his ideas about Mr. Tyler. If the police thought there was nothing in them, well and good. That was not his affair.

He leaned back comfortably and lighted a cigarette. There was another matter that engaged his interest, and he gave it his full attention for the next ten minutes.

At police headquarters they told him that Ormsberry might be found at Anstruther's apartment, so he had himself driven there, and met the detective just coming out.

"I won't keep you, Mr. Ormsberry," Sommers said, when he had introduced himself. "If you're going somewhere, let me drive you. We'll talk on the way. I need only five minutes."

Ormsberry was, in fact, on his way to his own office, his private sanctum whither he retired from the world in moments of necessary concentration. He gave the address and they got into Sommers's cab.

As the young man talked, the detective studied him thoughtfully. He was not much given to believing gossip, but as Sommers went on he made a mental note to investigate this affair. There was something very convincing in this bronzed, quiet young man with his reserved face and his method of understatement. Ormsberry couldn't, at first, place him; and then he remembered.

"You're the man whom Hennessey interviewed at the Fontenoy Club this morning," he interrupted suddenly. "You substantiated Reddington Johns's statement that he left the club at seven-thirty."

"Right," agreed Sommers amiably. "That's really why I came to you now. I would not, perhaps, have thought it any of my business to tip you off about Mrs. Tyler and Anstruther, except that I felt I'd more or less got myself into the case anyway."

"What do you know about Anstruther and Mrs. Tyler?" demanded the detective.

"A lot of gossip," said Sommers promptly. "They've been seen everywhere together, and people have been putting the usual two and two together."

"That's no good to me," stated Ormsberry.

Sommers laughed.

"Right-o!" he assented amiably. "How's this, then? Day before yesterday—the day before he was killed—Anstruther took passages for two on the *Meringian*, sailing for England next week. I'm English, as you know, Mr. Ormsberry, and a pal of mine—Archie Blake—fellow I used to know at Oxford—is in the office of the White Cross, her owners. I dined with Blake the same evening, and he tipped me off about it. We'd been talking about Anstruther, of course. Everybody in our set has, I should say. You ask him about it."

Ormsberry made a note of the name and address.

"I'll verify it, of course," he agreed. "But you'll see it's not conclusive. Your theory is, of course, that he planned to take Mrs. Tyler with him and Tyler found out about it and got him?"

"Something like that," assented Sommers.

"In the first place," Ormsberry pointed out, "we'd have to prove that the second passage was intended for Mrs. Tyler. Then we'd have to show that Tyler had found out about it."

"Well," said Sommers slowly, "I can't help you there. That's your job, isn't it? But at any rate I've got it off my chest. If I can be of any service in clearing the thing up, I'd be glad."

Ormsberry was thinking rapidly. There was, after all, something in this. It was at least possible that this would explain Hatu's tall, dark lady.

"What does Mrs. Tyler look like?" he asked. "You know her?"

"Only by sight," said Sommers. "She's about thirty, I should say. A handsome woman—rather Junoesque in type. One of those clear, white complexions; very black hair—"

"Ah!" murmured Ormsberry thoughtfully. "I'm inclined to think you've hit on something. I'm much obliged to you."

"Not at all," murmured Sommers. "This your place?" he added, as the taxi came to a stop in front of a small office building on Madison Avenue. "Let me know if there's anything more I can do. You know," he confessed, smiling, "I'd jolly well like to do something. I feel the virus stirring in my blood, and all that. Devilish fascinating game—detecting."

Ormsberry laughed. He was well pleased with the world. Things, he considered, were looking up.

"Drop in in a day or two," he said. "I'll know then how things are going."

"Right-o!" Sommers shook hands cordially and departed.

When he had gone Ormsberry turned with a new jauntiness in his step and ascended to his office.

There he made some pretence of lunching on sandwiches sent in from the corner drugstore, issued orders that he was not to be disturbed, and settled himself to an afternoon's hard work on the Anstruther case.

The social intimates of the exquisite Van Dusen Ormsberry would never have recognised him in this alert, hardmouthed man in the bare, white-walled room containing only a battered desk and four stiff chairs. And yet it was here, if ever, that the real man could be seen, the man that lurked, alert and forceful, shrewd, vigorous, possessed of unfathomable energy, behind the suave veneered surface with which it amused him to mask his true countenance. But very few people ever saw him here. This was his own private refuge to which he retired when some knotty problem claimed his attention, requiring solitude and uninterrupted concentration. Hennessey had seen him here, and his chief from headquarters; almost no one else.

The room was pleasantly cool behind its striped awnings, after the oppressive heat and glare of the street. Mr. Ormsberry sighed and wiped his wet forehead with an immaculate English handkerchief. Then he drew the most uncomfortable chair in the room up to the desk, sat down, and endeavoured to organise his thoughts.

There were, he realised, three obvious lines of inquiry open to him, and, while none of them promised very much, they must all be followed up, as a matter of routine. First, the mysterious lady who visited Anstruther the night before must be traced. Secondly, Channing must be interviewed and asked to give an account of his proceedings. Thirdly, and most importantly, he must look into this affair between Anstruther and Miriam Tyler.

His mind hovered for a moment round Hatu. He had been able to form no satisfactory estimate of that smiling little man. Perhaps— But no; he could not possibly have been the man on the wall; he was entirely too minute.

Then there was the secretary. But, if the Newark police were right, he, too, might be counted out. Lastly there was that vague impression of Peter Jepson's of the man to whom Anstruther was talking in the club library. It seemed hardly worth while to waste time on so indefinite a thing, and yet it might be a good idea to send Hennessey up there again—talk to the waiters, and so on. Obviously, Anstruther must have been followed from the club, unless the meeting on the bus had been pure coincidence, which seemed hardly probable, in view of all the circumstances.

Absently Ormsberry noted down these possibilities on the pad before him. There was something else, he felt sure; something that had once crossed his mind and now eluded him. He reached for the 'phone, got headquarters on the wire, and started the machinery for tracking down the mysterious lady and investigating the Tyler menage. He was just about to ring off when that other idea occurred to him, full force.

"Just a minute," he said to the man at the other end of the line. "Hold the wire." He had it now. Before his mind's eye hovered the insolent, smiling face of Jerry Howard as he had invaded Mr. Speck's office that morning, and his talk with the lawyer after Howard had gone. Something in all that he didn't understand. Something worth finding out. He spoke again into the receiver. "There is something else," he said slowly. "I want a man shadowed for the next two or three days—until further notice. Put some one good on the job. It may be important. Name is Jerry Howard. You'll pick him up at the Fontenoy Club, or at his home." And he gave Howard's address. "Have reports sent to me morning and night." He listened to the brisk repetition of his directions and rang off. He did not feel particularly hopeful of results, but the thing was worth trying.

Once more he had recourse to the 'phone and this time got Mr. Speck on the wire.

"I wonder," he murmured ingratiatingly, "whether I could persuade you to invite Brian Channing to dinner this evening."

Mr. Speck laughed amiably at the other end of the line.

"I've anticipated you, my dear fellow. I was talking to Channing over the 'phone not ten minutes ago and arranged with him to dine with me at the Red Tape Club. Delighted to have you dine with us—if I may again anticipate your suggestion." And he chuckled.

"How well you understand me!" said Mr. Ormsberry admirably. "With and on you?"

"The same," said Charles Edward Speck. "But what's it all about, if it isn't indiscreet to ask?"

"I've got to question the fellow," complained the detective. "And I want to delude myself into thinking it's a pleasure and not a duty. Furthermore, I think—well, you'd better be there to advise him."

"The deuce you say!" exclaimed Mr. Speck. "Seven-thirty?"

"Sharp," assented Ormsberry, and rang off.

And then, suddenly, things began to happen. Hardly had he hung up the receiver when the bell rang, and the operator in the outside office announced a lady.

"Who is it?" he asked curtly.

"Won't give a name, sir," said the girl. "Says it's about the Anstruther case."

"Send her in," ordered Mr. Ormsberry. And he rose and drew up to the desk a second chair, turned carefully toward the light. There was a quick step outside, a faint rustle, the door opened, and a woman swept into the room.

In spite of the quietness of the day, her entrance had to drag back upon her magnificent figure in a wind of her own making. Her breath came and went hurriedly either from excitement or from rapid going. Her magnolia-pale face looked wan and pinched under the brim of her wide black straw. The astute brain behind Mr. Ormsberry's admiring eyes estimated shrewdly the formidable value of her simple black-and-white summer frock.

"I am Van Dusen Ormsberry," he said, coming forward politely, "at your service."

"Thank Heaven, I've found you at last," exclaimed the lady. "They told me you might be here, and I came straight on. I slept late this morning and only saw the papers about an hour ago. Oh, Mr. Ormsberry, you must find the murderer."

"Exactly," he murmured soothingly. "It would help me to understand you, madame, if you would tell me your name."

"Why, of course!" Her face, however, grew, if possible, a shade paler. "I am Mrs. Robinson Tyler."

He saw then that she was trembling, and politely urged her to sit down. After a moment she went on with some loss of assurance:

"You are the proper person, aren't you—that is—I mean—" She stumbled and then began again impulsively: "I've never had to do with the police before, and I don't quite know—"

Ormsberry interrupted her gently.

"Let me help you out. I am right, am I not, in supposing that you know something about the events of last evening—something, let us say, that you think may be useful to the police in tracking the man who killed Mr. Anstruther?"

"Yes, oh, yes; I'm sure I do," she cried.

"Then you're quite right to come to me with it," he assured her. "I am in charge of the case."

"I know." She dropped her eyes to her hands, which nervously twisting a handkerchief in her lap. "Mr. Ormsberry," she went on after a moment, "I can't, of course, command your discretion, but I have come freely, of my own accord, to tell you what I know, and I beg that you will involve me no more than is necessary."

Ormsberry bowed.

"You have my assurance of that. I dare say it will not be necessary to mention your name at all. In any case, I will do the best I can for you."

"Thank you!" She paused again, as though, now it had actually come to the point, she had not the courage to go on. Ormsberry waited patiently. He was tremendously sorry for this passion-racked woman, sincerely, honestly sorry, and yet all the while his mind was running over Hatu's description: "Tall, black hair, about thirty years of age." It suited her perfectly.

"You've doubtless heard," Miriam Tyler went on somewhat bitterly—"every one seems to have heard—that

George Anstruther and I—that we loved each other. Well, it is true, I see no reason to deny it. Robinson Tyler has given me again and again cause to seek my happiness else-where. And there was nothing in the devotion between Mr. Anstruther and myself of which either of us needed to be ashamed. As a matter of fact, we had tried to resist the attraction between us." She flushed a little, and Mr. Ormsberry, listening sympathetically, wondered if the "we" was strictly veracious. She did not look like a woman who would make any strong resistance against an impera-tive emotion. She went on:

"Mr. Anstruther had determined to go away shortly on an extended European trip. But yesterday afternoon things came to a crisis between my husband and myself. I decided definitely to leave him. In my distress and perplexity it seemed necessary for me to see Mr. Anstruther at once." She paused, seemingly unable to go on. Mr. Ormsberry prompted her gently:

"So you called up his apartment and were told he was out. And then later—about nine o'clock—you called there, in person."

"You know?" she breathed, startled.

"Only what Hatu told me. He told you that Mr. Ans-truther would not be in till late, and you said you would wait. He showed you into the drawing-room and left you. What happened after that? That was what you wanted to tell me, wasn't it?"

She looked at him uneasily, as though she wondered how much more he knew, but his sympathetic look seemed to reassure her.

"I waited until ten o'clock. I was getting more and more nervous, and had about despaired of his coming home, when the door bell rang. I knew, of course, that it could not be Mr. Anstruther, for he would have his key. I knew, also, that the curtains over the front windows absolutely shut in the light, so that any one standing in the street could not see whether or not there was any one at home. So I just waited while the ringing went on, for I could not, of course, open the door.

"Presently the ringing stopped, so I supposed whoever it was had given it up and gone away. I waited a few moments, and then, my nerves by this time completely shattered, I decided to go. I turned out the light, pulled the lace veil I was wearing down over my face as far as I could, and went out. It was only when I got the outer door fully open that I discovered that the man who had rung the bell had not gone away as I supposed, but was still lingering on the step, as though undecided what to do. It was too late for me to retreat, however, so I went out, hurried past him, and made off up the street as fast as I could go, praying that he had not recognised me as I did him."

"You knew him, then?"

"Yes, although I had not seen him for over a year."

Again that premonitory shiver ran down Mr. Ormsberry's spine.

"And it was—"

"Brian Channing." She then rushed on: "I read the account of the murder and the burglary very carefully, Mr. Ormsberry, and there isn't a shadow of doubt in my mind that he's the man you want. When I got to the corner I looked back and the step was empty. He had gone into the house."

"You are certain he had gone into the house?"

"Well, of course, I couldn't swear to it, but it seems likely. I didn't see him on the street, and he could so easily have slipped through the door I left open."

"To be sure." The detective rubbed his chin thoughtfully. "Now, one thing more, Mrs. Tyler. You say it was only yesterday afternoon that affairs really came to a crisis between you and your husband, in spite of the fact that—

as you say—he had already given you cause for serious displeasure. May I ask how that was? Why was it that you quarreled seriously—yesterday?"

She flushed angrily.

"I'm afraid that I can't see the connection," she began icily.

"Was it, perhaps," suggested Mr. Ormsberry, "that Mr. Tyler had discovered that you were planning to sail next week for England—with Anstruther?"

She grew deadly pale, but she rose to the situation with a dignity that compelled his admiration.

"The cause of my disagreement with my husband, Mr. Ormsberry, can have no possible bearing on the case. It had nothing to do with what you suggest."

The detective bowed.

"Of course," he said suavely, "I must take your word for that. Well, it is most generous of you to help me, Mrs. Tyler. What you've told me will be, I am sure, of material help to me in clearing up this matter. I'll ask you, if you don't mind, to say nothing about this to any one else for the present. I think I shall not have to bring your name into the case at all. Just do nothing further until you hear from me."

She had thawed progressively during this speech, look of intense relief took ten years from her age. She held out her hand.

"Oh, thank you so much!" Suddenly her eyes filled with tears and she added brokenly: "But if it can help you—to find—to find— I'd give anything—do anything—to bring to justice the man who killed him, Mr. Ormsberry."

Her lips trembled. Abruptly she turned and almost ran from the room.

The detective stood staring after her with a puzzled frown.

10

At about four o'clock on this same hot afternoon in the upper room of a speakeasy on Ninth Avenue, in the section succinctly described as Hell's Kitchen, sat a middle-aged man in a new, ill-fitting suit, with the prison pallor still on his face. He was a heavily built fellow with a bull neck and a head thrust belligerently forward—a man, clearly, of prodigious animal force and poise. His face, too, was remarkable, with its sharp, shrewd eyes, long, humorous upper lip, and powerful jaw. If it had not been for the extreme, loose-lipped weakness of his mouth, it would have been a likeable face, an invincible face.

This man was engaged in the interesting occupation of reading the newspaper notices of his own release from prison the week before, on the governor's pardon. One notice which had appeared in the *Sphere,* read:

> James Higgins, known as the "Scragger," was released from Sing Sing on a pardon granted by the governor. He has served five years of a life sentence for killing Clinton McGuire, late millionaire and oil magnate. It was thought at the time that he was only the tool of some person or persons higher up who desired McGuire's removal, but the police had been

unable to solve the mystery, owing to Higgins's invincible determination to hold his
tongue.

Scragger Higgins stopped reading, and his long humorous lip curved in a smile of genuine amusement. He had
gotten a good deal of fun out of bamboozling the police
about that affair.

"It's damn' right they never found out about that business," he muttered. "They never find out—about anything."

He picked up the pile of the morning s papers on the
table beside him and began to run through the accounts of
the Anstruther affair; and as he read he chuckled. This—
this was positively the best episode in a career that was
signally marked with colourful affairs. This was rich.

He followed the lines of type with a stubby forefinger.
Ah! The conductor of that bus had seen the fellow, had he?
He ran through the vague description:

"Average height, evening clothes, straw hat." A "good
dresser," the conductor had said. Scragger laughed again,
rose, and inspected himself in the cracked mirror on the
wall. Then, with another chuckle, he sat down again and
began to go methodically through each one of the princi-
pal morning papers, and all the evening editions yet out,
wading painstakingly through every word they contained
relating to murder.

At a quarter past four he rose and stood for some time
behind the drawn window curtain, peering out into the
street. Satisfied at last that there was no one on the watch,
he went down and repeated his tactics at the front door.
All clear. He went out, hailed a passing taxi, and had himself driven to the lower East Side. There he dismissed the
cab and plunged into the milling crowd on the sidewalk.
He wove his way in and out for several blocks, through

alleys he knew like the palm of his hand, always with a wary eye out for the possible trailer. At last, satisfied that he had shaken off any pursuer, even if there had been one, he got on an uptown elevated train, alighted, and took the Thirty-fourth Street crosstown, got off a block east of the Avenue, and walked uptown several blocks. Here, after a hurried look around, he plunged into the area way of a smart-looking brownstone house, rang the bell, and when a maid answered the ring, asked to see Mr. Robinson Tyler, privately and at once.

"He's expecting me," he added, seeing the maid about to protest.

He waited patiently in the little entry, happily unconscious of the irony of fate that had led him a dance through the broiling city in a quite unnecessary attempt to shake off a non-existent trailer, only to land him at last into the very arms, so to speak, of the man Mr. Ormsberry had set to watch the comings and goings of Robinson Tyler. As a matter of fact, the police were not—for the time being, at any rate—interested in the doings of Scragger Higgins, murderer. It was quite beyond his shrewdness to surmise that they might be—and were—extremely interested in the doings of Robinson Tyler. Clever as he was, he quite overlooked the inconspicuous figure of the man who stood well back in the doorway of the pharmacy on the corner, where he could watch through the glass the comings and goings from the Tyler house, and where, if need arose, he could be in quick touch with headquarters by means of the telephone booth behind him. A veteran of many man hunts was Plain-clothesman Smith. He knew his job.

Also, he knew Higgins. He had seen him after his conviction, and he had an excellent memory for faces. Furthermore, he was aware of Higgins's release from prison the week before. So he spotted him the instant he turned into the street and watched with interested speculation his entrance into Tyler's house. He was just debating whether it would be wise for him to leave his post long enough to 'phone the news in, when another arrival stayed him. A long, low, racy-looking car swung round the corner and drew up in front of the house. The driver, a blond, youngish-looking man, got out and rang the bell, and was immediately admitted.

Hennessey had primed Smith about the case, giving him a *précis* of the chief members of the cast, so that the detective had no difficulty in placing Reddington Johns.

This time Smith had no time for speculation, for a taxi drew up behind the car and a lady got out. So quickly did the taxi follow the roadster that Johns had hardly disappeared into the dimness of the hallway, and the maid had not yet shut the door, when the lady dismissed her taxi and began to climb the low steps. Clearly the maid recognised this visitor, for she waited, smiling, and holding the door wide. A moment later it shut behind them both.

Smith found that, by a little manoeuvring, he could, while standing in the 'phone booth, see a reflection of the Tyler house in the mirror over the soda fountain. He telephoned in to headquarters, and ten minutes later was joined by another unobtrusive man who fell, apparently, into casual conversation with him and then strolled in and imbibed a coca-cola at the fountain. When the Scragger came out a few minutes later, he was the subject of interested scrutiny by two pairs of eyes, and he was followed down the street by a shadow that never left him, and yet was never near enough to catch his eye, should he turn his head.

The Scragger, however, walked jauntily, with eyes front, entirely indifferent to possible pursuit. He walked east until he had passed the line of extreme respectability. Then he turned into a dairy lunch and ate a hearty meal.

Meanwhile, Yvonne Lorimer, following Reddington Johns in at the brownstone house, paused to speak a friendly word to the maid. She was too shrewd a woman not to realise the value of being on good terms with the servants in the houses she frequented.

"How hot it is," she said, smiling. "Is Mrs. Tyler in, Mary?"

"Yes, ma'am. She's upstairs in the sitting-room. Just step into the drawing-room, ma'am, and I'll tell her you're here." She turned toward the stairs.

"Oh, Mary," said Mrs. Lorimer softly. "Wasn't that Mr. Johns who just came in?"

"Yes, ma'am. He's with Mr. Tyler and—and—" She stammered and went on: "They're in the library, ma'am. Just wait a minute, ma'am, and I'll tell Mrs. Tyler." And she vanished up the dark stairs.

Mrs. Lorimer looked after her thoughtfully. Something in the girl's manner—a faint perturbation—caught her attention. Who was this third person in the library whose presence should cause embarrassment to this usually suave domestic? Without any very definite intent, moved by a mild sort of curiosity, she strolled down the dark hallway toward the closed library door.

The house was very still, and the deep hall carpet deadened her footsteps. She heard voices raised behind the panels: Tyler's voice and Reddington Johns's, and a third voice—a harsh, uncultivated voice using some abominable accent—she heard quite distinctly; and the sentence it carried caused her to glance hastily over her shoulder to make sure she was unwatched, and then creep forward and stand close against the door, heedless of any risk of its being opened, careless of everything, absorbed in the argument that was going on in the room beyond.

For perhaps two minutes she listened. Then the sound of a door opening upstairs sent her scurrying back into the drawing-room. When Mary came down she was standing sedately in the window, with no sign of anything untoward, unless it was a faint heightening of colour in her pale cheeks.

"Mrs. Tyler is having tea upstairs, and hopes you will join her," announced the maid, standing in the doorway.

Mrs. Lorimer nodded brightly as she turned to the stairs.

"Don't bother to come up, Mary; I can find my way very nicely."

Surely the hall was very cold, she thought, shivering a little as she went up. She wondered if, when the time came, she would really have the courage to play the cards that fate had thrust into her hands. For she had heard enough through the library door to set her trembling at the prospect of plunder spread before her dazzled eyes.

Climbing the stairs, she was already beginning to calculate and plan how to take advantage of this unexpected bit of information. It never for an instant occurred to her to hand over her knowledge to the police. She knew very well the monetary value of it, and she had no intention of losing any fraction of its purchase price. Predatory and unscrupulous by nature, she wasted no time in horror over the thing she had just found out, although the two conspirators were, as she would have said, friends of hers, but she was keenly alive to her own personal danger, once they discovered her eavesdropping. She laboured under no delusion as to the calibre of the men she had to deal with.

Blackmail in any ordinary sense would not do, she concluded, before she reached the top of the stairs. For one thing, both men together were not rich enough to pay her for the risk she would run in holding them up. No, the thing to do was to act quickly and daringly, get what she needed at one throw of the dice, and then go away—out of the country—somewhere that would give them definite

assurance that she meant to keep her part of the bargain—
silence. That way lay her only safety.

Her thoughts reverted to the rumoured merger in Heron
Oil and the humiliating outcome of her conversation with
Reddington Johns the night before. Apparently he had,
from the beginning, seen through her attempt to wangle
from him information on this point. There had been a
time when he would have told her anything she wanted to
know. Why, a year ago he would have handled her stock
himself— That was it! Of course, that was it! She smiled
to herself, stopping dead still halfway up the stairs while
she ran swiftly over the situation in her mind.

She was convinced that Mr. Johns, through his intimacy
with Joseph Kron, president of Heron Oil, knew whether
or not there was to be a merger, and that he meant to use
this information for his own purposes. And rumour had
it that there was, very shortly, to be a meeting of the directors that would formally decide the matter and publish
the decision to the world. Very good! This was her chance.

And then there was Jerry Howard, who had made it
very clear that he would value highly advance information
on what the decision of the directors was likely to be.

Jerry Howard! Yvonne's teeth closed with a little click.
The note that morning received from Jerry, telling her of
his success with Joan Archer, reposed in her handbag. She
clenched her hand on it and resolved again, as she had
resolved many times during the day, to settle that account
in full.

Meanwhile, there was this affair of the merger. She, as
well as Jerry, knew how valuable advance information on
this point might be. She would give him one more chance
to share it with her, and then— She figured rapidly. She
was to see Jerry at nine. She had called him up on receiving his note, and insisted on his giving a reluctant consent. She would, as she phrased it, "have it out with him"

then, and afterward, whether he proved tractable or not, she would see Reddington Johns—how and when would depend on how Jerry took her ultimatum.

Her plans made, she walked briskly down the upstairs hall, and went into Miriam Tyler's sitting-room.

11

Meanwhile, Brian Channing had spent a thoroughly wretched day. During the long year of his exile he had never allowed himself to doubt that when he returned to America he would find Joan restored to health both mentally and physically, restored to her normal point of view, and ready, please Heaven, to be won gradually back to a hopeful attitude toward the future and a kinder attitude toward himself. He was, it must be confessed, a rather naive young man as far as women were concerned. And when Joan said she could not think of marriage, it never occurred to him to doubt that she meant what she said.

He had always been a man's man, and the intricacies of the feminine mind and the tricks of feminine nerves were mysteries to him. A man more familiar with women would certainly have foreseen danger in allowing a year's absence to flow between himself and the woman he loved. He would have known that, in her overwrought state, her mind might play her strange tricks and lead her into extravagant actions. None of these possibilities, however, occurred to Brian. He had suffered by the long separation; he had suffered when his letters remained unanswered; he had feared, as the time approached for seeing her again, that he might find her love for him had changed; but he had never, it must be confessed, thought of returning to find her engaged to some one else.

The announcement had struck him temporarily oft balance; so much so that he did not at first pause to think whether there might be something behind that simple statement that it would be worth his while to know. Resentment, jealousy, and a genuine and terrible suffering clouded his mind and prevented any clear thinking out of the situation. In the first heat of his indignation, he determined to leave town immediately without seeing Joan again. But next morning he received a note from her begging him to call on her at four o'clock, and he knew that he could not go.

During his enforced waiting he called Mr. Speck and agreed to dine with that gentleman at his club. His professed motive in seeking out the little lawyer was to hear what, in his absence, had been done about the Fortescue case; but his real impulse was to find somebody to whom he could talk about Joan.

Beyond the lace, delicate as frost tracery on glass, that curtained the drawing-room windows of the Fortescue house, the park drowsed in a blue haze of heat. Awnings were lowered against the descending August sun, but the fingers of warmth seemed to curl under their faintly flapping edges, and press on heavy eyelids, heavy brains, muting the summer noises to a half-heard hush. Joan Archer moved from tea table to window, from window to chair, with the disembodied feeling of a ghost moving in familiar scenes made unfamiliar by some indefinable change.

Incredible that Brian's return should so have shattered the insecure peace she had won, filling her at once with delicious indecision and a dragging weight of terror. Her fingers twisted together nervously, and she stared out into the hot street, deserted at this hour except for the passing vehicles and an occasional dispirited passerby. Why didn't he come? Her note had mentioned four o'clock. Oh; the hateful notoriety that bound her hand and foot, that prevented her from seeking him out, whatever her need!

She tried to comfort herself with Jerry's assurance. Jerry had really been very sweet last night when he had brought her home, half hysterical, and had surprised her into admitting that she recognised Brian in Anstruther's apartment. Very gentle Jerry had been; very reassuring; very certain of his power to steer suspicion away from Brian. She had hated him, perversely, for binding her so much the closer to him and her bargain. But to-day—there had been something terrible about Jerry at lunch, something ruthless and subtly threatening.

Why—why had she chosen last night to draw her bonds closer, to shut more securely the door against escape? Was it because Brian's return had made her unsure of herself, uncertain of her power to carry through her determination never to involve the man she loved in the situation that made her own life a nightmare? Jerry was different. To Jerry she could give a *quid pro quo*. Jerry needed her money as desperately as she needed his protection—actual and spiritual; as much as she needed his help to shut out this horrible loneliness that was slowly, quite surely undermining her sanity. Jerry was a good friend. But was he? Was he? What was this new force that had entered into the relation between them? She trembled and tried to crush down her fears.

After all, nothing mattered now but Brian. Whatever her original motive had been in engaging herself to Jerry, she could not now go back on her word for Brian's sake. It even gave her a sort of fearful joy to be enduring this pain—for him. And she was to see him again, although only for a few moments, and for the last time.

And then suddenly he was there, coming to her with quick steps on the cool, bare floor.

She half expected him to kiss her, but he did not—only looked at her with hurt, questioning eyes, as though afraid to so much as wonder what her note had meant until she told him what she wanted. The pain in her heart deepened with an unexpected agony. She realised fully, for the first time, that this was really the last meeting. Hitherto at the back of her mind there had been the thought that nothing was final; that she might be able to take him back. Now she saw clearly that, if she was going to do this thing, she must do it now. She could not keep him dangling. She must give him his warning and let him go. Her body was cold; her voice was painfully, horribly natural in her own ears. Glancing at herself in the mirror as she turned back to her chair, she saw that she was not even pale. It could not be apparent to him that she suffered, and she was at once glad and bitterly sorry.

She steadied herself, clasping her trembling hands in her lap.

"Shall you be going back to Europe?" she asked. "From what you said—we were so hurried—" She tried again: "I thought it possible you might be going at once, and I did not want you to go without my seeing you again."

"That was kind of you," he said.

"I was not being kind," she said softly. "I am sorry. I should like to keep your friendship, if that were possible, but I can see it would not be wise—just at first."

His tired face relaxed a little. He smiled wryly.

"I am not in a mood to deny you that consoling hope."

"You are cruel!" she cried.

But he looked at her. She wondered how it was he did not read the truth in that long, kind look.

"I think perhaps you'd better tell me why you sent for me," he said gently.

Once more that agonised contraction of the heart! This, then, was the end.

"Yes, I will tell you."

When she had finished he stood looking thoughtfully down at her.

"So you recognised me?"

"I—I thought so. I wasn't sure until I found that Jerry had recognised you, too."

"Did he tell you that he recognised me—I mean before you told him?"

"I think so—I don't remember—I can't be sure. It was all so confused."

"I see." He paced once, thoughtfully, the length of the room and back. "I'll see Speck at once about it."

"Brian!" Joan was on her feet and had caught at his arm. "I told you so that you could leave at once. You're going abroad anyway. Why not go now—without saying anything—to any one?

"Run away? H'm! There might be something in it if there was anything to run away from."

"You mean it wasn't you?"

He looked at her with astonishment. Then suddenly he caught her shoulders and looked searchingly into her face.

"You didn't think it was—really?"

"Of course I don't think you murdered Mr. Anstruther," she cried indignantly.

"Thanks! But you think I may have burgled his rooms?" A healthy rage was stirring in Brian, clearing his brain of its fog of bewilderment. He began to realise there there was something he did not understand.

"But you might have had some—some good reason for—burgling," she murmured faintly.

"Do you think I did?" he demanded. "Look me in the eye and tell me: do you think I did?"

She smiled at him—such a look as few men get from more than one woman in the course of their lives. When she spoke her voice answered every question in Brian's mind, resolved every doubt he had or could have.

"I'm waiting for you to tell me." Joan had forgotten subterfuge; forgotten her elaborate and futile plans; remembered nothing but the need of showing the man she loved the faith she had in him. And this time Brian understood. Intuitive wisdom descended on him. He knew that he must not betray his knowledge then. He chose to answer her question plainly and simply as she put it.

"You were mistaken when you saw me in Anstruther's room. I was not the man."

"Well," said Joan, with a gallant lift of the head that he remembered, "then I can see it would be stupid for you to run away."

He studied her carefully for a moment, watchful lest he betray the triumphant laughter that was in him. The ridiculous child! The darling little goose! What an idiot she was—what a beloved, priceless little ass! But he only said:

"If I ran away, they'd take it for a sure sign of guilt, you see."

"Yes, I see," she said gravely, a worried frown on her pretty brow. "But, oh, please, see Mr. Speck right away and get his advice. I shall worry so—I really shall."

He told her he was dining with Mr. Speck and would lay the matter before him.

"After all," she comforted herself, "I don't see that any one need ever connect you with the burglar. Neither Jerry nor I would ever tell that we thought it was you in that room. Wasn't it funny, by the way, that Jerry thought he recognised you, too?"

"Perhaps," suggested Brian gently, "the man really looked a good deal like me. I wish you could remember whether it was you or Howard who spotted me first."

"I don't know—I really don't. I was so—so frightened and confused, Brian." She flushed deeply and averted her eyes. Brian longed to take her in his arms and tell her that he quite understood, that he saw through the barrier she was willfully erecting between them, but caution bade him wait awhile. He only said tenderly:

"It is very good of you to be so concerned about me. And very good of Howard," he added dryly, "to lend himself to your deception."

She looked up quickly, doubtfully, and found him regarding her with eyes full of laughter.

"You're laughing at me," she cried reproachfully.

"Perish the thought!" He strove to meet her gaze with gravity, but laughter shone and sparkled in the back of his eyes. "But you've given me an idea—an idea, by Jove, and it's a pippin."

She laughed—a little uncertainly, perhaps, but with a leap of the heart; her first spontaneous laugh for many hours.

"What on earth are you talking about?"

"Don't you wish you knew?" cried Brian teasingly. He was frankly laughing at her now. "Oh, boy!—as I hear they say in these United States—don't you wish you knew?"

He rose and, seizing her hands, drew her to her feet. She saw by his eyes that he was very near kissing her, but he did not.

"My dear child," he said gently, "I want you to promise me not to worry any more. It's quite possible that I may be connected with the case, for I did actually go to Anstruther's house after I left you last evening—although I didn't actually go into his apartment—and somebody may have seen me. But if I am involved, I shall know how to extricate myself." He laughed again teasingly. "I'm a big boy now; I can take care of myself—and of you, dear heart." He lifted her hand to his lips and left her.

Curiously enough, when he was gone, she felt no inclination to give way to despair. Tragedy did not seem to loom with such fatal inevitability.

As she dressed for dinner, she sang a little for the first time in months, and even looked with a demure interest at the reflection in her mirror.

"Dear heart!" she repeated softly to herself, and laid the hand he had kissed softly against her cheek. It must be confessed that, for the moment, she completely forgot that she had sent him out of her life for ever.

Just then the maid came in to announce that there was a reporter downstairs, asking for her. The colour faded from her face with a rush.

"you should have told him I could not see him."

"I did, ma'am; but he said it was something about that awful murder last night, ma'am—something about Mr. Channing—so I thought—"

"I'll see him at once," gasped Joan. "Ask him to wait."

When she came downstairs, she was outwardly quite composed—too composed, thought Caruthers, veteran reporter for the *Sphere,* as he came forward to meet her.

"You wanted to see me?" she asked in a cool little voice.

"We want your corroboration of a story that has come into the office," he said promptly, with just the right touch of sympathetic understanding. "We have been told that the police believe you recognised the man whom you saw in Mr. Anstruther's apartment last night—and that the man was Brian Channing. Is this true?"

Joan felt as though the pounding of her heart would suffocate her. She must keep her head; she must think. She sparred for time.

"I can't understand how such a rumour got about," she said in a voice surprisingly firm. "I told Mr. Ormsberry that I did not recognise the man. You see," she added with great show of reason, "I only had the most fleeting glimpse of him."

"But I understand he passed very near you in getting away."

"It was quite too dark for me to see anything clearly."

"You could, however, make a shrewd guess at his identity?"

"I should not think of making a guess, as you say, in such an important matter."

Caruthers, in view of the source of his information, knew that the girl was evading, but he could see no way to get the truth from her. He doubted, as a matter of fact, whether the police would get anything from her she did not wish to tell. For all her look of fragility and helplessness, there was something in her face, a look of firmness, of character, that held out no hopes to any one seeking to penetrate her reserve. She suddenly carried the war into the enemy's camp.

"Where did you get this story about Mr. Channing?"

Caruthers found himself hedging in turn.

"We have our sources of information at headquarters."

"But the police knew nothing of this—" She bit her lip and grew desperately pale. Caruthers was frankly sorry for her.

"My dear young lady, don't be so concerned. We knew, of course, that you recognised Channing. It was, I think, fairly obvious. Your admission is a mere detail."

"I don't admit it!" she cried. "I did not recognise him. If you say I did, I shall deny it."

He looked at her with commiseration, bowed without speaking, and withdrew.

12

At eight o'clock, in the oak-paneled dining-room of the Red Tape Club, Charles Edward Speck, Brian Channing, and Van Dusen Ormsberry were dallying with coffee and cigarettes. Brian Channing, alone of the three, was quite at his ease. The two older men bore decided signs of strain. The late editions of the *Sphere,* carrying the report of Joan's identification of Channing in Anstruther's apartment, had put Mr. Ormsberry in a very difficult situation. He felt that his hand was being forced. He wondered if Jerry Howard, fearing that his tip about Channing was being suppressed, had taken this means of forcing the information into the light. He saw that Channing was far from realising the seriousness of his position, a circumstance that did not make things any easier for the detective.

They had been discussing Channing's interview with Joan.

"You see," the young man explained, "I had to tell her that I might be connected with the case, even at the risk of worrying her, for it was bound to come out that I had been to Anstruther's house, and it would have frightened her much more to come across the news casually in the papers."

"You say you didn't actually go into the house at all?" asked Ormsberry slowly.

"Certainly I went in," said Channing impatiently. "I rang the bell and no one answered. I was just about to go off when a woman from one of the other apartments came out. I caught the door before it shut, and went in on the chance that Anstruther's door might be unlatched. I thought, if it was, I'd go in and wait for him."

"And was it unlatched?"

"No. So I went out again immediately. I was—well, frankly I was in no mood for sleep, so I walked round for a while."

"Where?"

"Oh, just around. I don't know—didn't notice—" Suddenly Channing paused and looked from one to another of the grave faces opposite. "Say, what is this? A cross-examination? It's no use asking where I went. Even if I could tell you every step of the way, it wouldn't help any. I can't prove an alibi."

"Didn't meet anybody you know?" asked Mr. Speck anxiously.

"No." Brian frowned thoughtfully, "But I don't see why it's so serious. Joan only thought the man in the room might be me. She wasn't sure enough to swear to it."

"Jerry Howard would swear to it," said Ormsberry softly.

Brian glanced at the detective thoughtfully.

"I wonder if you have the same idea that I have about Howard. Since I wasn't in Anstruther's study, he couldn't really have recognised me. I'm inclined to think that he took his tip from Joan, and is trying to fasten the thing on me to get me out of the way. It may be far-fetched, but I believe the fellow's quite capable of it. And the motive is so obvious."

"The same idea occurred to me," confessed Mr. Ormsberry. "He's such a—pleasant animal. But that suspicion doesn't help us very much actually. For Howard would swear himself black in the face that it was you, and Joan would have to admit that, for the first few minutes, at least, she thought it was you, and you can't prove that it wasn't you. We've nothing but your word."

"But it's too silly. Where's my motive?"

"It might not be difficult to imagine one. For instance, why did you, practically the instant you were off the ship, go to see Mr. Anstruther?"

Brian looked at him uncomprehendingly.

"Why, that couldn't have anything to do with this affair. I went to see him immediately because I really came back to this country for that precise purpose. That is, I wouldn't have come quite so soon if it hadn't been for a letter Anstruther wrote me."

"What letter was that?" asked Mr. Ormsberry quietly.

"Before I went away—during Joan's trial and afterward—Anstruther and I had a number of conversations about the circumstances surrounding the murder of Mr. Fortescue. While Anstruther and I were never intimate, we saw a good deal of each other at one time. He was, as you may know, very much interested in every big murder case that came up; used to follow them closely in the papers, and often was present in the court-room. He got ideas for a lot of his mystery stories that way. Well, he was obsessed with the mystery surrounding Mr. Fortescue's death. Of course, he never for a moment believed that Joan was guilty. He was sure there was some hidden fact beyond and behind anything that came out in the trial; and he was sure that, if that one link ever came to light, it would be easy to find out who the murderer was.

"But, even failing that information, he was confident that the mystery could be solved by sheer logic. He evolved a dozen theories about it, but no one of them tallied precisely with all the known facts. I confess I hadn't much faith in his achieving anything useful. I told him so before I went away; and he said: 'Don't you believe it. It will come

to me suddenly. This business is like a cross-word puzzle
with the key word missing—find that, and all the rest will
slip into place. Some time I'll wake up in the middle of
the night with that key word. And when I do, I'll let you
know. I don't promise to follow up my conclusions. That
will be your job.' I told him, of course, that I'd come from
the ends of the earth for the pleasure of meeting Fortescue's murderer, and he promised me again that he'd let me
know if anything occurred to him.

"Well, two weeks or so ago I got a letter from him saying that he'd got the answer, and I'd better come home. I
took the first boat, and as soon as I got in I called Anstruther up. His Jap told me he was dining uptown at his
club and was going afterward to Mrs. Mortimer's. Well—"
Brian hesitated and flushed. "I'd already found out that
Joan was to be at Mrs. Mortimer's, so I decided I'd wait to
see Anstruther until I got there and not try to get round
to the Fontenoy, for I had a lot of little things to do before I started down. But at Mrs. Mortimer's I found that
Anstruther hadn't turned up after all. So when I—when
I'd seen Joan, I—I thought he might have gone back to
his house for something first, as he lived just round the
corner; anyway, I fancied that I saw a light in his rear window. So I went round to see. He was still out, so I went
away again. And that's all I know about it. Surely there's
nothing in all that to establish a motive for my ransacking
his apartment, to say nothing of murder."

"Putting that aside for the moment," said Ormsberry,
"what was Anstruther's theory of the Fortescue case?"

"I don't know."

"He never wrote you about it? Never dropped a hint?"

"Never. That one letter was the only one I received
from him while I was away. I don't know whether I kept it
or not—"

"It doesn't matter," interrupted Mr. Ormsberry. "We found a copy of it in the files."

"I see. Then you knew all this before?" Brian gave him a long, steady look.

"Not in detail, of course. We could only guess at it."

There a moment's pause. Then Brian said quietly:

"You said something just now about a possible motive for my killing Anstruther. I'm afraid I'm very stupid, but I don't see just what you mean."

"It's just this. Suppose you had killed Fortescue—"

"What?" Brian started and half rose from his chair. "Suppose *I* had killed Fortescue? What the devil do you mean?"

"Just a minute. I'm trying to present the situation as a prosecuting attorney might put it. Suppose you had killed Fortescue, and Anstruther had found some logical way of fastening the crime on to you. He writes you a letter so ambiguous that a clever criminal lawyer could persuade any jury that it was a blackmailing letter. You, receiving this letter, return at once to forestall the publication of Anstruther's theory, which he says he will not publish until you return; you start down-town at—when did you leave your hotel to go to Mrs. Mortimer's?"

"A few minutes after nine."

"And at nine-fifteen, or thereabouts, on top of a bus, Anstruther was killed."

Brian frowned thoughtfully.

"I see."

"An hour later his room was rifled and some manuscript was stolen from his files."

Once more Brian spoke thoughtfully.

"I see."

"And two people saw the burglar escaping over the wall. One is prepared to swear it was you, and the other thought so—at least for a few moments. And a third person—Mrs. Tyler—is prepared to identify you as the man she met at the door of Anstruther's house at approximately the time that the burglar must have made his entrance."

Mr. Speck leaned forward.

"By gad, this is cold-blooded—positively cold-blooded."

The other two paid not the slightest attention to him.

"There's just one other question I must ask you," the detective went on. "Where were you—what were you doing—on the night John Fortescue was killed?"

There was a long silence. It seemed as though the two elder men held their breath for Brian's answer Brian himself sat quietly, idly balancing an unlighted cigarette on an outstretched finger. It was possible to time the moment when actual, full realisation of his predicament came to him by the little convulsive twitch of his hand that sent the cigarette to the floor. He bent to retrieve it, and when he straightened his face was quite calm.

"Of course I remember that night—every detail—quite well. It was so much discussed. As it happens, I spent the evening at home, alone. No one came in and I talked to no one over the 'phone. That's the truth, but I wouldn't have the ghost of a chance to prove it."

Mr. Ormsberry sighed.

That puts me in a deuce of a hole. Now that this newspaper story is out, if I don't arrest you before morning—for the burglary, if not the murder—people will be asking why. And I shan't have any answer except that I don't believe you're guilty. And the answer of headquarters to that will be that I'm not paid my munificent salary for having opinions, but for producing facts."

"Then why don't you arrest me?" suggested Brian easily.

"Because it's a lot easier to get a man into jail than to get him out again."

"But listen to me," urged Brian earnestly; "you're going to have to arrest me soon anyway. Why not do it now, at once, and make it publicly clear that you believe you've caught the murderer? Then the other fellow, the real murderer, will think he's safe and perhaps—well, perhaps he'll show his hand a little, or give you some clue to hook him by."

"There's something in that, certainly."

"And then there's this point: this thing that you've been talking about as a possible motive for my killing Anstruther—why shouldn't all that apply to some one else? Perhaps he talked about his story to some one else—or his secretary might have talked."

"His secretary! By George!" cried Mr. Ormsberry suddenly. "I'd almost forgotten the fellow. He might at least be able to give us some idea of what this lost story of Anstruther's was about. I'll see him in the morning."

"If we could just get the plot of that story," said Brian, "it might give us the clue to the whole mystery."

Here Mr. Speck broke in with the suggestion: "Don't authors sometimes discuss the plots or their stories with their editors before actually starting to write them? I seem to have heard something of that sort."

"I'll see what I can do along that line, anyway," assented Mr. Ormsberry. "We know, at least, the name of the editor for whom the story was written—if it was, as we suppose, the last thing he wrote. Hatu mentioned that an editor called up during the morning yesterday and asked why he hadn't received it. Hennessey will have made a note of the name."

"It seems to me that this business of the lost story is our most hopeful point of attack," said Mr. Speck gravely. "From what you tell me, I think it very unlikely that Tyler had anything to do with the affair—at least, in the role of the injured husband. If he had, he'd have been interested in the letter files, not the manuscript drawers."

"Well, whoever he was, and whatever his motive, he'll be more careless if he thinks the police have a candidate for Sing Sing already in jail," said Brian dryly. "And I want him to get careless; I want him to be caught. I'd be willing to risk a good to help to catch him—if there's the slightest chance of his capture leading to the discovery of Fortescue's murderer."

"You agree with me, then," said Mr. Ormsberry, "that the two crimes are in some way connected?"

"It seems, in view of all this, extremely probable."

"H'm!" The detective stroked his chin thoughtfully. "Could you make it convenient to be arrested this evening, or would you prefer to wait until morning?"

"Better get it in the morning papers," suggested Brian.

An hour later Mr. Ormsberry, before leaving the club for headquarters, sent out a boy to buy Brian a toothbrush and notified the newspapers that an arrest had been made in the Anstruther case.

13

Meanwhile, another meeting of a very different nature was taking place. Having entered the portal—no less pretentious word describes it—of one of the more fashionable new apartment houses on upper Madison Avenue, and mounted aloft in the crystal-lined elevator that gave back from half a dozen angles the perfection of his turn-out, Jerry Howard surrendered his hat and stick to the butler who opened the door at precisely the right moment to admit him. Drawing off his gloves, he caught a glimpse through the wide archway of Yvonne Lorimer as she threw aside the paper she was reading and rose to meet him. The shaded lamp cast into vivid relief her look of unrestrained, welcoming ardour, utterly revealing because, as she thought, unobserved. The light blazed in her magnificent red hair and chilled on the sea-green fold of her gown, frosty with silver brocade.

Jerry knew that when she greeted him a moment later her manner would be the suave perfection of the sophisticated woman. That was as it should be. It pleased him; soothed his vanity without taxing his energies. Tactful woman, Yvonne! Well, it paid her well, after all. Because of it, she had held his roving interest longer than its usual span. He had had an uneasy feeling, however, that the end had almost been reached. Recently he had felt beneath the shell of her manner a dragging of chains, a stirring of tides. It was this affair of Joan Archer, of course. Women were so lacking—even the most sensible of them—in any grasp of the practical, once their affections were involved. What could she lose, after all, in his acquisition of the Fortescue millions? He shrugged, and went in to greet her.

"Jerry!" she cried, and her voice held only a shade more of warmth than convention permitted.

He smiled appreciatively as he bent to her fingers.

"I doubted a little in the wisdom of this meeting," he said, "under the circumstances, but now I'm delighted that I let inclination override prudence."

"Don't think for a moment that I mistake your real reason"—she laughed—"for overriding prudence." Her tone was light enough, but he fancied a sting under the banter. "Confess now! You're dying to know whether or not I found out anything last night from Reddington Johns."

"Naturally!" He laid his hand on hers where it rested on the shining edge of the piano, and looked deep into her eyes. It was no credit to Jerry Howard that his lashes were long and drooping and that the curve of them caught at the unwary heart. He knew, however, precisely the value of that look and counted on it. "As much for your sake as for mine," he said gently.

As a rule, women had believed anything he told them, spoken in that manner, with that look. Even Joan had believed him when he promised to help Channing. Joan, who, for some curious reason, did not love him. And yet he had a curious feeling that now Yvonne did not believe him—that she saw quite clearly through to his thought. She dropped her lashes, however, before he could read her eyes surely.

"And what, fair sir, is to be my reward?"

"The prettiest fortune I can make you," he assured her lightly.

"But," she demurred, "with the information I have, I could so easily make my fortune for myself."

A pulse quickened in him, and the only real emotion Jerry Howard ever experienced flared up in him. The mouth lost its smile and became cruel, predatory.

"Then he really told you whether there would be a merger?"

She studied him coolly.

"What will you give me if I tell you?"

"Give you? Good heavens, what do you want? I didn't know I was paying you for the information."

She moved away from him, and, he uncomfortably felt, took the advantage of the situation with her.

"No? Well, you are paying me, Jerry—in one way or another. I am just the least bit in the world tired of spying for you—for nothing."

"That's an ugly word, Yvonne."

"It's an ugly truth. I really didn't mean to let it drop so vulgarly, Jerry, but it's such a relief sometimes to be so vulgarly truthful. Perhaps I'm not as bad as I sound. I've been useful to you, haven't I?"

"Certainly," he said warily, studying her.

"And you've no intention of—dispensing with services, now that Joan Archer has taken you on payroll?"

"Yvonne!"

"This isn't a moment for heroics, Jerry. When first delivered your ultimatum, I thought I loved too much to lose you entirely. But, on consideration, I've decided that I love you too much to lose you at all."

"What do you mean?"

"Just this: either you give up Joan Archer, as you'd be perfectly able to do when we've cleaned up on this oil proposition, or I keep Reddington Johns's confidence to myself and—our ways part now!"

For a moment a red film of anger obscured Jerry's vision. Then his habitually cool mind regained control of the situation. He saw clearly the pallor of Yvonne's drawn face, the cruel little pulse racking in her throat. Bluff! She was torn with terror lest he accept her alternative. He smiled pleasantly. She was playing into his hands.

"Very well, my dear. I'm sorry you take this attitude, but, after all, the decision rests with you. Joan has set an early date for our wedding, and I dare say my funds will last out the interval. Keep your secret!"

He expected her to throw herself into his arms with self-reproaches and protestations. He was both surprised and disconcerted when she did no such thing. Instead she smiled and patted his arm.

"My dear," she said coolly, "in all my experience I never knew a man who ran more truly to form than you do. All one needs is the key; the rest is easy. And I think—I have the key."

Her hand fell lightly on the evening paper she had thrown down when he entered. She turned it over and went on in her odd conversational manner as though this were the most casual of all casual meetings:

"This Anstruther murder is a frightful thing, isn't it? Do you suppose it will involve Joan? I see here that she has admitted recognising the man in Anstruther's room."

"Yes," said Jerry coolly; "I was very much surprised. I understood last night that she meant to keep the matter dark."

"Then she told you last night that it was Brian Channing?"

"Yes," said Jerry, and added quickly—a little too quickly—"Of course, I knew it already. I had recognised him myself."

"Oh, of course," said Yvonne. "I'd forgotten." To herself she was thinking: "He's lying." Aloud she said: "I wonder how the papers got on to the fact that Joan had recognised the burglar." She paused the fraction of a second and then made her shot: "There really wasn't any one but you who could have told them, was there?"

"Well, I didn't tell them," said Jerry brusquely. "She asked me not to, and—what business was it of mine, anyway?"

"What indeed?" purred Yvonne. "Yet, considering the fact that she fainted on recognising the man, I can conceive that it might—interest you."

Jerry flung away from her and paced the length of the room in irritation. Yvonne studied him through her lashes.

"Come! I'm not criticising you, my dear. It's nothing but sentimental foolishness in her to want to shield a—well, a probable murderer." She smiled a faint, secret smile. "And, of course, it's only sensible of you to want to clear Channing out of the way where he—can't come back. I think—really I think you were only doing a public duty to publish the fact."

He looked at her dubiously, but said nothing.

"Of course," Yvonne proceeded, "there is no doubt that it *was* Channing?"

There was a barely perceptible pause before Jerry spoke, but Yvonne's quick ear caught it.

"No doubt at all."

"You really saw him, too?"

"I saw him, too."

"Well," said Yvonne pleasantly, "that will dispense with all possible opposition to your plans, won't it?"

"By Jove," said Jerry, "you are a sport, Yvonne. I don't blame you for getting upset, but I knew, when you'd had time to think it over, you'd be reasonable."

Yvonne threw back her red head and laughed.

"Funny how, when a man says that, he means: 'I knew you'd agree with me.'"

Jerry dropped down beside her on the divan and took her hand.

"But you do agree with me that the sensible thing to do is to make sure of the Fortescue millions?"

She evaded his question deftly.

"Do you think that you were taking no risks with—the Fortescue millions when you gave away Channing to the papers?" she asked softly; then, seeing him about to protest, she hurried on: "Don't you know that Joan would throw you over in a moment if she had the slightest suspicion of what you've done?"

"You forget," he said, "that it was not I who gave that tidbit to the papers."

"You're priceless, Jerry!" She laughed delightedly, and leaning over patted his hand. "Leave this business of Reddington Johns to me," she said gently, "I've always been your friend, my dear."

He went away satisfied a few minutes later. But Yvonne sat where he had left her, and her face wore again that oddly calculating look. Presently she rose and took the telephone from under its fluted shade. Bending to it with a pouncing movement that suited the barbaric quality of her, she gave Reddington Johns's number. It was high time for her to have it out with Mr. Johns.

As she waited for it, however, she was not thinking of that. She was trying to recollect whether a certain charming young man, whom she had recently met and flirted with at dinner, was on the staff of the *Globe* or the *Sphere*. She was fairly sure it was the *Sphere*. And it was that newspaper that had carried the paragraph about Joan's admission that it was Channing whom she recognised in Anstruther's apartment. She seemed to remember, now she thought of it, that the young man had left the party about eleven o'clock to go on duty. She glanced at the little clock on the mantel and then, still holding the receiver in one hand, rang with the other for the butler.

Just then she got her number. An unknown voice at the other end of the 'phone said:

"Fontenoy Club."

"Mr. Johns, please."

While she waited, she looked up and saw Harper standing in the doorway. He was a big, stalwart fellow; one would, had he not been so impeccably the butler, have taken him for a promising pugilist. Yvonne looks at him for a moment appreciatively.

"I shall need the car presently, Harper," she said briefly. "About eleven. Oh, and I am expecting visitor—in half an hour or so. When he comes, bring him in here and wait in the pantry. Close the door, listen closely for the bell. If I ring, come at once, do you understand? Immediately!" She turned away, adding with grim meaning: "I may need you."

"Yes, madame." Harper permitted himself the faintest of hopeful grins, and withdrew.

For a moment Yvonne sat drumming her fingers on the desk. Then Johns's voice came to her distantly, distinctly. Harper, lingering for a moment in the hall before retiring to his pantry, smiled with some amusement as he listened to her crisp sentences. He opined that the fellow at the other end of the 'phone must be having a bad moment.

Yvonne herself opened her door to Reddington Johns fifteen minutes later. She had, in the interval, changed into street dress, but she looked no whit less the barbaric queen. There was something venomous, something deadly in her jade-green eyes, in the metallic glint of her flaming hair, the ivory pallor of her skin. The line of her mouth, accentuated with a scarlet stain, was predatory, cruel. Studying Johns under the brilliant lamplight in the foyer,

she saw that he was shaken beneath his assurance, and her
courage rose. Deadly as she knew him to be, she held the
whip hand. She wasted no time in amenities. She led the
way directly into the drawing-room and motioned him to
a chair.

"I've decided," she said in a cool, composed voice, "to
allow you to handle my stock to-morrow. I don't know
whether there is to be a merger or not, but you do, and
you will know how to play it to the best advantage. Of
course, the more you clean up the better I'll be pleased,
but I don't advise you to risk too much because, you see,
it would be so unfortunate—for you—if I were to lose."

There was a murderous gleam in Johns's eyes.

"Just precisely what game are you playing?" he demanded. "I'm quite aware that, for some time past, you've been
trying to hypnotise me into handing you out some free
information about that merger, but I thought I'd given
you clearly to understand that there was nothing doing. If
you want some one to handle your stock to-morrow, go to
a broker, I'm not in the habit—"

"Quite so," murmured Yvonne sweetly. "But fortunately
habits can be broken, and I'm sure you'll break this one
for me. You see, as I hinted over the 'phone, I happen to
know that the man Higgins, sent up for murder five years
ago, had been pardoned and is in New York."

"Why not? It was announced in every New York newspaper. What then? What has all this to do with me?"

"That you'll have to explain, of course," said Yvonne
gently. "Doubtless you can explain why, at five o'clock
this afternoon, in the Tylers' library, you and Robinson
Tyler paid Higgins twenty-five thousand?"

She thought Johns was going to faint. He grasped the
chair back to steady himself.

"You're insane—inventing the wildest nonsense."

"Not at all. It is quite simple, really. Miriam Tyler and I, as you know, have been intimate for years. I had gone to tea with her and was waiting in the hall while the maid went up to announce me when I overheard voices in the library. I was able to hear quite clearly what you were saying. And the maid would be able to identify Higgins. I do not, of course, know your motive, but I dare say the police—"

As he sprang toward her, her hand touched the bell on the table beside her. Before the sound died away Harper stood in the doorway.

"Show Mr. Johns out, Harper," she said quietly; and then to Johns: "I'll see that you have my stock before opening time to-morrow." As he was going out, she stopped him. "By the way let me know as soon as possible how things go, for, if all goes well, I'm planning to—to go abroad for an indefinite stay. In fact, I doubt"—she hesitated, watching him closely—"I shall ever come back to this country." Then she added with a little laugh: "Especially if you make me enough to buy a palace on the Riviera."

For a moment they studied each other. Then Johns nodded shortly.

"We'll have to see what can be done."

As the door clicked behind him she drew a long breath. So far so good. She fancied he would not make her any trouble. But there was still something more to be done before she slept that night. She called Harper and told him that she was ready for the car. On being informed that it was already waiting, she went into her own room, put on hat and wrap, and picked up her gloves. In the hall she paused.

"On second thoughts," she said, "I think you might come with me, Harper." She was thinking of a certain nasty look in Johns's eyes.

"Yes, madame."

She had herself driven downtown to the offices of the
Sphere. Here, after a little inquiry, she found her way to
the reporters' room and sent her card in to Mr. Spencer.
In a few moments a young man came out whom she recognised as her vis-a-vis at dinner. It was clear that he, too,
remembered her, for he came eagerly, with a fine flush of
excitement on his face.

"By Jove, this is fine! What can I do for you, Mrs.
Lorimer?"

She smiled at him ravishingly.

"I have a rather extraordinary request to make. Perhaps
it will be quite impossible for you to get me the information I want . . ."

This piqued his professional pride. He was a very young
reporter, and he hated to admit that anything was beyond
him.

"Try me!" he suggested, smiling. "Want me to burgle
the office safe for you?"

She laughed.

"Well, not quite. But I do want you to steal something
for me. I'm very anxious to find out—for a purely personal
reason—who it was who 'tipped you off,' as you say, to the
fact that Miss Archer recognised Mr. Channing last night.
Would that be possible?"

The young man looked doubtful.

"I'll see what I can do," he said. "One of the boys told
me Caruthers got the tip in a note, and—"

"A note?" cried Yvonne. "Oh, I'd love—I'd just love to
have it."

"Well, I don't know why not," said Spencer thoughtfully.
"It may be on his desk. Wait a moment. I'll see what I can
do."

In ten minutes he came back and handed her a note in
a blank envelope.

"For the love of Mike, don't ever tell where you got it. I'd be fired sure if it came out."

"I won't," she promised. "And if you're interested in knowing what I want it for, come up to tea some afternoon soon and I'll tell you the whole story."

"I'll be there," promised Spencer, who found the lady much to his taste. He stood staring after her as she moved gracefully away down the dingy hall.

"Gee, some baby!" murmured a snub-nosed office-boy behind him, and began to hum the first bars of a certain popular song: "Yes, sir, she's my baby!"

Spencer turned briskly and made a dive for the boy's head. Missing that agile youngster by about five feet, he resumed his ruffled dignity and stalked back to the reporters' room.

In her car speeding homeward, Yvonne spread out the note on her knees and smiled as she saw Jerry's well-known handwriting. Her face wore the look of one who finds a theory borne out by the facts. She debated briefly whether it was too late to go at once to Joan Archer, but, seeing that it was after twelve, decided to postpone her visit until the morning.

She leaned back luxuriously as the car sped up through the deserted streets. Things were going very smoothly— very smoothly, indeed.

14

When Reddington Johns left Mrs. Lorimer that Wednesday evening he was in a mood to commit any indiscretion. His temper, once it slipped its leash, was both venomous and uncontrollable. He was completely at its mercy. His rage whipped his taut nerves with a thousand separate stings. As he flung off down the Avenue he had no clear idea except to get in touch with Robinson Tyler and arrange to end the persecution which seemed to be closing on them both.

By the time he had walked a dozen blocks, however, sanity began to return to him. It occurred to him that, under the circumstances, it might be just as well not to go direct to Tyler's house. He did not, after all, know how many people were in Mrs. Lorimer's confidence. He paused on a corner and looked about him. Across the street was a drug-store. He went in, shut himself up in the 'phone booth, and called Tyler's number.

Twenty minutes later he strolled into a little French restaurant on Lexington Avenue, picked out a table in a far corner where he could command a view of the room and the door into the street, and sat down on the upholstered settle that ran around the wall. Except for Madame, sitting behind the little counter near the door, and a waiter languidly serving supper to a bored-looking couple on the other side of the room, the place was deserted.

Presently the waiter strolled over and laid a menu card on the red-and-white checked tablecloth of Johns.

"I'm waiting for a friend," Johns told him. "I won't order just yet."

"We close at midnight," the waiter stated coldly.

"That's all right: he'll be here at any—"

At this moment Robinson Tyler came in from the street. He nodded coolly to Johns and sat down opposite him across the little table. They ordered something and the waiter departed, still languidly.

"Well," said Tyler, in a flat voice that had less carrying power than a whisper, "what's up?"

He leaned back, lighting a cigarette and staring thoughtfully at his friend through the smoke. There was something formidable in him as he leaned there at ease, his lids drooped over blank eyes that had a strange, opaque look as though a film had been drawn over them. For all the sleekness of black hair and boots, the effeminate cut of the attire that gave him the appearance of a too well-groomed lounge lizard, he gave the impression of being far more deadly than Johns. Perhaps it was the absolute lack of humanity in his cold, dark face.

Johns told the story of his interview with Mrs. Lorimer, a recital punctuated with pauses while the waiter brought their sandwiches and white wine. At last the waiter withdrew to the other side of the room and left them to themselves.

Tyler rubbed out his cigarette slowly and thoughtfully. His gesture conveyed, oddly, something of the character of the man, calculating, ruthless. Presently he said:

"Just how much of our conversation did Mrs. Lorimer overhear?"

"Enough," said Johns bitterly, "to know that we paid the Scragger twenty-five thousand."

"Does she know what for?"

"I'm not sure," murmured Johns, his eye on the waiter. "She didn't, at any rate, put it into so many words."

"You should," stated Tyler coldly, "have found that out."

"How could I? If she didn't really know, but was only guessing, I'd just have given the show away."

Tyler shrugged and returned to his consideration of the tablecloth.

"I think," he said at last, "that you were just a trifle hasty all along the line. I begin to see, now that I've had time to think over it, that there were a good many weak points in Miriam's story."

"It's a fine time to think of it—now," commented Johns disgustedly.

Tyler paid no heed to him.

"For instance, she told me that she overheard a conversation between you and me, in my library, five years ago, which betrayed her to the fact that we 'knew something about' the murder of old Clinton McGuire. I didn't question the statement at first because I remembered very well that on one occasion we had begun to talk on that subject, and I had a sudden feeling that there was a third person in the room and changed the subject abruptly. I remember very clearly the feeling I had. But nothing happened and I forgot about it until Miriam recalled it to me yesterday.

"Well, I've been thinking it over, and I don't believe we said anything on that occasion that could possibly have given more than the barest suspicion of a hint to an eavesdropper."

"How can you tell?" demanded Johns. "That was five years ago. You can forget a lot in five years. I'm sure *I* couldn't swear to just what was said."

Tyler drew a thoughtful ring on the tablecloth with a prong of his fork.

"I've something more reliable than my memory to go by," he said softly. Until three years ago—two years after she overheard this conversation, mind you—Miriam and I were on very good terms. In fact, we didn't quarrel until she found out about Kitty Thomas." He grinned. "And even then she had nothing to say about McGuire. It was only when she wanted to go off with Anstruther that *that* came out."

"I don't see what that proves," asserted Johns. "Or at least it only proves that when she overheard the conversation Miriam was still in love with you. When woman's in love—"

But Tyler interrupted him sharply.

"We're not talking about women—in general," he reminded his friend. "We're talking about Miriam. You've got to remember," he said dryly, "that she's one of these 'good women.' If she'd really believed, at that time, that I had had any hand in bumping off old McGuire—or in getting the Scragger to bump him off, she would not have touched me with a ten-foot pole. She's that kind. No, the truth of the matter is—and I'll take my oath to it—she wanted to force my hand yesterday. She wanted to make me agree to her terms, and I, like a fool, fell into her trap. She stampeded me into believing that she really knew something about that old affair. But she didn't, Red. She couldn't have. And consequently she couldn't have passed any information on—to any one else."

Johns grew slightly pale.

"Then you think—"

"I think," Tyler repeated softly, "that we have been just a trifle hasty."

Johns's face looked rather green in the glaring light.

"Here! pull yourself together," Tyler commanded. He pushed the wine glass into the other's nerveless hand, and waited while he drank it off. Then he went on implacably: "What is it Mrs. Lorimer wants you to do for her?"

Johns told him, his confidence returning as anger surged through him again.

Tyler considered for a moment.

"Well," he said at last, "why not? Let's take it she means what she says and nothing more. You make her enough money to live comfortably abroad, and she goes over to France—and stays there. I think you'd better take her at her word, Red."

"I'm hanged if I will," said Johns violently.

"You'll be hanged," Tyler reminded him dryly, "if you don't. Or—no; it isn't hanging in this state."

Johns clung to the table edge.

"If you think I had anything to do with—"

But Tyler cut him short, His tone commanded attention, yet he spoke so softly that no one ten feet away could have heard a word.

"Listen to me, Red," he said. "It's no good our thinking anything. How far we may be involved in the matter you speak of, neither of us, as a matter of fact, knows. I have my own ideas on the subject, I confess," and he looked at his friend with cruel eyes that seemed to penetrate to his very soul. "I've no doubt you have yours. But we've got to remember that, as far as the police are concerned, we both have motives for wishing Anstruther out of the way—that is, if they can induce Miriam and Mrs. Lorimer to talk."

"*You* have a motive," Johns interrupted sullenly. "Every one knows he was Miriam's lover."

Tyler's look was murderous.

"And *you* have a motive," he said softly. "If the police get at Miriam and hear her story about McGuire."

"We were both in on that," blustered Johns.

"My dear Red!" Tyler's manner reproved his heat. "If we keep our heads, there is no reason why either of us should be in on anything. As far as that goes, motive or no motive, we can both establish our innocence of Anstruther's death. We've both got air-tight alibis."

They glared at each other, testing, feeling each other out like antagonists in some primitive jungle, circling warily.

"And furthermore," Tyler went on, "I'll make a shrewd guess that the Scragger has an air-tight alibi, too. All the same," he added slowly, "the fewer questions asked, the better. Whatever the truth of the matter is, we don't want them to find it out. I think we'd better square Mrs. Lorimer."

For a long moment they stared into each other's eyes, beast fronting beast. Then Johns shrugged.

"Why not?" he said as Tyler had said before. "In that case, I'll get on. It might be just as well for us not to be seen together any more than is necessary." He rose, and stood looking down at the other man. "I hope," he said courteously, "that your alibi is a good one." Then he took up his hat and departed.

Tyler sat looking after him, an unpleasant grin on his thin lips. He wondered how much Johns knew and much he suspected. He thanked God piously for his own shrewd and clever brain.

15

The morning papers carried the news of Channing's arrest. The prisoner himself, reading the front-page article over an early and appetising breakfast, sent in at the express order of Mr. Ormsberry from a nearby restaurant, wondered which man, of all the thousands that surrounded him, was reading that item with a sense of relief, of release from terror. He noted that the evidence leading to his arrest was only sketchily touched on, and the possible motive for his connection with the case was not mentioned at all. It was hinted that the police knew a great deal more than they disclosed.

The gravity of his situation could not fail to impress a man of Channing's intelligence, but his face bore no trace of strain or sleeplessness. He looked vigorous and alert. It is true his heart contracted with pain when he thought of Joan's suffering when she should hear of his arrest, but, mingled with the pain, was an exultant joy that she could still suffer for his sake.

It was in this frame of mind that Ormsberry found him. That dapper gentleman looked immaculate as ever, despite the hour, and the fact that nothing but a cold plunge, a rapid change, and a hasty breakfast intervened between the morning and a sleepless night. Channing had been taken into the attorney's room for the interview, and the two men shook hands cordially.

"Speck will be along shortly to arrange bail for you," Ormsberry told the young man. But Channing would have none of it.

"Nonsense, my dear fellow. I'm quite comfortable as I am."

Ormsberry stared at him.

"You don't mean that you're going to refuse bail?"

"I mean that you're going to see that I'm refused bail. Look here! I thought one of the big ideas of this dramatic incarceration was to give our murderous friend the impression that the police believed they had actually nailed the guilty party. A fat chance you would have of making him believe that, if you let me out of jail. Not much! I'm not striking any heroic pose, or anything like that. The only way I'm going to be cleared of this mess is for you to find the man who really killed Anstruther. Well, go ahead and find him. I'll stay here until you do."

Ormsberry shrugged.

"You win," he said. And then for a minute he busied himself quite unnecessarily with some papers which he took from his pocket. If the truth must be told, he—the case-hardened Mr. Ormsberry—dared not, for the moment, trust his voice. There was something about this whole affair that got under his skin, he told himself crossly. He was afflicted with poignant and painful memories of Joan Archer. He knew too well the peril in which this youngster before him, with his blind, romantic courage, was standing. He became very businesslike.

"Well," he said, "I've been through every paper in Anstruther's rooms—Hennessey and I spent the night at it!—and there's not a thing, so far as I can tell, that bears the slightest relation to the Fortescue case except this, which doesn't get us anywhere. I found the clipping in a notebook he sometimes carried round with him, to judge by the worn cover. Here it is."

Brian bent over the slip eagerly. It was dated the year before.

CROSS-EXAMINATION OF ESTELLE FORTESCUE

Q.—As I understand your statement, on the morning of the murder you arrived, on the *Kent,* from England, and went directly to your brother's house? *A.*—Yes.

Q.—And within a few minutes of your arrival you quarreled with your brother? *A.*—Yes.

Q.—On what ground? What was the subject of your quarrel? *A.*—I have already answered that question.

Judge Jackson.—The question is allowed.

Q.—I merely want to be quite clear in the matter. Why did you quarrel with Mr. Fortescue? *A.*—I quarreled with him because of the position he was permitting Joan Archer to assume in his house.

Q.—And what was that? *A.*—He was allowing her to take the position of mistress of the house—a part quite unsuited to a young girl. I assured him of this and he lost his temper—he was always irascible—and told me he knew his own business best.

Q.—And for that reason you left his house? *A.*—Yes.

Q.—Although you had lived there for many years, you left because he wanted to make his daughter the mistress of his house? *A.*—She was not his daughter, although she disliked it very much when any one recalled the fact.

At this point the clipping was cut off short. Channing looked up blankly.

"What do you make of that?"

Ormsberry shrugged and put the little book back into his pocket.

"The point is, what did *he* make of it?"

"It's evident that he didn't feel that it reflected on Joan," murmured Brian thoughtfully, "for he always maintained that Joan was innocent."

"Well," said the detective, "if he felt it reflected on Miss Fortescue, he was barking up the wrong tree, for I did my best to puncture her alibi last year, and it was absolutely air-tight."

"But it was queer—her going off like that, just because of a tiff about Joan," said Brian thoughtfully.

"It's my impression," insisted Ormsberry, "that Miss Fortescue is capable of much queerer things than that. It's my guess that she's got a devil of a temper. I wouldn't put it beyond her to have murdered her brother, except for the fact that she really was in Philadelphia at the time the crime was pulled off. The police had affidavits not only from the friends with whom she was staying, but from three guests—none of whom she had ever met before, so there could be no motive for collusion—who came into dinner and spent the evening. And to cap the climax, there was a maid who swore she took ice water to her room at twelve-thirty, and saw her at that time. And the doctors agreed that Fortescue was killed between eleven and twelve."

"Then why did Anstruther keep that clipping?"

"We'll have to know more about it before we can guess that. I'm on my way to headquarters now, to meet Hennessey and see if he's been able to round up Anstruther's ex-secretary. He may be able to throw some light on this for us."

"Did you get in touch with Anstruther's editor?"

"Yes, but he wasn't much help. He says Anstruther told him he was working on a mystery story founded on the Fortescue case, and promised it to him on the day he was murdered, but the story never turned up. I've set the post office to tracing it, but it's my bet that it will never be found. There's absolutely no doubt left in my mind that that's the story Anstruther was working on the day he was killed, and that it has been destroyed."

"Well," said Channing cheerfully, "there's still, the secretary. He is sure to know something about it."

But when Ormsberry got to headquarters he found a disconsolate Hennessey waiting for him. Roberts, Anstruther's ex-secretary, had left his lodgings in Newark the night before and had not been seen since. It seemed quite clear that he had disappeared!

The news of Channing's arrest affected a dozen people in as many different ways. Estelle Fortescue read it with pleased surprise. She had never ceased to hate Joan Archer. Miriam Tyler read it with the bitter rejoicings of satisfied revenge. Yvonne Lorimer, dressed for the street as she ate her early breakfast, perused it quietly, as something she had quite expected to find among the morning's news. Gregory Sommers studied it with amazement. Reddington Johns unfolded his paper with unsteady hands and laid it down with the look of a man reprieved.

Jerry Howard, waking later, read the news in bed. He reached for his bedside 'phone and made two calls. The first was faintly peremptory and mentioned that he would be lunching at his club at one o'clock. The second number was Joan Archer's. When he got the connection, however, Joan's maid said she had already gone out.

"The deuce she has! Well, tell her Mr. Howard called, and will call again." He rang off and returned to a more careful reading of the article.

The paper had been brought to Joan on her breakfast tray. One hurried glance had sent the fresh colour from her face. As she read, her horror deepened. The depression of the year before, which she had only begun to throw off, returned to her a hundredfold, for it was not now her own security that was threatened, but Brian's—Brian, from whom, for some insane reason no longer very clear to her, she had separated herself.

Her instinct was to go to him, but she had learned caution in a very hard school, and she did not know how she might involve him by such hasty espousal of his cause. She was a marked person wherever she went and the mystery still surrounding her past shadowed her most casual move.

But action of some sort was imperative. She must see Mr. Speck and make sure that everything possible was being done for Brian.

She was dressed for the street and on the way downstairs when a maid brought her Yvonne Lorimer's card with a hasty word, "Important," scribbled across it. But for that she would have excused herself, but some premonition caused her to direct that Mrs. Lorimer be shown into her sitting-room.

Perhaps even Yvonne was touched by the look Joan's pale, strained face; perhaps it was only consummate acting. At any rate, her glance softened and she took her hostess's proffered hand in both her own.

"You poor child! You must not worry so! I'm sure everything will be all right."

"You're very good," murmured Joan, "but—"

"But it isn't my business?" interpolated Mrs. Lorimer. "My dear, it is my business this far: I know positively that it was Jerry Howard who told the police that you had recognised Channing in Anstruther's apartment, and who sent the reporter to you last night."

Joan shook her head gently. She remembered gossip of Mrs. Lorimer's regard for Jerry.

"You're mistaken, I'm sure. Jerry was most kind. Mr. Channing himself went to the police."

"I knew, of course, that you wouldn't take my word for it," Yvonne went on quietly, "so I stopped late last night at the office of the *Sphere*. A reporter friend of mine gave me the note that Mr. Caruthers received by messenger yesterday afternoon—from Jerry."

Joan read the proffered note and gravely returned it. Her voice when she spoke was oddly unlike her own.

"It does not matter." She turned away, and after a moment spoke over her shoulder, "I suppose—in doing this—you serve your own ends. Nevertheless, I am grateful to you. But I wish—you'd—go!"

She hardly heard Yvonne's quiet departure. Her world was indeed crumbling round her. Whom was she to trust? In all the world, it seemed to her at that moment, there was no one. And yet, strangely, she was conscious of release, of a lightening of the spirit. It remained only to write a few words to Jerry.

She wrote them in her precise schoolgirl hand, ordered her car, and drove downtown. On the way she stopped at a corner mail box and dropped into it the note breaking her engagement to Jerry Howard.

16

In Charles Edward Speck's dignified offices on lower Broadway, Joan Archer was a frequent and popular visitor. The old clerk in the outer office had cause to remember her for many secret benefactions, and he greeted her warmly as she stepped out of the elevator a few minutes later.

"No, miss," he replied in answer to her question; "he isn't engaged now. You can go right in." Every employee in the office was aware of the "old man's" partiality for this daughter of his old friend, and red tape was automatically abandoned for her benefit.

So it happened that Joan was a witness of a highly undignified scene which was taking place in Mr. Speck's office at the moment of her entrance. She had knocked softly and, hearing Mr. Speck's voice, had assumed that he was giving her permission to enter. She opened the door and stood amazed.

Mr. Speck, in his shirt sleeves, was kneeling on the floor, pummeling in a highly scientific manner a punching bag which hung on a metal frame protruding from an open closet door. Opposite him stood the Admiral, likewise in shirt sleeves, his hair tousled, his freckled countenance flushed with exercise and excitement, his absorbed gaze

fixed on his employer. Neither of the pair was conscious
of an audience.

"There," said Mr. Speck, sitting somewhat gingerly
back on his heels. "That's the way it goes. Now you try it."

The bag had evidently been hung for the Admiral's
benefit at the proper distance from the floor to suit his
height. At Speck's command the boy charged in, attacking
the bag with such ludicrously accurate imitation of the
little lawyer that Joan, in spite of her grief and anxiety,
could not restrain a laugh. The two looked up and saw her.

"Well, by Jove," cried Mr. Speck, staring. Then he remembered his manners and got to his feet. "You've caught
us fairly, my dear," he said, reaching for his coat. "'Ten-
tion, Admiral. Ladies aboard."

"Yes, sir," said the imp, and slipped into his jacket in a
manner so studiously copied from his employer that once
more Joan had all she could do to restrain her merriment.

Mr. Speck looked at her with twinkling eyes over the
boy's head.

"The Admiral is going to be a detective when he grows
up, and we are laying the—er—groundwork," he informed
her gravely. "Put the ball away," he said to the boy. Then
he turned to Joan. "Now, my dear, sit down and tell me
what is wrong." He swung his desk chair toward her and
sat looking at her with kind, comprehending eyes. "It's
Brian, of course," he said when she hesitated. "We're doing everything we can for him, Joan. He asked me to tell
you not to worry about him."

"You've seen him then?" she asked eagerly.

"This morning."

"Have you arranged bail for him?"

"That was my intention," said the lawyer, "but he
wouldn't have it. He thinks if he is locked up in jail the
real murderer will be more likely to show his hand." Mr.
Speck's private conviction was that, the evidence against

Brian being what it was, he would not in any case have been released on bail, but this he did not mention, noting the girl's strained look.

Joan sprang to her feet and moved about the room like one who finds it impossible to sit still. Neither paid the slightest attention to the Admiral, busy returning the punching bag to its closet. Neither noticed the extremely slow and methodical way in which the boy performed this office.

"But they can't hold Brian," cried the girl desperately. "There can't be anything against him—nothing but the glimpse Jerry and I had of the man in the apartment, and that was so quick, so uncertain. Of course I know now that I was mistaken—and I'm sure Jerry didn't recognise the man at all—he just said he did. Do you know, by the way, that it was Jerry who gave that away to the papers? After he promised me he'd do everything he could to help Brian?"

"I was quite sure of it," said Mr. Speck. And then, in response to her amazed look, he told her about Howard's visit to his office the morning after the murder. "Are you really engaged to him?" he asked at length.

"No," stormed the girl furiously. "Of course not. As soon as Mrs. Lorimer told me that it was Jerry who had told the *Sphere* about recognising Brian, I—"

"Mrs. Lorimer?" cried the lawyer. "Where does she come in?"

Joan flushed.

"She seems to be—interested in Jerry. But what she said was quite true. She showed me Jerry's letter to the paper. As soon as she had gone I wrote to Jerry and broke my engagement. I don't know now why I ever got engaged to him—except that I was so—so lonely." Tears were very close now, but she blinked them resolutely away.

The Admiral stared at her with bright, excited eyes. Copying Mr. Speck in all things, he found it very easy to fall in with his devotion to Miss Archer, particularly when he remembered the shiny and efficient pair of skates that young lady had bestowed on him the preceding Christmas. Now he was divided between sympathy for her obvious distress and excitement at an idea that had just materialised in his mind—an idea closely allied to his reigning ambition to be a detective when he grew up. He listened closely to what was being said while he pretended to be still busy shutting away the punching bag.

"I want to help Brian," Joan was crying desperately. "I want everything to be done for him that can be done. You must tell me exactly what they have against him. You must tell me everything and not hold things back for fear of worrying me."

Mr. Speck looked at her closely; then, as though his mind were made up, he nodded.

"Very well, my dear," he said briskly. "Sit down and compose yourself and I'll tell you the whole thing—although I'll probably get the very deuce from Brian when he hears I've done it."

Joan managed to respond with a pale smile.

"Well," she said, "at any rate he can't prevent your telling me."

The Admiral flattened himself against the wall, scarcely daring to breathe. Unless they turned their heads they could not see him. He hoped they would not turn—yet.

Briefly, in his most vivid court-room manner, the little lawyer sketched the progress of events, exaggerating nothing and omitting nothing. When he had finished Joan sat for a long time staring thoughtfully at the floor.

"Then they think," she said at last, "that Brian might have killed Mr. Anstruther to suppress his solution of the mystery about father's death?"

"Yes, my dear, that's it."

"Why don't they get hold of this man Roberts, Mr. Anstruther's secretary? Surely he'd be able to tell what the missing story was about."

"So we all thought, my dear. But Ormsberry called me a short time ago and told me that Roberts has gone—disappeared."

"They can find him," she cried.

"They've put out a drag net for him all over the country."

She wrung her hands impatiently.

"If Brian could prove he had no connection whatever with father's death, this case against him would fall down?"

"It would certainly be materially weakened. But, unfortunately, Brian can't prove an alibi on the night your father was killed." There was another painful silence, which Mr. Speck broke almost unwillingly. "And we must face the fact, my dear, that, after all this time, and the exhaustive investigation that was made last year, it is very unlikely that your father's murderer will be found."

"Unless," said Joan, and her voice was hardly more than a gasping whisper, "unless he—or she—should confess."

Some implication in that gasping voice reached Mr. Speck's nerves before it reached his brain; it pulled him to his feet and left him staring down at that slender, shaking figure; it left him with an icy band around the heart.

"Is it really so," Joan's curious, dry, gasping voice proceeded, "that a person once acquitted of a crime—cannot be tried again?"

Mr. Speck did not answer. He found the floor oddly unsteady under his feet, and the firm edge of his desk on which he leaned seemed for the moment unsubstantial. But presently he was able to say in his accustomed manner:

"Of course, it would help Brian if the person who killed your father confessed, but only if it were some one in whom Brian had no personal interest—whose name he could have no motive in defending."

Again that horrible, nerve-racking pause. Then Joan's new voice:

"I see. Yes, of course you are right. It would have to be some one—in whom he had no—personal interest."

"My dear," said Mr. Speck, and he sat down suddenly, "what we need at this point is a swig of good pre-war."

The Admiral, sensing the psychological moment, made his reappearance on the scene with a squat bottle and two glasses.

"There are," said Mr. Speck, when he had duly ministered to the glasses, "times when it is advisable to wink at the law. This is one of them. Your health, my dear!"

The whisky brought a faint colour into the girl's face.

"Thank you," she said faintly. She looked apologetically at her old friend. "I'll try not to lose my head. But I must see Brian. You must see him and arrange it for me. You will, won't you? Please say you will."

Mr. Speck looked at her with a fondness he made no attempt to conceal.

"I'll do my best, Joan," he assured her.

"And we've got to find Roberts," cried the girl. "Promise me that you'll spare no expense to find him He's our best hope."

Mr. Speck promised.

Neither paid any attention to the Admiral, stealing from the room with the portentous gravity of a miniature Sherlock Holmes on his freckled countenance.

17

It will be remembered that Mr. Ormsberry, with his inveterate habit of investigating everything he did not understand, had requested that headquarters should put one of their good men on the trail of Jerry Howard. The detective had no great hopes that anything of moment would come of this precaution, but he had not been able to think of a reasonable explanation of Howard's behaviour on the night of Anstruther's murder and the morning following, and Mr. Ormsberry had an insatiable curiosity about things he did not understand. Wherefore, Plainclothes-man Reilly was put on the job.

The first twenty-four hours produced nothing of interest, and the first day's report included little more than Jerry Howard's lunch with Joan on Henri's roof and his visit to Mrs. Lorimer's in the evening. Nor did the second day—Thursday—begin any more encouragingly. Plainclothes-man Reilly, lounging in a doorway opposite the block of exclusive bachelor apartments that housed Mr. Howard, yawned extensively and cursed the stupidity that had led him to embrace so unadventurous a career. And then, promptly on the stroke of one, Mr. Howard issued forth.

Reilly, instantly alert, dropped inconspicuously into his wake, but once again disappointment awaited him. His prey, it appeared, was bound around the corner to the Fontenoy Club for lunch. Thither the officer followed him and fell into discreet conversation with the door man.

And then suddenly, quite without warning, one of those little incidents occurred that test the quality of the inspired man hunter. So slight a thing it was that only some sixth sense, that ever-watchful instinct that made Reilly a quiet celebrity in his own field, enabled him to grasp his opportunity before it passed him by.

The door man was called inside to the desk, and at that exact instant a leisurely messenger boy ascended the steps with a letter in his hand. Reilly, acting on some obscure impulse, with a quick glance over his shoulder, opened the glass door and held out his hand.

"Who for?" he asked, and glanced at the address "I'll sign for it."

Clearly the boy took him for a person in authority. He presented his book and departed. The little man, again assuring himself that he was unobserved, stepped across the street to a cigar store on the corner and drew behind him the door of a telephone booth. Then, with infinite solicitude, he opened the flap of the carelessly sealed envelope. Inside he found a typewritten note, unsigned, and several folded bills of large denomination. The note puzzled him. He read it three times and then copied it carefully on the back of a dirty envelope.

> "I enclose bills covering in full my indebtedness following on our poker game of Tuesday last. As you justly observe, it's no use trying to bluff the man with four aces. However, I give you fair warning—and you are in a position to know that I am a man of my word— that I will not play with you again. This settles *in full.*"

"Whew!" The little man whistled softly. "I should say it would!" He stared open-mouthed at the figures on the bills. Then he sealed up the note and enclosure, walking up Madison Avenue to a Western Union station, and waited until he saw a boy go out again with the letter. Then he returned to his post.

Thus it was the unsuspicious Mr. Howard made that afternoon a sizable addition to his bank balance.

That same evening, Mr. Ormsberry, sitting over a late dinner solicitously served to him in his comfortable sitting-room by Johnson, his pluperfect valet and house man, painstakingly studied the evening papers. A faint breeze blew in through the wide windows overlooking Gramercy Park and carried the smell of green growing things, but the detective's usual epicurean pleasure in these delicate nuances of sensation, and in the modest luxury of his surroundings, was, on this occasion, conspicuously absent. So absorbed was he that he positively overlooked an exquisite chicken in aspic, until Johnson's horrified cough recalled him to himself.

Seeing that his master momentarily laid aside the papers and directed his attention to his dinner, Johnson ventured another faint cough and said gently:

"There was a young person to see you this afternoon, sir—a young boy—about twelve years old I should say, sir."

"To see me?" cried Mr. Ormsberry, amazed.

"Yes, sir. He said he would return, sir."

"What name?"

"Well, sir," Johnson hesitated and looked, actually, a little embarrassed. "I asked his name, sir, and he said, very haughty like: 'In our profession—Mr. Ormsberry's and mine—we don't use names any more than we can help. Tell him a friend called. That's it—a friend.'"

The detective laughed heartily and helped himself to chicken in aspic.

"Some kid that's been reading Sherlock Holmes," he surmised.

"Yes, sir," agreed Johnson.

Mr. Ormsberry returned to his reading, frowning over the spread page. Scare heads screamed across the eight columns. There had been a minor panic on the Street, temporarily driving to second place the Anstruther affair. A rumour had gotten about that an expected merger between several large oil companies had fallen through. There had been heavy selling and mysteriously steady, scattered buying at almost nothing. The stock had fallen thirty points, and when, just before closing, the announcement was made that the merger was an accomplished fact an almost hysterical mob, sure of nothing but heavy losses, began to be aware that somewhere, somehow, a fortune had been made—by whom it was not quite certain. In the later editions it became clear that it was Joseph Kron, president of Heron Oil who had staged the coup; and that Reddington Johns, said to be his only personal friend and intimate, had also been in on the ground floor and had made a neat fortune for himself and for some mysterious third party whose name was not mentioned.

Mr. Ormsberry laid down the paper and picked up the reports that had come in from his operatives during the day. He flicked through them and saw that Hennessey had gotten a confirmation from Archibald Blake, employed by the White Cross Line, of Sommers's statement that Anstruther had taken two passages for England on the day before his death. Surely, despite her denial, that second passage had been meant for Mrs. Tyler!

He re-read carefully the report from Plainclothes-man Smith, who had been detailed to watch Robinson Tyler's house. This report had come in early in the morning. He had had no opportunity to more than glance at it, but that glance had sufficed to point his interest in Mr. Johns's financial transactions. One paragraph of the report especially caught his eye.

> "At four-forty-five Scragger Higgins came around the corner from Madison Avenue and rang the basement bell. He was admitted after a short conversation, but I could not see who admitted him. At four-fifty a man whom identified as Reddington Johns drove up in a roadster and was admitted at the front door by the maid, moment later a red-haired woman, probably Mrs. Yvonne Lorimer, drove up in a taxi. The maid saw her coming and held the door open for her. She was admitted without question. At five-ten Higgins came out at the basement entrance. I had in the meantime telephoned to headquarters and they sent Jones out. He followed Higgins when he left Tyler's house. At five-twenty Reddington Johns came out. At six-five the maid came out and hailed a taxi for Mrs. Lorimer, who got in and drove away."

"Reddington Johns and Robinson Tyler," murmured Mr. Ormsberry. "And Robinson Tyler had a possible motive for killing Anstruther, and Johns was almost the last man to see him alive. And they're hobnobbing with Scragger Higgins."

He turned up the card of the man who had trailed Higgins but found nothing to interest him in Higgins's doings of the night before. An entry made just before the report was handed in, however, caused the detective to raise his brows and pause in the middle of a bite. For it seemed that as soon as the banks were open in the morning, Scragger Higgins had sallied into the sacred precincts of the Trust and Bond and opened an account, under another name, to the amount of $25,000.

"The deuce!" exclaimed Mr. Ormsberry. "Sharp work for a man who's been out of jail a week! And there hasn't been a big robbery since then either. Blackmail!" murmured the detective, and he stared thoughtfully at the ceiling. "I think," he told himself approvingly after a moment's reflection, "I did quite right to tell Hennessey to find out whose stock it was that Reddington Johns was manipulating to-day."

He returned to a perusal of the reports, and smiled a little over Reilly's grimly worded account of the pursuit of Jerry Howard. The copy of the intercepted letter he read again and again. It might, of course, be what it purported to be, but, if it was, why did the writer omit address and signature? "Our game of Tuesday last." It was on Tuesday that Anstruther was killed.

He drank the last of his coffee. His sleepless night was making itself felt. His head was heavy and dull. He was about to summon Johnson to remove the tray when the telephone rang on the stand behind him. Coming in the absolute stillness, the sound startled him. He got suddenly to his feet, spilling newspapers and reports to the floor. He bent to retrieve them, and as he did so one of the spread pages caught his eye. The *Sphere* had fallen open at the society page and he saw prominently displayed a photograph of Estelle Fortescue.

"Darn the woman!" he exclaimed wrathfully. "Hasn't she got taste enough to keep out of the papers?" He swept the page up and glanced at the caption under the picture. "Miss Estelle Fortescue, whose engagement has recently been announced."

He flung the paper impatiently aside. In his interest in the Tyler-Johns combination he had managed to forget momentarily that wretched Fortescue affair, and here it was being thrust under his nose. Dash it all! He never could manage to quite hate the woman, for all her miserable treatment of Joan; she was such a self-tormented, wretchedly disillusioned creature.

The 'phone rang again and he picked up the receiver. It was, as he expected, Hennessey on the wire.

"Yes, sor," said Hennessey in response to his chief's query, "I got in touch with one of the clerks from Bruce and Bruce, which was the broker Mr. Johns did most of his business with. The clerk didn't want to talk at first, for it seems Johns was very particular that his doings was to be confidential, but I told him we wouldn't bring him into it."

"Quite right," murmured Mr. Ormsberry.

"Yes, sor. Well, it seems that this morning Johns appeared with power of attorney from Mrs. Yvonne Lorimer, and—"

"Mrs. Lorimer!" exclaimed Ormsberry. "H'm! Well, go on."

"He sold a large block of stock belonging to her, and then, with the cash, he began to buy Heron Oil, which had already fallen twenty points or so. He worked through half a dozen brokers. Want the names?"

"No," said Mr. Ormsberry. "Did he buy this stock in his own name or in Mrs. Lorimer's?"

"In Mrs. Lorimer's, sor. He bought a lot in his own name, too, but that was a separate transaction."

For a long moment Ormsberry ruminated. Then he said gently to his assistant:

"I rather think I'd like to know what Scragger Higgins was doing on Tuesday night, about the time Anstruther was murdered. Pick him up, if you can, and find out."

"Yes, sor."

"And you might call me back here and let me know."

"Yes, sor."

"Sorry to keep you at it so late, Hennessey."

"Glory be, sor!" cried the Irishman fervently. "Sure, 'tis not till ten of an evenin' I begin to wake up, sor."

Ormsberry chuckled as he hung up the receiver, but the smile faded as he stood thoughtfully staring out of the window. His habitual, good-humoured look was conspicuously absent; there were harsh, bitter lines at the corners of his mouth, and his eyes were steely and sharp. This was Ormsberry, the man hunter. He was thinking rapidly, fatigue forgotten in the excitement of the chase.

So his hunch had been good after all, and Yvonne Lorimer was implicated in this affair, whatever it was. Whatever it was? Why, what could it be but the Anstruther affair? He began to reason it out, step by step.

First point: Mrs. Tyler had admittedly had an affair with Anstruther—an affair which was a matter of common gossip—and had quite probably intended to sail with him shortly.

Second point: Robinson Tyler might very easily—very probably—know about it. This, thought the detective, accounts for Tyler's motive, but where does Johns come in? However, we will leave that until later.

Third point: Higgins, sentenced to Sing Sing for murder, is released a week before Anstruther's death. How he and Tyler got together is as yet undetermined but get together they did, as witness Higgins's visit to Tyler's house.

Fourth point: Reddington Johns dined with Anstruther the night he was killed and knew about the novelist's intention to go to Mrs. Mortimer's party, and probably the approximate time at which he meant to leave the club. Query: Where was Johns after he left the club, and did he get in touch with Tyler or Higgins?

Fifth point: Jerry Howard said he recognised Brian Channing in Anstruther's rooms the night of the murder, but Brian said he was not there and Mr. Ormsberry believed him. Did Howard really recognise the man in

Anstruther's rooms, and could it have been Reddington Johns or Robinson Tyler? Howard knew them both.

Sixth point: Jerry Howard, according to gossip, was very intimate with Mrs. Lorimer. Did he tell her who it was he had seen in Anstruther's apartment, and did she go to Tyler's house to blackmail Tyler and Johns? Was that the reason Johns made a fortune for her in Heron Oil? Or was she in some way actually involved in Anstruther's death? Ormsberry thought this unlikely. Blackmail was much more in her line, he felt sure.

Seventh and last point: Might not the note and money, intercepted on its way to Jerry Howard, be Howard's share of the hush money?

By Jove! Mr. Ormsberry squared his shoulders and a pleasurable thrill ran through him. This looked promising. There were lots of holes in the evidence, he realised, but on the whole things worked together pretty well. It looked—yes, it really looked as though theft might be something in it. He'd like to give that cat Yvonne Lorimer a taste of the third degree, but realised he'd have to know more before he could proceed to action. The handsome Yvonne would not talk unless he could force her hand.

How to go about it, then? His mind flashed back to Miriam Tyler and her obvious evasion when he had questioned her about her quarrel with her husband. That was the point of attack, of course. She had loved Anstruther. If he could make her see how important the point was, she would come clean.

He glanced at his watch, but just as he had made up his mind that it was not yet too late to call on Mrs. Tyler the door bell rang, and he heard Mr. Speck's excited voice in the hall.

18

The little lawyer came bustling into the room with every button fairly shining with excitement.

"Ah, there you are, my dear fellow!" he cried. "I know it's a disgraceful hour to intrude my personal affairs on you, but—"

"It is," murmured the detective, smiling, "and, furthermore, I was just going out," he added resignedly.

"But this can't wait," objected Mr. Speck. "It's that imp of mine—the Admiral—Mona Adams's boy Bill."

"What's he been up to?" asked Mr. Ormsberry, interest waking in his languid eye.

"He's run away," cried the lawyer tragically. "Run away—to be a detective!"

"What? To be a— Here, wait a minute!" Mr. Ormsberry strode to the door. "Johnson! Johnson!" he called.

The pluperfect valet appeared, his dignity deftly rebuking his master's excitement.

"Yes, sir?" murmured Johnson, with just the right shade of patronage.

"What was that boy like—the one that came here and asked for me this afternoon?"

"Fair-haired little chap, sir, very freckled; about twelve, I should judge, sir."

"That'll be him," said Ormsberry ungrammatically. "Did he say where he was going, or what he wanted to see me about?"

"Said he wanted to see you about a matter of business, sir, and that he'd be back."

"Did he say when he'd come back?"

"No, sir. He said he'd be back when he had some information to impart. Those were his words, sir—information to impart."

"Nick Carter," groaned Mr. Speck.

"I expect so," assented the detective. "That will be all, Johnson."

Johnson departed, bearing the dinner tray, and the two men were left alone.

"When did this happen?" asked Ormsberry, pitying his friend's anxious face.

"About noon. The boy went out as usual for his lunch, they tell me. I had gone to the Tombs to see young Channing. When I got back, after lunch, I found this note on my desk." And the lawyer threw a note across to his friend.

Mr. Ormsberry examined it with his habitually quick, careful scrutiny. It was enclosed in an office envelope and written laboriously on Mr. Speck's best stationery. It read as follows:

"Mr. C. E. Speck.
"Dear Sir,—I am very sorry about Miss Jone. Please tell her I am sorry about her. She says she wants Mr. Roberts. Well, I am going to get him for her. I will come back when I have some infomashun to impart.
"Very trewly yours,
"William Adams.

"P.S.—Mr. Roberts and me are frens and I know all about him, so I can get him easy."

"I thought, of course, the boy would go home this evening, but I went over there when I left the office and his mother hasn't heard from him. She's half frantic. I stayed with her for a while, thinking the little monkey would come in; but at last I notified the Newark police and came straight to you."

"What's this reference to Joan?" demanded Ormsberry, still scrutinising the note.

"Why, Joan was in the office this morning, and the boy was in and out. I suppose he heard us talking about Channing and wishing we would get in touch with Roberts."

"How does it happen the boy knows Roberts?"

"Billy was with us last year during Joan's trial, and Anstruther and his secretary were for ever in evidence. Anstruther went to court every day, you know, and he often had this Roberts with him to take notes. The boy was in and out on errands, and of course he was up to the ears in excitement about it.

"Then Roberts lives in Newark, you know, and so does Mrs. Adams. Bill used to go home on the ferry with him. Apparently Roberts chummed up with the kid. I don't know whether he hoped to get office details from the boy, or whether he just liked him. But, anyway, I gathered from Bill that they used to hold long, man-to-man conversations about the case."

Mr. Ormsberry flipped the letter over, looking at it this way and that, half resentfully, as though expecting it to impart further information.

"My guess is that the boy's all right and that we'll hear from him as soon as his pocket money gives out and he gets hungry. He's probably having the time of his life pretending to be Sherlock Holmes. At the same time—h'm!"

"Well?" demanded Speck impatiently.

"At the same time, if the kid really should happen to cross the trail of the person or persons interested in this

affair . . ." Ormsberry paused thoughtfully, and something
in his silky voice sent a shiver up the little lawyer's spine.
"I think," the detective continued more briskly, "I really
think we'd better look into this." He went to the 'phone
and gave some brisk orders.

"That's about all we can do to-night," he told his friend.

"So you won't go yourself?" asked Speck.

There's nothing I can do—yet. In fact, I doubt if anything can be done to-night. We'll have to trace the boy. I
don't know much about the hours of ferry-house employees,
but I think it's highly probable that the men on duty this
afternoon, when the kid probably crossed, have gone off by
now and we shan't be able to reach them until morning."

"Good Lord," groaned Mr. Speck. "I hate to face his
mother with nothing more than that."

Mr. Ormsberry looked with genuine pity at his friend.
"Tell her we're doing everything that's humanly possible,"
he said gently. "It will be true."

Mr. Speck wrung his hand and after a deep drink of
Scotch, which did not seem to improve his spirits much,
went away.

After he had gone the detective stood for a moment in
the centre of the room, running his hand back over his
forehead as though to clear his head of the fatigue that
seemed to lie like a tangible weight on his brain.

"Poor little shaver," he whispered.

Then he rang for Johnson.

"Let me have some more coffee at once," he ordered crisply; "a pot of it. This is going to be an all-night session."

Then he got Newark on the wire.

It was one o'clock when Hennessey called him.

"No luck yet," that officer reported. "But we can't lose
Higgins with Jones trailing him. We'll be hearin' from
Jones in the morning, and then I'll pick him up."

"All right," said Ormsberry. He had almost forgotten about Scragger Higgins. "Now go and get some sleep. In the morning I want you to run over to Newark and see if you can't put some pep into those fellows over there." And he told him about the boy's disappearance. "I want you to see that everything's done that can be done. I can't go myself. I've got a very important interview."

After Hennessey had rung off Ormsberry still sat at the phone, answering calls from the Newark police, who were stirred to action by the weight and importance of the Ormsberry name. Twice Mr. Speck called from Mrs. Adams's house, and the second time the boy's mother came herself to the phone, begging for news which Ormsberry was obliged to deny her. At three o'clock he acknowledged himself beaten for the moment and called off the chase until the morning.

Standing in his window in the soft darkness just before the summer dawn, he said to himself:

"When this case is over I am going to retire to the country and raise chickens. My heart is too doggone soft for this game." And he sighed deeply as he got wearily into bed.

19

Meanwhile, Robinson Tyler had spent the day very busily with his own affairs. In the morning, following hard upon his conversation with his dear friend Reddington Johns the night before, he had done some careful and accurate thinking. He was, as he was well aware, in serious danger from several sources and for several different reasons. He did not blink the fact that, if his complicity in the murder of old Clinton McGuire became known, through his wife's revelations, he would not escape trial even at this late date. Murder is never outlawed, and the New York law has an inconvenient way of looking at the accomplice as equal to the actual murderer in guilt. The fact that Scragger Higgins had been pardoned and released after serving five years of his sentence for second-degree murder, owing to some faint doubt as to the validity of the case against him, would not at all mitigate the severity of the law as toward himself, Robinson Tyler.

But he could not see how suspicion was to be directed against him—unless Miriam talked. The only other people aware of his connection with that old crime were the Scragger himself and Reddington Johns. The Scragger, Tyler was well aware, did not talk. Not even to save himself had he breathed a word against the men higher up. He had stood his trial grimly, humorously, taking a saturnine pleasure in defying the police. No, the Scragger did not talk.

About Johns he was not so sure. As long as it was to his interest to be silent, silent he would be. But if he were fearful for his own safety, driven into a corner, what then? He was a weak man and a coward, and no one knew this better than his dear friend, Mr. Tyler. On the other hand, Johns could not very well implicate Tyler in McGuire's death without implicating himself. No, on the whole, there was not a great deal to be feared in that direction.

As for Miriam, he fancied she could be managed. There had been a time when he had known how to manage her.

He gave his attention to the Anstruther affair.

There was a good deal about that that he didn't understand; much that he would be glad to know. His mind reverted again to Reddington Johns, and his teeth came together with a little click as he thought of the possibility that he had been double-crossed. Something had happened, he was sure, more—or less—than he had intended. In some way his plans had been altered without his knowledge or consent. But by whom? And why?

It was the uncertainty that made him uneasy. Things he could see and feel he did not fear. He had his own way, at once bold and subtle, of handling obstacles he could grasp. It was the vagueness of outline, the confused proportions of the present situation, the uncertainty from which direction the danger would come, that filled his mind with a dim prescience of panic.

He put the thought from him. Panic was the last thing he had time for now. He set himself determinedly to perfect his plans.

At noon he sent word upstairs to his wife that he would be glad to see her, but she put him off with a headache. He thought for a moment of insisting, but remembered in time that it was persuasion and not force that the situation demanded. When he went out after lunch, en route for his bankers, he ordered a box of roses sent in from a nearby florist.

Miriam appeared at dinner, pallid but remarkably handsome in an ivory-coloured dinner gown. Her husband studied her thoughtfully across the roses in the centre of the table, and in spite of his irritation with her and—yes, his fear of her—his pulses leaped. Gad, what a stunning creature she was with that burning, haunting glow in the back of her eyes and her fine air of a bereft queen. He lifted his glass and nodded to her across the flowers.

"I haven't acknowledged your—thoughtfulness," she said with a wan smile and a gesture toward the roses. "It was—quite sweet of you," she conceded.

He saw that she was puzzled as to his intent, and that pleased him. All the better if she were a little bewildered.

"I was distressed to hear that you were suffering," he said calmly.

Her brows went up, but the maid was changing the plates and she said nothing.

After dinner she would have gone straight to her room, but he asked to speak to her and she, persuaded perhaps by his offering, perhaps by that vague bewilderment that confused her, moved without a word to the drawing-room. He followed her at once and closed the door.

"It is good of you," he said, "to regard my wishes."

"Why not?" She looked up at him curiously from the divan on which she had seated herself. "I do not in the least mind speaking to you."

"I don't mean only that," he corrected her. "I mean, it is good of you to—accede to my wish to keep up—appearances."

"Not at all," she murmured. "After all, it's only—a temporary arrangement."

He came nearer to her; stood beside her, looking urgently into her eyes.

"Why need it be temporary?" he asked. "If we've been unhappy together, Miriam, it's been largely my fault. And I'm willing to mend my ways. You used to—care for me. I could make you care again, if you'd let me."

She looked down coldly at her folded hands.

"It's quite too late for that," she said.

"Anstruther's—dead, Miriam."

The hands clenched themselves. He could not see her face. He went on:

"When you told me the other day that you wanted your freedom, I was—well, I was beside myself with jealousy and rage. Of course, in a way, I deserved it, but—I suffered all the same. I swore to myself I'd keep you—against Anstruther and any other. And then, because I was so upset, I allowed you to bluff me with that bit of scandal you'd picked up about my knowing something of old McGuire's death. Well, I did know something—but not in the way you thought—not guilty knowledge."

Still she made no move; said nothing. He tried again.

"Can't we start again?" he begged. "I'll take you away. We'll go abroad—"

He saw that he'd said the wrong thing even in the same moment that he remembered that she was to have gone abroad with Anstruther. She rose; he saw that her face was bloodless, her eyes black with some terrible emotion. She was beautiful to him as she had never been before.

But his instinct, so subtle with women, warned him not to touch her now. He only looked at her with burning eyes. She spoke then, with difficulty, as though her voice were partly paralysed.

"I will think of what you say," she said. "To-night I am not—able. Another time."

She fled from the room and he made no attempt to follow her or stop her. She would come round, he fancied.

That night, or rather about one o'clock the next morning, the man on guard outside the Tyler house heard the click of metal on metal as the latch of the area gate was raised. The sound came to him distinctly across the silent street. Instantly alert, he shrank back into the shadow of the high stoop against which he leaned, and watched.

A dark figure came through the gate and stood for an instant, looking back, as though fearing pursuit. He saw then that it was a woman and that she held in her hand a small handbag.

After that breathless pause she turned away from the house and hurried up the street, her heels tapping the pavement with the irregular, uncertain sound of one walking in terror.

The man pursed his lips in a silent whistle. There could be no doubt as to her identity. As she turned, the light from the street lamp had fallen full on her face. Where, at this time of night, alone and secretly, could Mrs. Tyler be going?

Cautiously, with the cunning of the trained man hunter, the shadow followed her up the street.

20

In the morning Mr. Ormsberry was at once informed of Miriam Tyler's change of base. She had, so the report said, gone direct to the St. Angelo and engaged a suite. Ormsberry had, in any case, meant to interview her at the earliest possible moment, but now, spurred on by this unexpected move, he lost no time in calling her and arranging to see her immediately.

Instructing Hennessey to keep in touch with him as to the progress of the search for Billy Adams, he put that affair as much as possible out of his mind and went grimly about the business of tracking the man behind all these manifestations.

Mrs. Tyler received him without delay in her private drawing-room, crossed at this hour with slender shafts of morning sunshine. In the clear light he saw that her face was ravaged with grief, drawn with sleeplessness. It looked grey above the pallor of her stark white gown. But she forced herself gallantly to composure. He met her with a disarming frankness.

"I've come to you for help, Mrs. Tyler," he told her. "You said I might." She said nothing, but a hunted look came into her eyes. He went on remorselessly: "I've stumbled on a tangled intrigue that may—if I can straighten

it out—lead me to the man who was guilty of Mr. Anstruther's death." Two hectic spots of colour began to burn
in her cheeks, and he saw a cruel little pulse beating in her
throat. "I think you can help me to untangle the threads."

"I will, of course, if I can; but I told you everything I
know—everything I could think of."

"Pardon me, Mrs. Tyler; you didn't tell me why you
quarreled with your husband on the day that Anstruther
was killed?

Her hands tightened on the arms of her chair. For a
moment it seemed as though she would refuse. And then
suddenly she capitulated.

"Very well," she said; "I will tell you, although I cannot
see that it has any bearing on the case." She twisted her
hands together nervously and seemed to be considering
how she should begin. Then suddenly she broke into her
story and told it straight through, almost without pause,
and as though anxious to get through with it.

"I told you, I think," she began, "that Mr. Anstruther
had decided—very suddenly—to go away for an extended
European trip. I led you to suppose that—that he was running away from the situation that existed between us and
that I had agreed to the separation. This was not, however,
the fact. He had taken passage for me, too, and I was
determined to go with him. I saw that, if I allowed him to
go alone, I should—I should—"

Her lips trembled and Mr. Ormsberry supplied sympathetically:

"You feared you would lose him entirely."

She nodded and rushed on:

"I decided to have things out with my husband. If he
would allow me to go to Paris and enter an uncontested
divorce suit, I would persuade Mr. Anstruther to delay his
trip until we could marry. If my husband refused—well,

I don't know what I would have done. I would probably have sailed with Mr. Anstruther.

"On the day Mr. Anstruther was killed, in the afternoon, I told my husband that I wanted my freedom and asked him to give it to me. He laughed and said he was quite satisfied with things as they were. If I wanted my freedom, I could take it. As a matter of fact, I could have taken it, but he knew how I would detest the publicity of a contested divorce, and he took this means of tormenting me. Then I—well, I did something that I can hardly defend, perhaps, and yet—

"You don't know me, Mr. Ormsberry, and I can't expect you to look with leniency on what I am about to tell you, but bear in mind that I was very hard-driven. I was really desperate. Then I remembered something that happened five years ago, at the time this man Scragger Higgins, who has just been pardoned by the governor, was convicted of the murder of Clinton McGuire, the oil man. He refused, if you remember, to implicate the men higher up."

"I remember," murmured Ormsberry.

"Well, shortly after Higgins's conviction I chanced to overhear a conversation between my husband and Reddington Johns. It wasn't much, but it was enough to make it quite clear to me that they knew a good deal about the murder of McGuire. I didn't say anything then or later, because, after all, Robinson Tyler is my husband and I couldn't inform against him. I've never said anything about it to any one, until last Tuesday afternoon, and then, in the middle of something particularly horrid that Robinson said to me, this thing popped into my mind, and, without thinking what I was doing, I suddenly flashed out at him and told him he'd better be careful what he said, because I knew about Clinton McGuire.

"Well, the minute I'd said it, I knew I had a way of making him do what I wanted. He stopped in the middle

of a word and got as pale as—as white as this dress. He
wanted to know how much I knew. Well, as a matter of
fact, I knew almost nothing, but I wouldn't abandon my
advantage. I saw at once that he knew more about it even
than I had guessed, and I let him suppose I knew the
whole story.

"Really, Mr. Ormsberry, for a moment I was afraid for
my life. He looked at me so terrifyingly that—well, I lost
my nerve and did a dreadful thing. I protected myself in
the only way I could think of at the moment. I told him
that I had already told Mr. Anstruther all I knew about
the matter, and that he thought the affair could be proved,
and that he would take it up with the police if Robinson
Tyler would not allow me to get my divorce in peace. On
the other hand, if he would consent to that, we would, of
course, let the matter rest.

"Fortunately for me, he believed me. He agreed to let
me take my freedom, insisting only that I should stay in
his house until arrangements could be made for my sailing, and that I would avoid any overt scandal. But to-
day—well, I felt I couldn't stay there any longer, so I left
and came here. That is all I know. I have already told you
about my visit to Mr. Anstruther's apartment."

Mr. Ormsberry considered her for a moment under
lazily drooping lids. Nothing of his inward excitement
was apparent to her. His mind was seething. It all fitted
together so well. The weak point in his explanation of the
Tyler-Johns conspiracy had always been the lack of any
understandable motive on Johns's part. It was easy enough
to believe that Tyler might have killed Anstruther because
of jealousy, when he discovered the affair between the
novelist and his wife. But it had seemed fairly clear that
Johns was concerned in the matter too. Several things
pointed to it: his manipulations on the stock market in
behalf of Yvonne Lorimer; his presence in Tyler's house

when the gentleman was interviewing Scragger Higgins and paying him twenty-five thousand; the fact that he had dined with Anstruther on the night he was killed, knew that he was going to Mrs. Mortimer's and when, and had ample opportunity to pass the information on to Tyler or Higgins.

If Mrs. Tyler's story was true—and Mr. Ormsberry was prepared to believe her—Johns's connection with the plot was easily understandable. If Tyler and Johns had had a hand in the murder of Clinton McGuire, and believed that Mrs. Tyler had told Anstruther about it, certainly neither of them would rest until Anstruther had been silenced for ever. And what more natural than that they should pick Scragger Higgins to do the silencing?

Ormsberry ruminated. How much did this woman really know about the affair! She had lied before—or at least inferred a lie. Could he depend on her statement now?

He looked at her pale, beautiful face, so clearly stamped with suffering. His instinct was to pity and believe in her. But he knew his own weakness for a lovely face. When he spoke it was to shoot at her a ruthless question:

"Why was Scragger Higgins in your house at five o'clock on Wednesday afternoon? And why did your husband pay him twenty-five thousand?"

She stared at him blankly. Then the meaning of his question began slowly to filter into her understanding. She got to her feet and stood swaying, her face bloodless, a dazed, incredulous expression in her eyes. He thought she was about to faint and sprang to assist her, but she was made of sterner stuff than that, and she thrust him from her impatiently.

"I can't answer your question," she said hoarsely, "for I didn't know Higgins was there."

Ormsberry believed her. He saw the horror of growing realisation in her eyes.

"I take it you think, then," she went on in the same toneless voice, "that my husband hired Higgins to get rid of Mr. Anstruther—because of what I told him?"

"I think it quite possible," said the detective coolly.

She began to laugh. She laughed and laughed, while Ormsberry tried desperately to think of some way of shutting off that horrible sound.

"Oh, God," she whispered, "I might as well have stuck a knife into him myself!" She stopped laughing as suddenly as she had begun and stood looking calmly at Ormsberry. "I was going to ask you to safeguard me—not let any one know where you got this information, but I've changed my mind. I hope Robinson Tyler does call on me."

And to the detective's immense astonishment, she dismissed him with a perfectly composed inclination of the head.

He had an overwhelming impression of seeing a woman die before his eyes and be replaced by a perfectly correct, utterly lifeless automaton. He left her with a feeling both of admiration and of horror.

Ormsberry emerged from the immense lobby of the hotel into the clear brilliance of a perfect summer morning in a more cheerful frame of mind than he had known for several days. It seemed to him that he could see his way at last to clearing Brian Channing of the charge that hung over him. Surely Mrs. Tyler's revelations could have only one meaning. Tyler—and Johns—but especially Tyler, wanted Anstruther out of the way and hired Higgins to kill him. Higgins had done so and collected his wages. Jerry Howard had recognised either Tyler or Johns in Anstruther's apartment, had told Mrs. Lorimer, and they were both collecting blackmail.

It was all clear, and yet—hang it! There was something fishy about it, too. Under this hypothesis, how was he to explain the rifling of Anstruther's rooms? What papers could they have wanted? If it was Tyler who was almost caught there, and he was looking for his wife's letters to her lover, why hadn't he looked in the letter files instead of the manuscript drawers?

He tried to clarify his own faint impression of the man he had seen escaping over the wall. Tall, well-built, probably dark, although in that faint light it was impossible to be sure—the meagre details would have fitted either Tyler or Johns—or fifty out of every hundred men you might meet on the Avenue. Well, he would check up on the story to the last detail. And he would have some serious converse with Higgins—although, in view of that gentleman's reticence at his trial, he had doubts that he would get very much out of Higgins.

He hailed a taxi and had himself driven to headquarters. Here he was met with the information that Jones had brought Higgins in and they were waiting for him in his office.

Higgins, it seemed, when asked to say where he was during the evening when Anstruther was killed, had burst out laughing.

"Trying to pin it on me, boys?" he had asked. "Where do you reckon I could have got me a dress suit?"

"Come on!" Jones had urged. "Come clean. Spill the works. We got the goods on you."

But Higgins had obstinately refused to open his mouth.

"I ain't forgot," he had told them, "that anything I say can be used against me. Boys," he had said impressively, "this is big dope. If you want it, you'd better take me and introduce me to the big cheese. I ain't gonna waste it on little fellers like you."

So they had brought him in to Ormsberry.

The detective hesitated.

"Well," he said, "tell Jones I'll be there in a few moments, and meantime see if you can get me a minute with the chief."

Being one upon whom the blight of an inferiority complex had never settled, Mr. Ormsberry waited with perfect composure the result of his request for an interview.
He knew, to the hairbreadth of a degree, his value to the
department and to the personal ambitions of Police Commissioner Reagan. And he was quite accustomed to being
received in these purlieus with what amounted to a modest
fanfare of trumpets. He was not surprised then, when, on
approaching the sacred portals, Reagan himself came with
dignified condescension to the door to meet him.

The commissioner was a large, portly man, with a
hearty, jovial manner oddly at variance with his exceedingly shrewd, cold, and calculating brain. People were apt
to forget the man in the manner, but Ormsberry never
made that mistake. Perhaps that was on reason that he got
on so well with his chief.

"Well, Ormsberry, I hear you've met your match again,"
the commissioner greeted him cheerfully, closing the door.

"Your hearing, sir," murmured the detective, grinning,
"is not as good as usual."

"Got your man, have you?" It was more a statement
than a question.

"The trouble with this case is," Ormsberry complained,
"that I have got too many men."

"Have a cigar," suggested the commissioner, "and tell
me all about it."

"You know I never smoke," the detective mourned.

"Have a drink, then."

"Tut, tut!" murmured Mr. Ormsberry, with gentle re-
proof. "Really, commissioner!"

Reagan, bottle in hand, looked at him reprovingly.

"This is pre-Volstead," he said severely.

"Oh!" said his guest, relieved. "Then that puts another
face on the matter."

They pledged each other good-naturedly, and then Ormsberry, with the concise directness of which his ordinary manner gave no indication, outlined the progress of the case. The commissioner knew better than to interrupt. When the detective had finished he smoked for several moments thoughtfully. Then he asked:

"Why are you so sure Channing is innocent?"

"Because," said Ormsberry instantly, "I know the boy."

"H'm!" The commissioner gave that reason its due weight. He was not by any means a fool, and he knew his Ormsberry. "Still," he said slowly, "you must remember that that is not a very solid reason—from an outsider's point of view—mine, for instance."

"I intend," said Ormsberry grimly, "to furnish you with a better one."

"Very good," said Reagan. "Now, about Tyler and Johns. I gather that that is what you want my opinion on. I don't see any reason why you should walk warily in that connection. Let's haul them in and give them a grilling, anyway. You've plenty of evidence for that."

"Righto!" assented Ormsberry.

"In fact," said the commissioner slowly, as a man who weighs his words, "let me make it clear to you that you have a very free hand in clearing this matter up. I am tired of being asked whether this department is dead from the neck up. I want the man who killed Anstruther, and I want him pronto. If he is, as you suspect, the man who killed Fortescue, I want him all the more. It would give me a very pretty come-back to some of the sweet little remarks that have fallen from time to time from the lips of my political enemies. I want him rather badly, see?"

He looked Ormsberry in the eye, and Ormsberry saw.

"I guess," he said casually, "you want him about the way I do, chief."

The commissioner ruminated again.

"It's my impression that you'd better get hold of this secretary fellow—Roberts. It strikes me that his importance has been rather underrated."

"The drag net's out for him all over the country, sir. We'll get him, but it may take time. Meanwhile, we'll get after these other fellows. I haven't much faith that we'll get anything out of Higgins, but we can try."

"Have him in here." suggested the commissioner. "I'd rather like to talk to Higgins."

Ormsberry thrust his head out the door and gave an order. A moment later Jones and his prisoner entered the room.

Higgins entered jauntily, his wide, humorous mouth twisted in a quizzical smile, his shrewd, deep-set eyes twinkling.

"Well," he exclaimed, "if it isn't my friend Mr. Ormsberry! And Commissioner Reagan! How are you, commissioner?"

"Sit down, Higgins!" said the commissioner easily. "Have a cigar."

"So bygones are to be bygones!" murmured Higgins, grinning. "That's handsome of you, commissioner."

Reagan's jovial countenance beamed on him.

"Always ready to give a man a helping hand, Higgins."

The gunman burst out laughing.

"Sure!" he said. "But if it's free board and lodging you're offering me, commissioner—well, I can do without, thank you."

"That's as may be." Reagan's eyes were exceedingly sharp behind his smiling look. "I hear you have something rather good for us."

"So that's the ticket," murmured Higgins thoughtfully. "Well, I've nothing to hide. Shoot the works!"

"You went to Robinson Tyler's house at about a quarter to five last Wednesday afternoon?"

Higgins looked at him admiringly.

"Now how the devil did you know that, commissioner? Smart work!"

"Never mind how we knew it," interrupted Ormsberry grimly. "You were there?"

"I was there, all right," assented Higgins.

"By appointment?"

"Well, you might call it appointment. I called up and said I was coming. Mr. Tyler didn't like it very well, but he couldn't help himself."

"Did you also ask Mr. Johns to meet you there?"

"No; that was Tyler's idea. He telephoned Johns."

"H'm!" The commissioner took up the questioning. "What happened during the meeting between you and Tyler and Johns?"

"Well, now," objected Higgins, "you can hardly expect me to tell you that, commissioner."

"I'll tell *you* what happened, if you prefer," countered Reagan dryly.

Higgins glanced from one to the other and grinned.

"No, you don't," he murmured. "I've played poker myself, chief. I'll see you."

"I'm not bluffing," Reagan assured him. "Tyler and Johns between them paid you twenty-five thousand for killing Anstruther."

Higgins's grin widened automatically into a laugh but there was a sudden tightening of the eyes. All he said was:

"I'll ask you, commissioner, to prove them remarks."

"Where were you on Tuesday night between nine and ten o'clock?" Reagan shot the question at him sternly, his air of benevolent joviality suddenly gone.

Higgins glanced from one to the other, and this time his amusement seemed quite genuine.

"Well, now," he drawled, "I'll be right pleased to tell you where I was. I was in Scipio's Pool Room on Avenue A, from eight o'clock until midnight, playing pool with Officer O'Hara and a bunch of the boys. Laugh that off, commissioner."

Reagan and Ormsberry exchanged glances, and with a little nod Ormsberry slipped from the room.

"He'll find it's O.K., chief," said Higgins easily. "It's a 100-per-cent.-pure alibi—and, what's more, it happens to be true."

Reagan looked at the gangster thoughtfully. He believed him, but he also knew his man. He motioned Jones to leave the room.

"Of course," he said slowly, when the door had closed on the plainclothes-man, "there's something phony behind all this. If you didn't kill Anstruther—and I'm prepared to accept, for the moment, your statement that you didn't—then you know who did it; I don't exactly picture either Tyler or Johns passing out twenty-five thousand—for nothing."

"Smart work, commissioner!" murmured Higgin again with intense admiration.

To his annoyance, Reagan found himself losing his temper. He controlled himself with an effort.

"Spill the whole story to us, Higgins," he suggested, "and we may be able to do something rather handsome for you."

Higgins looked him up and down coolly.

"I should think," he said "you'd know better than that. You've had dealings with me before."

"Perhaps," suggested Reagan, "you'll feel differently about it to-morrow."

"You haven't a thing to hold me on," Higgins protested.

Reagan laughed.

"I'll think up something. Meanwhile we'll just stick you away as a material witness. That'll do—until to-morrow."

21

Meanwhile the search for Billy Adams went on with unabated zest. Hennessey, at Ormsberry's direction, had gone to Newark early in the morning to put himself at the disposal of the Jersey authorities and to keep his chief constantly in touch with new developments. But at noon, when he called the detective at headquarters, no further trace of the boy had been found. A guard on a ferry boat remembered seeing the youngster on an early afternoon crossing the day before, but from the time the boat touched the Jersey shore all trace of the Admiral was lost.

"Try the house where Roberts used to have a room," directed Ormsberry. "The kid may have gone there."

But when he rang off he sighed. He had no real faith that anything would come of the search. As he turned from the 'phone he found some one waiting to tell him that Reddington Johns and Robinson Tyler had been brought in.

"Show 'em in," he ordered; and while he waited, he stood staring blankly out of the window, ordering his thoughts for the ensuing interview.

Slowly he felt his mind, disturbed by his anxiety about the fate of the Admiral, begin to turn again like a well-ordered engine. This situation, demanding all his mental adroitness and acumen, was something he knew how to handle. He turned his back to the window and faced the two men who entered. Rapidly he summed them up.

Robinson Tyler, from his too-glossy black hair to his too-shiny black boots, was the image of self-possession. A hard nut to crack, Ormsberry decided. Reddington Johns, on the other hand, for all his insolent bearing, was decidedly rattled. He was in the grip of some powerful emotion; anger, Ormsberry guessed offhand; and consequently he could be made to talk. A man who allowed himself to lose his temper was easy prey to a shrewd cross-examiner, as the detective was well aware.

So this was the pretty pair whom Scragger Higgins had been blackmailing, and from whom Jerry Howard and, in all probability, Mrs. Lorimer, had been levying toll. The smooth Ormsberry brow was crossed by a single thoughtful wrinkle. He could not, somehow, picture either of these men as driving a dagger into Anstruther's throat, or having the nerve to enter and rifle Anstruther's rooms. Arrant cowards, both of them, if he knew anything about human nature. But even cowards have been known to fight when cornered, and, if Mrs. Tyler was to be believed, these two had thought themselves in a very desperate situation indeed.

However, Ormsberry's manner betrayed none of these things. He greeted them affably.

"Good-morning," he said cheerfully. "Do sit down."

But Reddington Johns showed a regrettable lack of appreciation of this courtesy. He leaned across the desk and scowled at Ormsberry.

"Will you be good enough to tell me to whose good offices we owe the outrage of this arrest? I suppose it is an arrest?"

Ormsberry regarded him in silent astonishment for a moment. Then he shrugged.

"Certainly it is an arrest. What did you think it was? A social call?"

"Don't get funny," Johns warned him furiously, his colour almost apoplectic. "I want to know upon whose accusation we have been brought here?"

Ormsberry studied him with some amusement for a moment: then, very delicately, he planted his stroke.

"I suppose," he murmured, "if I were to say—Mrs. Lorimer—"

"By heaven!" cried Johns furiously. "I knew that woman—"

But at this moment a cold, swift voice cut through this speech—a voice so cold and swift that it gave the effect of a sword flashing down between them.

"Let me remind you, my dear Red," said the self-possessed Mr. Tyler, "that he has not said that it was Mrs. Lorimer—or any one else." And he looked Ormsberry in the eye. "My impression, in fact," he went on after a moment, "is that Mr. Ormsberry simply wishes to—question us rather more particularly about our knowledge of what happened on the night that Mr. Anstruther was—most regrettably—killed."

Ormsberry bowed politely.

"Admirably put!" he applauded. "I find there are two or three little things I'd be glad to know before I go any further. Shall we say, to start out with, where you were, and what you were doing, between nine and ten-thirty on Tuesday evening last?"

"If you mean," shouted Johns, "to accuse me of having anything to do with Anstruther's death—"

"Just a moment, Red!" Once more Tyler's smooth voice interrupted him. "Mr. Ormsberry hasn't accused us of anything, I believe." For a moment his opaque black eyes met the detective's alert gaze steadily. Then he went on: "I am quite willing to answer any questions you may care to ask, Mr. Ormsberry."

"Good!" cried the detective cordially. "I see we shall understand each other."

"But," concluded Tyler, "I really can't help you much. I dined with some friends on the Square—the Van Delfts—at seven-thirty. I left there at nine sharp—they will remember, for it was the striking of the clock on their mantel that recalled to me the fact I had another engagement that evening. Then I walked directly round the corner to Mrs. Mortimer's. I fancy she, too, will recall the time, for she glanced at the clock as I went in, and reproached me for being five minutes late; we had had some joke about the inability of the average man to arrive on time at an evening affair."

"H'm!" Ormsberry considered him thoughtfully. "Did you receive or send a telephone call during the time you were at the Van Delfts'—or on the way to Mrs. Mortimer's?"

Tyler's brows lifted in suave surprise.

"No; certainly not."

Ormsberry shifted his attack to Reddington Johns. "Where were you between the time you left Mr. Anstruther at the club after dinner and nine o'clock when, I am told, you arrived at Mrs. Mortimer's?"

"I was on my way down from the club."

"From seven-thirty until nine? Oh, come now, Mr. Johns."

"I didn't leave the club that early."

The detective glanced at the slip of paper in his hand. "Seven-thirty," he repeated, "according to the doorman."

"Well, it may have been. I walked down."

Mr. Ormsberry grinned at him.

"Really," he remonstrated, "you must give me something more plausible. If you remember, it was pouring rain that evening until very nearly nine o'clock."

Johns glared at him.

"What the devil is it to you where I was?" he demanded. "Anstruther wasn't killed until after nine, and I've a perfectly good alibi for then."

"You didn't by any chance," the detective insinuated, "keep an appointment with Scragger Higgins between seven-thirty and nine?"

Once more Johns seemed about to explode, and once more Tyler interposed quickly and suavely. But this time he looked sharply at his friend, ignoring Ormsberry.

"You remember Higgins, Red?" he said, and his voice seemed to underline his remarks. "He was the man they sent up for murder five years ago. The police tried to get him to talk, but he never would; and he never has; and he never will," he added emphatically, and he looked the detective in the eye good-humouredly. "Checkmat!" his look seemed to say.

Ormsberry conceded the point with a shrug.

"As a matter of fact, Higgins hasn't talked—yet. But I've only had one conversation since they brought him in. I confess there's a point I'd be glad to have him clear up—or perhaps you can help me out. Why did you and Mr. Johns pay him twenty-five thousand on Wednesday afternoon?"

So genuine did Mr. Tyler's surprise appear to be that only a confirmed sceptic like Mr. Ormsberry could possibly have doubted him.

"I don't," he stated, "know what you are talking about."

Mr. Ormsberry sighed.

"Very well; have it your own way. Perhaps you will be good enough to tell me why you left Mrs. Mortimer's at a few minutes before ten, and where you went."

A momentary look of something that might have been uneasiness passed across Mr. Tyler's well-groomed countenance.

"I remembered that I had left my cane at the Van Delfts' and I went back to get it."

"Then undoubtedly there would be a maid, or a butler, to verify your statement."

"No." Tyler seemed for the first time to hesitate. "No, I decided I wouldn't bother them again that night after all, so, as it had turned into a lovely evening, I walked home."

The detective tried a bold move.

"On the other hand, Mr. Tyler," he suggested softly, "I fancy you walked round to Mr. Anstruther's house on the Square, entered his apartment with a duplicate key, and—were recognised through the window by Jerry Howard, who has been blackmailing you ever since."

"Ah!" It was a long-drawn breath of relief—or was it gentle mockery? Mr. Ormsberry could not for the life of him determine which. "I do not think you will hold me long on the evidence of Mr. Jerry Howard."

For a long moment the detective stared at him. Then he abandoned the contest for the moment. He perceived that his bluff had been called and he had no intention of disclosing to the astute Mr. Tyler the real grounds on which he was being held—Mrs. Tyler's story. Ormsberry pressed the buzzer on the desk and summoned the officer who waited in the corridor outside

22

Gregory Sommers, turning into the Fontenoy Club for lunch, was accosted by a newsboy with very red hair and very blue eyes.

"Wuxtry! Wuxtry!" shouted this enterprising youth. "Read all about the latest arrest. Anstruther's murderer caught!"

Sommers tossed a dime to the boy, and received in return the paper, its headlines blurred and groggy where the wet ink had rubbed.

"Here you are, sonny," he said. The boy went on and he stood for a moment on the step, eagerly scanning the running lines of type.

POLICE ARREST TWO SUSPECTS
Tyler and Johns Behind the Bars
Charged with Complicity in Novelist's Death

"Well, I'll be damned!" murmured Sommers, and he walked into the club with a warm glow of triumph in his veins. So this was what had come of his tip!

In the entrance hall of the club he found half a dozen men, all buried in open newspapers. Even George, the impeccable doorman, for once forgot his duties in an open effort to read the headlines over a shoulder of one of the members. He reddened and stiffened under Sommers's amazed glance.

"Fearful thing—this, sir. Bad for the club, sir. I see you've read the news, sir," he stammered.

"Ah!" murmured Sommers non-committally. "Mr. Jepson in?"

"Yes, sir, just went up, sir," George assured him. "Said he'd wait for you in the lounge, sir."

Sommers nodded, gave his hat to the attendant, and proceeded upstairs. He was glad he'd arranged to lunch with Jepson. He liked the fellow—found him invariably amusing. When he reached the top of the stairs the lawyer came forward immediately to meet him. He was a slight, lithe man, something over medium height, with a clever, pleasant, plain face, just alive now with interest.

"Seen the news?" he demanded, as they made their way to the dining-room and sought out a table in the window. "You hear nothing else talked about here now. The whole club's turned detective. Old Stokes is making up a memorandum for the police commissioner, and George looks at every one who comes in as though he were a potential murderer. I expect him to search me for concealed weapons at any moment."

Sommers laughed.

"Well, I'm thinking of becoming a sleuth myself," he confessed. "As a matter of fact"—he spread the newspaper out on the table before him—"I rather fancy that this"— nodding at the text—"can be laid to my door."

"No!" Jepson was immensely interested. "How do you come into it?"

Sommers related his interview with Ormsberry.

"I fancy," he concluded, "he found there was something in my suggestion about Anstruther and Mrs. Tyler, after all. I'll admit he didn't sound much impressed at the time, but it's part of the game these johnnies play, never to seem impressed with anything, what?"

At this moment the waiter arrived to take their order. When they were served Jepson came back to the point.

"What I can't see," he said with some perplexity, "is how Johns gets into the mess. Let's suppose you're right and that Tyler killed Anstruther because he's discovered his affair with Mrs. Tyler—what about Johns? Where does he come in?"

Their waiter, Jules, an anaemic, wizened little creature, leaned over at this moment to fill their glasses. His gaze, usually submissively drooped, seemed drawn by some strange attraction to Peter Jepson's face. The lawyer went on:

"I don't believe Johns had anything to do with it. He's a yellow cur, if ever there was one. It takes a man of iron nerve to do a thing like that, to carry it on his conscience and not give himself away."

The carafe shook in Jules's nervous hands and some of the water spilled on the tablecloth, but in their absorption neither man noticed it.

"Well," Sommers argued, "Tyler has nerve enough, Lord knows."

"Of a sort," agreed Jepson. "But I'm betting it's not this sort. Tyler's nerve is the nerve of the cornered rat. But this was an altogether different thing—called for an altogether more sturdy sort of courage—the courage of the aggressor. I picture it to myself this way: Imagine following the man you meant to kill, seeing him on the street and following him, or perhaps following him from this club; getting on to the same bus; finding the top was empty and sitting down near him, perhaps behind him, perhaps even beside him, if the murderer knew him to speak to; talking to him perhaps; picking a deserted part of the Avenue; cutting his throat very neatly; getting off the bus quite coolly. That's a different sort of nerve. Tyler hasn't—"

He broke off. A crash beside him and a startled glance from Sommers arrested his imaginary flight. He looked round. Jules, the waiter, had dropped the carafe and drenched the new green carpet with water and pieces of broken glass.

"Sorry, sir," stammered the unfortunate waiter. "It—it slipped." He knelt down to pick up the broken pieces, bending his head so that Jepson should not see his ashen face.

When they had finished their lunch and Peter Jepson had departed, Sommers strolled back to the dining-room and waited until he caught Jules's eye. Then he beckoned to the man and stepped back into the hall. After a moment Jules joined him there and followed him silently into the deserted library.

Sommers threw himself into a chair and looked curiously at the trembling waiter.

"Come," he said kindly. "Don't get into a stew, you know. What's up? What do you know about all this?" Jules was evidently too frightened to speak, so he added, smiling: "It's not so bad as all that, you know. Everybody in the club knows something about Mr. Anstruther's death— or thinks he does," he wound up with a grimace.

"Y-yes, sir," gulped Jules. "But not me, sir. I don't know nothing about it, sir."

"No? Then why did you drop the carafe just now when Mr. Jepson was talking about it?"

Jules glanced fearfully over his shoulder, as though even in the quiet security of the library he expected the hand of the murderer to reach out and crush him.

"It—it slipped, sir," he wailed miserably. "Honest to Gawd, it slipped."

"Ah!" agreed Sommers, smiling. "To be sure, it slipped. But why did it slip—just then?"

Jules looked at him piteously.

"It fair give me the creeps to hear him talkin' that way, sir, and me seein' him—"

"Seeing him where?" Sommers prodded. "Come, don't be afraid. No one's going to hurt you. If you know anything about this, you ought to tell, you know," he advised. "Otherwise you might get into trouble."

"I don't know nothin', sir, honest," Jules protested, almost in tears. "But I been thinkin', ever since I seen Mr. Jepson goin' off with Mr. Anstruther, sir, and the police sayin' he was followed from the club—"

"Sommers looked at him sharply.

You saw Mr. Jepson go off with Mr. Anstruther the night he was killed?"

"Yes, sir."

"And that was all?"

"That was all, sir.

Sommers considered for a moment.

"Oh, rot! There's nothing in it, of course," he said at last.

"No sir," agreed Jules. "Confession had, apparently, been good for his soul. He was breathing more freely. After a few more words Sommers dismissed the waiter, went downstairs, reclaimed his hat, and left the club. He walked slowly, meditating with some uneasiness. He liked Jepson. Amusing fellow! And, after all, it was certainly not his job to prod the police. Let them do their own sleuthing. He'd done his bit.

23

That afternoon Mr. Ormsberry himself interviewed the Newark authorities and went over the reports of the various operatives detailed to the search for Bill Adams. Inquiry at the house where Roberts, Anstruther's secretary, had roomed brought the information that a boy, answering the description of the Admiral, had called there late the afternoon before and asked whether Mr. Roberts had left any forwarding address when he went away. On being assured that he had not, the boy departed. The landlady thought she remembered seeing him hanging around on the sidewalk for a while afterward, but she could not be sure. That was all. From that point, apparently, Bill had vanished into thin air.

Mr. Ormsberry arranged for a general broadcasting of the boy's description, and, after a hasty and painful interview with Mrs. Adams, in which he attempted to give her a confidence he did not feel, he went home to a cheerless supper, which he found himself too tired to eat.

Johnson, that pluperfect manservant, protested gently.

"Really, sir, you'll make yourself ill."

Mr. Ormsberry regarded him sombrely.

"You are right, Johnson, quite right. We shall fall ill and sicken and die, and nobody will send us flowers. And quite right, too, for we are among those who cumber the earth, who follow after vain shadows, and who know not what they do."

Johnson was not quite sure what was required of him. He ventured a sympathetic cough and found to his satisfaction that it sufficed perfectly.

"To-morrow, Johnson," the detective proceeded dreamily, "I would have you get in from the corner bookstore all current publications having to do with horticulture, particularly—er—petunias and er—asphodel. Has it ever occurred to you, Johnson, how fascinating might be the study of the youthful and—shall we say—the adolescent petunia?"

The harassed Johnson fumbled the coffee things He feared that his master was trying to be funny, and he suspected humour in any form.

"N-no, sir," he managed at last.

"As soon as this disastrous affair is over—drained to the bitter dregs—Johnson," proceeded the detective, his eyes twinkling under drooping lids, "it is my intention to retire to some congenial spot in—what one might call—the wilderness, and grow flowers."

"Certainly, sir," murmured the imperturbable Johnson. "Anything else, sir?"

"No," said Mr. Ormsberry with a sigh, "I fear not."

He sat moodily at the window while Johnson cleared the table. Where, after all, had the day brought him? Still no trace of the Admiral. Tyler, Johns, and Higgins under lock and key, and precious slim evidence to hold them on, unless Mrs. Lorimer could be induced to turn State's evidence. And at that, he doubted if the murder could be traced to that combination. A conspiracy of some sort, certainly. Very probably, in fact, it was Robinson Tyler in the novelist's rooms, and yet— Who had killed Anstruther? The question remained as obstinately unanswered as ever.

His thoughts turned to the vanished secretary. Could it be that he had underrated the importance of that young man? Why, after all, if he was innocent, had he not come forward? He could hardly have fane to know that the police wanted to question him. His name was in every paper. Unless he was dead—

At this point the detective's meditations were in interrupted by a sharp ringing of the telephone. He reached a long arm for the instrument and heard Joan's anxious voice over the wire.

"Is there any news?" the girl wanted to know. "I saw you arrested Mr. Tyler and Mr. Johns. Does that mean that Brian—"

Ormsberry temporised.

"I think it certainly means that the case against Brian has been weakened, but we can't be sure of anything yet."

"And the Admiral?" she begged. "Surely you've found some trace of him? I feel so terribly guilty—I'm sure it's something I said that sent him off like that."

"Oh, as for him," Mr. Ormsberry was boundlessly confident. "Don't worry about him. He's a smart little shaver. He'll take care of himself, and come home when he gets good and ready."

"You're just trying to cheer me up," she complained.

Ormsberry laughed, and even Joan failed to catch the forced note.

"Remember, Miss Joan, I've been a boy myself, and I've run away, too, more than once. He'll be all right."

"Well," she conceded; "but you'll let me know when you hear anything?"

"Word of honour," Ormsberry assured her.

When she rang off, he took himself severely in hand.

"This will be about enough nonsense from you," he told himself. "You're getting an inferiority complex about this case. In fact, you're acting like a nervous woman. And

all because you didn't find Fortescue's murderer. The idea!
Every one fails sometimes." But now a shrewd, sure little
voice answered him: "But you haven't failed yet. You have
all the threads in your hands now. This time you're going
to find him."

Comforted by that secret voice, the great Van Dusen
Ormsberry went at length to bed.

He was roused in the middle of the night—roused from
vast depths of sleep—roused by a little, odd sound. He
came struggling up out of a deep sea of unconsciousness,
realising before he was fully awake the need of extreme
caution. For the sound he had heard was the faint impact
of an unwary shin against a chair

He was broad awake now, but he feigned sleep, breathing heavily, threshing about a bit to account for that momentary interruption in his breathing. His mind turned
to that fire-escape window in Johnson's pantry, but in all
the years Johnson had been with him he had never once
forgotten to adjust the protective device with which the
window was fitted. Mr. Ormsberry was not unaware that
he was an object of dislike to certain gentlemen of the
underworld, and he had chosen his apartment in full consciousness of that fact. There was no means of entrance
except through the two doors into the public hall and the
window opening on the fire-escape, all three protected by
an electric burglar-proof device. Except—

Mr. Ormsberry listened intently. Not a sound. Nor,
peering cautiously under slightly lifted lashes, could he see
anything but impenetrable blackness, cut by the slightly
lighter square of the open window.

No, it wasn't possible. He had himself inspected that
narrow coping that ran around the house at the level of
the windows. Nothing larger than a monkey could have

made that transit; and there was a sheer drop of five stories to the pavement below.

And then, against that pale patch of window, something
moved. The detective's hand slid cautiously, inch by inch,
under his pillow until it encountered and grasped his automatic. Then he sat up suddenly, his left hand against the
wall button, flooding the room with light.

"Hands up!" he said curtly.

There came a gasp from the direction of the window
and two grimy hands sought the ceiling, while to Mr.
Ormsberry's astounded gaze was revealed the countenance
of the Admiral, his freckles almost obliterated by two day's
grime, his blond thatch erect and tousled.

"Well, by—ginger!" murmured Mrs. Ormsberry.

The Admiral gulped and looked with a combination
of alarm and delighted excitement at the weapon in the
detective's nerveless hand.

"Yes, sir," he gasped at length.

Ormsberry laid the revolver on the table beside his bed.

"How did you get in?" he demanded.

"Through the window," the boy explained. "I climbed
up the fire-escape and crawled round on the stone shelf
outside."

"Great Caesar's ghost!" murmured the detective devoutly, turning faintly dizzy at the thought. "What will
your mother say to me?" He reached over and dragged the
boy to him. "You haven't hurt yourself?"

"Gosh, no!" Bill Adams laughed. "Couldn't very well
do that—unless I'd taken a header into the street, and—"

"Never mind about that," interrupted Ormsberry hurriedly. "What on earth induced you to come in that way?"

"Well," said Bill, making every effort to be reasonable
with this obtuse and elderly person, "I came up on the
dumb waiter first, but the door was fastened on this side

and my jimmy wouldn't open it, so I had to go down again and come up by the fire-escape."

The detective clutched his forehead.

"You came up on the dumb waiter?"

Bill nodded.

"But—but the rope might have broken! You might have— Good Lord!"

"Oh, no, sir," the boy assured him. "I tried the rope first, before I started up."

"But—but," stuttered Ormsberry, "why didn't you come up and ring the front door bell?"

The boy grinned.

"Not much! There was a cop outside in the street. I knew if he once got his lamps on me, I was a goner."

The detective followed this reasoning with lagging brain.

"But why not—I mean why? Why shouldn't a policeman have seen you?"

Solemnly the Admiral winked at him, as one man of the world to another.

"The bulls have been after me for two days," he informed the paralysed Mr. Ormsberry. "You know how they are—always trying to get the credit for what we fellers do. I wasn't goin' to let 'em get me till I'd seen you. You see"—Bill lowered his voice and looked about him with great effect—"I have some information to impart."

Ormsberry reached for his bathrobe and swung out of bed.

"Very well, young man," he said grimly. "I have some information to impart, too. Just wait till I get your mother on the wire."

"Gosh, Mr. Ormsberry!" cried Bill despairingly. "Can't you leave her out of it for a minute? I tell you I've got something big for you."

The detective paused in the doorway and looked back. Something in the alert, eager face, the tense, excited figure, recalled to him the bitter seriousness of his own childhood—a thing he had long forgotten. And hang it all! For all the preposterous prologue, there was something efficient and convincing about this youngster. Ormsberry dropped his manner of *de haut en bas* like an unnecessary garment.

"Come in here, Bill," he said. "We'll talk this over." And he led the way into the living-room. "Now," he said, "tell me all about it."

The boy sat down, crossing his legs carefully in exact imitation of Mr. Ormsberry's manner.

"Well, you see, it's like this," he began. "Mr. Speck is always saying that I ought to be a lawyer when I grow up, but I want to be a detective, sir; but he an' mother keep thinkin' how a feller that's a detective is likely to get shot up, an' all, and mother gets to worrying. You know how it is, sir."

Ormsberry nodded sympathetically, and Bill went on. "So I've been thinking I'd just show 'em what I could do when I got a chance, and then along came Miss Joan yesterday and I heard her say to Mr. Speck that you simply had to find Mr. Roberts so you could prove that Mr. Channing hadn't killed Mr. Anstruther. Well, you see, sir, I know Mr. Roberts very well. He and I used to talk over the murder of Mr. Fortescue going home on the ferry evenings. You see, he used to go to the trial with Mr. Anstruther."

"And I suppose," said the detective severely, "you used to tell him what Mr. Speck was doing about the case."

The Admiral looked at him with shocked surprise.

"Oh, no, sir. I never gave away any office secrets. We just talked about the case, you know. He'd say what he thought ought to be done, and then I'd tell him what I'd do if—" The boy broke off for a moment, flushing uncomfortably.

"If what?"

"If I was—the detective—on the case," he finished faintly.

"Oh! So you didn't like the way I was conducting the investigation?"

"Oh, yes, sir!" The Admiral's eyes shone with enthusiasm. "I—I—" But he found it hard to put his admiration into words, "That was what made me want to be a detective, sir—seeing what you did. Before that," he confided, "I wanted to be an engineer on a train—but that was when I was a kid," he added hastily.

Ormsberry rose somewhat hurriedly and crossed the room to the window. He had developed, it seemed, a sudden interest in the view. But when he turned back after a moment, his face was again quite composed.

"Well," he said, "go on. You say you knew Roberts well. How well?"

"He let me go home with him two—three times, and oncet he took me to dinner at the cafeteria he always went to." The Admiral's eyes were snapping with excitement. "And that time I saw a man named Mr. Thompson that was a friend of his, and they used to go there every night at six-thirty and have dinner together."

Mr. Ormsberry drew a sudden breath. He came forward and sat down near the Admiral.

"Yes?" he said quietly.

"Well, sir, I figured the police wouldn't know about this man Thompson, and maybe he'd have a line on where Mr. Roberts had gone, so I thought I'd just go and see. Well, I got over to Newark pretty early, so I went to Mr. Roberts's boarding house first, and talked to the landlady.

Gee! She'a tough nut all right." The boy grinned delightedly at some reminiscence. "Well, I gave her as good as
she sent, anyway," he announced complacently. "And I did
get one thing out of her. She said there wasn't any mail for
Mr. Roberts. He used to get mail—lots of it, she said; but
not a single letter since he went away."

The boy stopped and stared at Ormsberry, his eyes shining with excitement. The detective leaned forward tensely.
They had quite forgotten the difference in age between
them.

"I see," He nodded briefly. "So you think—"

"Well," said the Admiral, "whenever mother and I move
anywhere, she always gets a slip from the mail man and
sends the post office our new address, so letters will be
forwarded. So I thought maybe Mr. Roberts had done the
same thing. You see, it was kinda funny having his mail
stop all of a sudden like that. He couldn't have let all his
friends know he was going away—specially if he went off
in a hurry, like his landlady said!"

"By Jove!" murmured Ormsberry. "By Jove!" It was a
tribute to superior intelligence, and the boy understood it
as such. He flushed deeply under his freckles and grime.

"Yes, sir. So I thought I'd talk to the mail man, but he
didn't come along and he didn't come along, and it got to
be nearly half-past six, so I went to the Milford Cafeteria—that's the one I told you about—and hung around till
Mr. Thompson got there."

Bill was going strong. This was better than his dreams—
better than his wildest anticipation. Mr. Ormsberry—the
great Van Dusen Ormsberry—was actually hanging on his
words!

"Well, sir," he went on, his eyes shining, "Mr. Thompson recognised me all right, and when I told him that I
was investigating the Anstruther murder, he invited me

to have some dinner with him. Gee, and he sure fed me, you bet! Well, he tol' me that Mr. Roberts had a letter the day after Mr. Anstruther was killed. This letter was from his brother Sam in Chicago, and said for him to go there right away, because he was in a big real-estate deal, and he wanted Mr. Roberts to go in with him. You see, sir, Mr. Roberts had written to his brother before that he had had a quarrel with Mr. Anstruther, and didn't have any job."

"Yes, yes," said Ormsberry impatiently. "Go on!"

"Well, sir, Mr. Thompson tol' me that Mr. Roberts decided he'd go right away. He called Mr. Thompson up on the 'phone and told him about it, and said he was going to leave that afternoon. And Mr. Thompson asked him what his address was, and he told him, but Mr. Thompson couldn't remember it, and anyway. Mr. Roberts said he'd write to him, so he didn't pay any attention. You know how it is, sir."

Ormsberry nodded.

"Go on!"

"Yes, sir. Well, that was about all Mr. Thompson knew, so I went back to Mr. Roberts's house and waited for the mail man. That was when the cops started getting on my trail. Gee, I was lucky, though. I spotted the cop before he spotted me, so I cut down the street and waited in an alleyway. I would have gone home last night, but I knew they'd catch me if I did, so I just slept out in a lot. It was plenty hot."

The detective groaned but made no comment.

"Well," the boy went on, complete self-satisfaction visible in every feature, "pretty soon the mail man came along, so I asked him if Mr. Roberts had left any address to forward mail to, because I wanted to send him a letter and tell him his mother was dying; so the mail man said, yes, Mr. Roberts had left an address, but he didn't know what it was, because all he had done was to give Mr. Rob-erts a blank to fill out and then he had left it at the post office. So he said if I was to go to the post office maybe they would give me the address, but it was too late to go that night. So I gave him a tip, and told him not to mention it to any one, and he said he wouldn't."

"Of course," said Mr. Ormsberry gravely, "the department will take care of your expenses during this investigation."

"Well, sir, that's all right," said the boy. "So I couldn't see anything else to do that night, so I climbed over the fence into a lot and went to sleep. So this morning I went to the branch post office this man told me about, and I told them I wanted to send a letter to Mr. Roberts that his mother was dying and would they please give me his address, but I don't think they believed me, sir." The Admiral looked at Mr. Ormsberry gravely. "The man laughed and said it was all right and to run along. And so I got hold of the coloured man that washes out the post office, and I told him I wanted the address of a gentleman who had gone to Chicago, and his mother died and I wanted to write him a letter, and where were the addresses kept, and could I get a look at them. And I gave him a tip, too."

"Great Caesar's ghost," murmured Ormsberry again, head in hand.

"Well, sir, this coloured man, he got me in back behind the counter and things, but just when he was goin' to show me the file cases along came the same guy that told me to run along, and he—he threw me out, sir. I kicked his shins as hard as I could, and I hit him the way Mr. Speck taught me to hit the punching bag, but he threw me out just the same." Shame suffused the Admiral's countenance, but it was clearly for the impotence, not for the violence, of his performance. Mr. Ormsberry perceived that here was no budding pacifist.

"Hard luck, old fellow!" he murmured. "Never mind. You've done wonders. We'll set the police after that post office fellow and he'll give up the address all right."

"Gosh!" wailed the Admiral. "You ain't gonna hand this over to the police, Mr. Ormsberry! I fixed it all right."

"The devil, you did!" Mr. Ormsberry sank back again into the chair from which he had half risen. "I might have known it. What now?"

"Well, sir, I got hold of that coloured man again. He was kinda sore because he'd been fired, you see, for letting me in. But I gave him another tip, sir"—the boy's chest was fairly swelling with importance—"and he said if I was to write to Mr. Roberts at his old address in Newark, and leave the letter at the post office, marked 'Air Mail,' they'd send it on quick, and he'd get it pretty near as fast as a telegram. So I did it. I tol' Mr. Roberts that I wanted him to come right back."

"You—you—" gurgled the detective. "Oh!" He subsided weakly. "When do you think he'll get here?"

"Well," said the boy cheerfully, "I kinda think he'll be here Monday."

"That's settled, then," said Ormsberry briskly. "Good work, Adams."

The boy beamed, partly at the praise, partly at the official and manly use of his surname.

"Now," the detective went on, "the next thing is bed. I think we'll put you in the room Johnson uses when I want him to stay the night. You will be O.K. there." Ormsberry inspected his visitor critically. "And now, how about a hot bath, eh? A hot bath before I turn in always makes me feel great after a hard day's work."

The boy yawned.

"You bet," he said. "Gee, I wanted to come in before, but I was afraid they'd get me, if I tried to make it by daylight."

Ormsberry's capacity for amazement was exhausted. He shut his guest in the bathroom and mixed himself a large whisky and soda. Then he went to the 'phone and notified Mrs. Adams and the Newark police that the boy had been found. Then he got hold of Hennessey.

"Find the man that runs the branch post office nearest Roberts's boarding house, get Roberts's forwarding address, wire it to Chicago, and tell them to see that he gets headed this way by the quickest train they run. I need him."

Then he went to tuck his guest up for the night, arming himself first with a glass of milk and a huge slice of cake filched from Johnson's pantry, and reflecting, meanwhile, with some satisfaction, that the stone coping did not run under the window of Johnson's room.

The boy was already in bed, his cherubic face staring sleepily up from the white pillow, the freckles once more visible. He accepted and devoured with sleepy dignity Ormsberry's offering. Then the detective bade him goodnight and switched off the light. From the darkness a faint voice followed him into the hall.

"Please, sir."

"Yes?" He paused, attentive.

"Did you—did you tell mamma I'm here?"

"Yes, I told her."

A long yawn from the darkness—a long, deliciously relaxing yawn.

"Tha's—good," murmured the desperate detective, and with a deep sigh settled himself for sleep.

With a very light step Mr. Ormsberry betook himself down the hallway to his own room.

24

Mr. Speck arrived at the Gramercy Park apartment next morning before Ormsberry and the Admiral had finished breakfast. Clearly the little lawyer was not disposed to take any chances of the boy's disappearing again. And yet, for a man who had put in a very painful two days in consoling a despoiled and stricken mother, he looked very chipper. In fact, on his way over in the cab, he had debated the propriety of offering the prodigal a substantial reward for his escapade, for had not Mona Adams been nicer to him, Mr. Speck, during these past two days than ever before? And had she not, turning from the telephone after receiving Ormsberry's reassuring message, flung herself into Mr. Speck's arms and wept on his shoulder? From that point the lawyer's reflections ceased to be logical and became purely lyrical. He only knew that somehow, through the agency of the Admiral's most regrettable behaviour, everything had been satisfactorily settled between Mona and himself. His instinct was to scatter largess, but that, he realised, would not do.

Wherefore he schooled himself to severity and spoke reprovingly to Bill, who was perched on the pinnacle of bliss, hardly able to support the combined ecstasies of breakfasting with the great Van Dusen Ormsberry and being allowed to eat all the waffles and drink all the coffee he could hold. But when Mr. Speck had heard the full and complete epic of Bill's performances he permitted himself to soften. Where, after all, he reflected, on the wide face of the earth could be found another boy such as this?

Ormsberry watched his friend dubiously, conscious, from the moment of his entrance, of a new quality in his manner. He chuckled softly to himself as he realised the absurdity of the comparison that sprang, unbidden into his mind. The metamorphosed Mr. Speck was like a barren field on which, overnight, had sprung up a crowd of spring flowers. There was, under his accustomed dry brittle manner, a radiance that nothing could conceal. The detective, guessing rightly at the source of that radiance, was delighted. He wanted to clap his friend on the back and tell him how pleased he was, but he did nothing of the sort; only wrung his hand warmly at parting and watched the boy and the man go away together with a look of such gentleness as his carefully schooled countenance seldom wore.

Johnson's respectful voice recalled him to the business of the day.

"Mr. Hennessey is downstairs, sir."

"Eh? Oh, to be sure. Ask them to send him up."

Ten minutes later he was closeted with Hennessey and the day's routine was under way.

"I wired Chicago last night, sor," Hennessey was saying. "And I'd a wire first thing this morning that they were on the job. It seems the address this man Roberts is staying at is somewhere out in the suburbs and it will take them a bit of a time to get at him, but they'll send him on as soon as possible."

"H'm!" murmured Ormsberry. "Saturday! Well, he probably won't make it before to-morrow night or Monday morning, even if they get him right away. That'll have to do. Now, meanwhile—have they got anything out of Higgins yet?"

"No, sor. Nor Johns nor Tyler neither. Johns looked like an easy nut to crack, but Tyler seems to have put the fear of Heaven into him, for he hasn't opened his mouth—except to curse. He's done plenty of that."

"Well," said Ormsberry thoughtfully, "I'll have a go at Mrs. Lorimer. It's clear she knows something about that gang, because Johns nearly had a fit when I suggested she had something to do with their arrest. Then I suppose we might have a go at Howard. By the way, speaking of Howard, what were you able to find out about that letter Reilly intercepted—the one with the money in it?"

"Nothing to speak of, sor. It was sent out from the Western Union office in Grand Central. Nobody there remembers it particularly, or could undertake to identify the person who sent it. This guy is smart—you have to admit that."

Ormsberry nodded absently, drumming with his fingers on the table.

"We'll see how clever he is after we've had a talk with Roberts. Meanwhile, there's another thread we've been overlooking, and that's the man this fellow Jepson saw Anstruther talking with in the library of the Fontenoy Club just before he was killed."

"He didn't see him talking to any one, sor," Hennessey corrected him. "He said he saw him standing on the hearth in such a way that he *might* have been talking to some one."

"And that he bent forward and spoke to some one sitting in a chair by the fireplace, before he went out to speak to Jepson," the detective insisted.

"Yes, sor; he did say something like that. At least he said that was his impression, sor."

Ormsberry ruminated.

"Do they keep any sort of list of the members who visit the club in the course, let us say, of an evening?"

"I thought of that, sor, and I asked about it, but the only list I could get was the list of the men who had dined there on Tuesday evening. They keep that, of course, because most of them have their dinner charged up to them. And I got the hall porter to write down the names of any one else he could remember had been there that night. Here it is, sor."

Ormsberry studied the list Hennessey gave him.

"H'm! Doesn't help much. However, it may suggest something to Jepson. I'll take it along." He folded the paper and thrust it into his pocket. Then he rose and strolled to the window, staring down into the gardens below. "If Roberts can't help us," he said slowly, "I'll have to turn Mrs. Tyler loose on that pair. . . . And Higgins. I promised her I'd keep her out of it if I could, but it looks as though it wouldn't be possible."

"There's Mrs. Lorimer," suggested Hennessey.

Ormsberry stroked his chin thoughtfully.

"Ever seen her?"

Hennessey grinned.

"Yes, sor."

His chief looked at him amiably.

"I'm a timid man, Hennessey," he murmured. "I should say that Mrs. Lorimer is much more likely to get something out of me than I am to get anything out of Mrs. Lorimer."

At this moment the telephone rang and Hennessey, answering it, handed the instrument to his chief.

"It's the commissioner," he said softly.

Reagan was clearly upset.

"Tyler's lawyer has been pitching into me for an hour," he complained. "Wants to know what the heck we're holding them on. Remembering what you said, I tried to put him off, but it's no go. He's going to start things if we don't come through. Which is it going to be? Do I let 'em go, or do we make our case? I'll hold 'em if you say so, but I don't like Johns's close connection with Joseph Kron. It may mean a hell of a lot of trouble for us."

Ormsberry reflected rapidly.

"Let 'em go," he decided; "but have 'em trailed. It's highly probable that Johns may lose his nerve and try to make a bolt of it. Also, better put Jones to look out for Mrs. Lorimer. They may make trouble for her."

"Right!" The commissioner seemed vastly relieved. "How I do hate these legal fire-eaters!" And he rang off.

When Hennessey had left him, Ormsberry went downtown and sent in his card to Peter Jepson, attorney-at-law. Jepson received him immediately.

"By Jove, I'm glad to see you," he greeted his visitor cordially. "I've been awfully interested in this case, you know. Feel a sort of personal connection, you might say, seeing that I was practically the last to see the poor chap alive. What luck are you having?"

Ormsberry told him briefly such facts as were public knowledge, and for a few minutes they discussed the matter. Ormsberry was considerably impressed with the lawyer's shrewdness and good sense, and he was the more inclined, therefore, to believe in his impression of the mysterious unseen in the club library. He led the conversation skillfully in that direction.

"The more I think of it," Jepson said earnestly, "the more certain I am that there was some one there."

"You're certain you didn't see him? Not even a shoe showing beyond the chair?"

Jepson considered.

"No, nothing of the sort."

"Yet you're sure there was some one there?"

"Positive. You see, I saw Anstruther lean forward and speak to some one before he came out to meet me."

Ormsberry produced the list Hennessey had given him.

"Can you suggest which, if any, of these men it might have been? What I mean is, I wish you'd run through this list and check the men you are sure were not in the library at that particular time. You say you'd been strolling through the other rooms just before you stopped to speak to Anstruther—"

"I see what you mean." Jepson took the list and studied it, crossing out immediately a dozen names. "These," he explained to Ormsberry, "were in the cardroom, and these were still in the dining-room when I went upstairs." Gradually, after some thought, he reduced the list to half a dozen names. "These I do not remember seeing," he confessed.

Ormsberry thanked him and put the paper in his pocket.

"What are you going to do about it?" asked Jepson, seriously.

"I'm going to see whether these gentlemen can furnish an alibi."

The lawyer nodded, looking speculatively at the detective.

"Forgive me if I'm stupid," he said at last, "But just why—if it isn't impertinent to ask—do you put so much importance on this little episode?"

"Well," Ormsberry hesitated, smiling down at Jepson as he rose to depart. "It really isn't fair to ask a man to betray himself, but, since you ask, I don't mind telling you. Of course, it's possible that the man whom you didn't see—the man to whom Anstruther was talking—may figure in the murder, since it is probable that whoever committed the crime followed the novelist from the club. But the main interest I have in the incident is, frankly, that I don't understand it." At this point the detective grinned engagingly. "And I have always hated things I did not understand."

And with that he took his leave of the lawyer in the friendliest possible fashion.

In a public 'phone booth downstairs he called headquarters and read the list Jepson had given him, supplementing it with certain directions. Then, having consulted his watch and decided that, by this time, even so fashionable a lady as Mrs. Lorimer might reasonably be expected to be on view, he went uptown, and, not at all overawed by the marble-and-gilt magnificence of the entrance hall of her apartment house, caused his name to be sent up to her.

The announcement caught Mrs. Lorimer, so to speak, in mid flight. She was actually in the very act of putting on her hat to go down to a cab, which was to take her to a ship, which, in turn, was to carry her to Europe. The announcement of Ormsberry's name sent a thrill of terror through her. For the last two days—ever since her final interview with Reddington Johns when he had turned over to her the profits of his Wall Street coup—there had been a cloud of fear hanging over her. She knew it to be quite unreasonable, especially now that Mr. Johns and Mr. Tyler were under lock and key in jail; but there it was. He had been so terribly angry. Suppose he should take it into his head to think she was in any way responsible for his arrest? No, she decided to put as much distance as possible between herself and Reddington Johns before he got out on bail, or something.

And now, here was Ormsberry, the detective in charge of the case, to bar her departure. For once in her well-poised life, Yvonne Lorimer knew panic. So far, she had managed to keep clear of the case, but now— What did he want? Would he try to prevent her departure? Would they try to make her give evidence? And how much did he know anyway? Could she be called an accessory? For the first and only time in her life Mrs. Lorimer lost her head.

"Tell them," she said to Harper, who had brought the message, "tell them to ask Mr. Ormsberry to be good enough to wait downstairs for a few minutes. Then take my bags down in the service elevator and put them in a cab, and wait till I come."

"Yes, madame." Harper was halfway to the door when he turned back and said respectfully: "Beg pardon, madame, but do you think it is advisable? I understand that Mr. Ormsberry is in charge of the Anstruther murder case, madame, and—"

Yvonne turned her strange green eyes wrathfully on the butler.

"Please do as I ask, Harper," she said.

"Yes, madame."

Unwillingly he went to do her bidding while she hurried her maid with the final preparations.

Meanwhile Ormsberry, downstairs, was wrinkling his brows over her message. After a moment's reflection, he strolled over to the girl at the switchboard.

"Is it usual," he asked her, "for Mrs. Lorimer to ask her guests to wait down in the public hall?"

The telephone girl, a strawberry blonde of the most superior refinement, raised mascaraed eyebrows at him.

"How do you get that way?" she asked with interest. "Think I'm an information bureau?"

Mr. Ormsberry flipped back the edge of his coat displaying a certain emblem.

The girl's eyes widened and her eyebrows came down.

"No, sir," she said faintly. "I've never known her to ask anybody to wait down here before."

"H'm!" Ormsberry considered for a minute. "Know whether she's planning to go anywhere—leave town, I mean?"

"Yes, sir," stammered the girl. "She's going to Europe. Her trunks went out early this morning."

"Where's the service entrance?" The detective shot the question at her like a bullet from a gun.

"Around the corner to your left as you go out."

Almost before she had finished speaking the detective rushed across the foyer and, without waiting for the dignified doorman, wrenched open the door and darted down the street. At the corner he paused, and with well affected unconcern, looked down the side street. There, sure enough, stood a cab, its motor chugging, and a tall man, who looked like a butler, was putting several travelling bags into it.

The detective hesitated. Suppose the telephone girl were to warn Mrs. Lorimer and she slipped out the front way after all, while he waited for her at the back. Yet, if he stood where he was, she could easily get into the cab and away before he caught her up. He looked about for a policeman, but there was none in sight.

Ormsberry stepped back out of sight of the man in the cross street and summoned a passing cab. When it drew in to the curb he bade the driver wait, and resume his sentry duty at the corner, where he could watch both entrances. At any rate, he now had a means of following if Mrs. Lorimer escaped him.

But the telephone girl, it soon became clear, had been overawed by the badge of authority, for a few minutes later Mrs. Lorimer, followed by her maid, came precipitately out at the servants' door and got into the taxi. Clearly the man had already received his orders, for the machine started forward almost before the door was closed. Ormsberry sprang back and got into his own cab, just as the other swerved into the Avenue.

"Follow that cab!" he said to his driver. "And if you get a chance, draw level with it at the first traffic stop."

The two cars swept down the Avenue before the green traffic lights, and as the red came on the cab ahead swerved into a side street, going west. Ormsberry's driver, coasting a car that had swept in between them, and scraping the mud-guard by a bare inch, followed and drew up beside the other cab as it was held up at the next corner. Ormsberry thrust a bill through the open window into his driver's hand, stepped out, opened the door of Mrs. Lorimer's cab, and got in.

"I am sorry," he said courteously, "to take this unconventional means of seeing you, but I really couldn't wait until you got back from Europe."

Yvonne's face went ghastly white under the brim of her smart straw.

"Get out of my cab," she said, "or I will call a policeman."

"Pray don't trouble yourself," murmured Ormsberry. "I am a policeman myself—of sorts. Allow me to introduce myself." And he offered her his card.

But by this time she was regaining her self-command. "What is it you want? I may be wrong, but I fancy that even a policeman must have some valid excuse before forcing himself into a lady's presence."

"Quite so," agreed Ormsberry. "I have a valid excuse. I want you to tell me what you know about the Anstruther murder."

Mrs. Lorimer's surprise was a triumph of histrionic skill.

"What I know about— But I don't know any thing."

"Then why did you run away from me when I called at your house just now?"

She bit her lip.

"I was afraid you would delay me so that I should miss my boat."

"I'm sorry," the detective regretted, "but I'm afraid you will have to postpone your sailing."

"You can't stop me," she protested desperately. "It's imperative for me to sail, and you've nothing to hold me on."

"Come, come," deprecated Ormsberry gently. "You are labouring under a serious misconception of the power of the police department. I can hold you, if you force me to it, but I'd much rather have you stay of your own free will, to help us, as I'm sure you can."

She stared out of the window, biting her lip. Ormsberry studied her with interest. Here was a woman driven by abject terror, if he ever saw one. But terror of what? There he could not be sure. Was she in some way actually involved in the murder and afraid of police investigation on that account, or was she afraid of? Mr. Ormsberry had a momentary picture before his mind's eye of Reddington Johns's face when he mentioned this woman's name. He had a shrewd idea that that was what she feared. He spoke reassuringly.

"You needn't be afraid to tell anything you know," he said. "We'll see that you have adequate protection."

She looked at him quickly, and he perceived that she was quite herself again. Her green eyes glinted at him through her lashes, and she smiled a strange provocative smile.

"You leap to conclusions, don't you?" she murmured sweetly. "Well, I surrender, since I must. What do you want me to do?"

He leaned forward and spoke through the window to the driver.

"We'll just drop in at my office for a few minutes," he told her. "It's near by and we can talk less—conspicuously. You can send your maid on to make arrangements about having your trunks returned to you."

"I warn you," said Mrs. Lorimer, "that I know nothing about all this. I shall not be able to help you."

"I'll take my chance of that," said the detective.

But, ensconced in his shady office, exerting all his professional skill to trick and confuse her, he could get nothing out of her. She adopted an air of sweet candour, and he could not break it down.

"What is it you want to know?" she asked. "I'll help you if I can."

"I want to know what happened in Robinson Tyler's house on Wednesday afternoon at five o'clock."

She raised her oddly tilted brows.

"My dear man, how should I know? I can tell you what I did, but as to what—if anything—was going on in the house—well, really!"

"You went in about five?" he prompted her. "Why?"

"Why? I went to tea with Miriam Tyler, of course. We've been friends for years."

"Who else was there?"

"Who else? Why, no one—that is, as far as I know. I saw no one."

"Reddington Johns was not there?"

"He may have been. I didn't see him."

"How did it happen that Mr. Johns handled your stock in his recent coup in Wall Street?"

Even this did not faze her. She answered readily enough:

"He is an old friend of mine. He did it to help me out."

"Just friendliness?" Ormsberry's tone was dry.

"Just friendliness," she smiled.

He studied her coolly for a minute.

"Just what is Mr. Howard's connection with this affair?"

The only sign of emotion she showed was a taint hesitation before she answered.

"As far as I know, he has no connection with it."

But Ormsberry had caught that faint hesitation. And he had heard the gossip linking her name with Howard's. He said thoughtfully:

"I am under the impression that Howard knows far more than is good for him about Anstruther's death. I'll even go so far as to say that he is in grave danger of arrest, unless we can prove something against Tyler and Johns."

But Mrs. Lorimer smiled at him.

"Do you really expect me to fall for that, Mr. Ormsberry?" she said sweetly. "There simply isn't any way at all in which you can be sure whether or not I know anything about this business. You haven't any real right to keep me from sailing to-day. It's just bluff on your part. Do you think for a minute that I'd believe you'd do a thing like that unless you wanted information pretty badly? You don't really know anything, do you?"

Ormsberry laughed outright but said nothing.

"If you can prove anything against Mr. Howard," she went on, "go ahead and prove it. But you can't. I happen to know, because I was at Mrs. Mortimer's party at the time Mr. Anstruther was killed, and so was Jerry Howard. I saw him."

Ormsberry laughed again.

"*Touché!*" he admitted. "And you were at Mrs. Tyler's when Robinson Tyler and Reddington Johns paid Scragger Higgins twenty-five thousand for killing Anstruther—and you know that, too."

The thrust was so sudden that she half rose from her chair. The laughter was gone from Ormsberry's face. His eyes bored through her.

"Don't lie to me, Mrs. Mortimer. And don't console yourself with the idea that I don't know anything about this case. I want the truth and the whole truth. You knew about this transaction, didn't you?"

"No!" she gasped. "I swear I didn't. I—I don't believe it."

"You knew about it," he repeated, standing over her. "And you used your knowledge to force Reddington Johns to work for you on the Exchange."

"No, it isn't so!"

"And you're afraid to admit to this knowledge because, for one thing, the law may hold you accessory and for another, Johns may—kill you."

"No! No!" She put her hands up. "You've no right to say these things. It's not true."

"You're afraid to tell, Mrs. Lorimer; but you know." He spoke more gently. "Tell me, and I personally will guarantee that you come to no harm."

He was thinking of Brian Channing and Joan. He was merciless for their sakes. Mrs. Lorimer began to laugh hysterically.

"You can't bluff me, Mr. Ormsberry, and you can't scare me or coerce me. I'll tell what I see fit to tell, and no more. What are you going to do about it?"

He stared thoughtfully at her. Then he said:

"I'm going to call a cab and send you home." And when she looked at him in astonishment, he added: "Don't try to run away again. It wouldn't be—wise."

As he put her into a cab he added a last word:

"Reddington Johns will be released this afternoon. The commissioner tells me we can't continue to hold them on the evidence we have. When you want my protection—you have only to ask for it."

He smiled and bowed politely, and closed the cab door on her terrified face.

25

So far so good! Ormsberry glowed with satisfaction as he returned to his office. He was fairly well convinced that these people between them—Reddington Johns, Tyler, Higgins, Mrs. Lorimer, Jerry Howard—knew why Anstruther had been killed and who had killed him, and soon he, too, would know. He had put the screws on Yvonne, and, unless he was grievously mistaken, by Monday she would be ready to talk. He had no fear of her escaping him. He had taken every precaution against that contingency. If he felt a twinge of conscience about exposing her to danger from Mr. Johns, he dismissed it by assuring himself that she was quite safe with Plainclothes-man Jones on guard.

And then to-morrow—or Monday at the latest—Roberts would arrive from Chicago. Surely, he, too, would be able to throw some light on the situation.

Ormsberry thought regretfully of young Channing in jail, and comforted himself with the thought that, at any rate, it would not be for long. Monday—or Tuesday at latest—should see him free again.

Meanwhile, there was the week-end to get through. He felt himself full of nervous energy, a suspense, an odd inexplicable uneasiness that would not let him rest. Suppose, after all, Roberts's contribution to the evidence should point to Brian? Ormsberry thrust the thought from him, but it persisted. It wasn't possible that Anstruther could really have believed Brian guilty of Fortescue's death, and yet—there was that letter written to Brian in Paris. Certainly, twist it as he would, Mr. Ormsberry could not deny that it was capable of two interpretations. And yet surely Anstruther was too keen a judge of character to suspect young Channing.

Ormsberry shuddered and once more put the thought resolutely from him. To steady himself he ran over in his mind any loose ends that might require attention before Roberts's return. But the only thing that occurred to him was Jepson's meeting with Anstruther at the Fontenoy Club, and the little incident of the man in the overstuffed chair. He had already given instructions about that, but, moved by a sudden impulse, he decided to go up to the club himself and look into the matter. Clapping on his hat, he went into the outer office, left word with the telephone girl where he was to be found, went downstairs, summoned a taxi, and had himself driven to the Fontenoy Club. On the way up he decided that he would leave to headquarters the search into the alibis of the men whose names figured on the list Jepson had given him. He himself would devote his attention to a general canvass of the personnel of the club, hoping in that way to come across some clue to the identity of the mysterious unknown.

He sent in his card to the steward and was immediately received by that worthy in his little office behind the cloak-rooms.

M. René was round, bald, and very French. Also, he had an almost apoplectic respect for the law and was, consequently, most eager to be of service to the great Mr. Ormsberry, whom he evidently considered its ornament and crown.

"So Monsieur would find the name of the unknown gentleman in the libraree, eh?" he asked, when Ormsberry had stated his business. "Very difficult, but not impossible—for Monsieur," he added with a quick little bow, "Monsieur is of those who read finger prints and foot marks as I read the headlines of the papers, not so? Eh, monsieur, but I am a great reader of detective stories. I know—I, René—how you find the whole history of a crime in the dust caught in the groove of a penknife!" And he folded his hands on his well-filled waistcoat and beamed excitedly at Ormsberry.

The detective laughed.

"Well," he said, "I've never done just that trick, although I've no doubt it's possible. This, however, is much more prosaic." He took from his pocket the list Hennessey had procured and spread it out on the table. "Tell me, if you can, which of these men are in the habit of spending much time in the library. I'd like a word with the likely ones."

"Me—I cannot tell that, monsieur: but I shall speedily find out for you. Jules, one of our waiters, also has charge of the library, and he will know. In one little instant Jules shall be here."

But Ormsberry interrupted René's sudden rush for the door.

"Suppose we go upstairs and find Jules," he suggested. "I should like to have a look at the library."

To this René immediately assented. They went upstairs together, and, passing down the wide hallway, turned into the library. It was a big room, pleasantly and luxuriously furnished, and done in shades of dull brown and plum colour. At the far end a huge fireplace filled almost the entire wall, flanked with book-cases that extended the whole length of the room, broken only by two enormous windows in one wall. On either side of the fireplace, and turned toward it so that only their backs were visible from the doorway, stood two huge, overstuffed chairs, with reading lights conveniently at hand. When they entered the room was empty, except for a slight, emaciated-looking man of indeterminate age, dressed in a rusty black, who was arranging some books on a shelf.

"Ah, Jules!" said M. René. "Come here a minute."

Ormsberry, meanwhile, was inspecting the room with interest. He turned now to Jules.

"Be good enough," he said crisply, "to sit for a moment in that chair by the fire—the one to the left."

Jules, reassured by a nod from his employer, obeyed, and Ormsberry noted that Jepson was right. A man standing in the doorway could not tell whether there was any one sitting in that chair or not.

"All right," he said. "Now, come here. I want to ask you some questions about the night Mr. Anstruther was killed. You know what night that was?"

Jules's pale, frightened-looking face seemed even more frightened.

"Yes, sir. It was Tuesday night," he managed to stammer.

Ormsberry looked at him kindly.

"Don't be afraid," he said. "I just want to ask you some very simple questions, and there'll be something in it for you afterward."

"Yes, sir; thank you, sir," gasped the man.

"I want you to tell me, as far as you can, the names of any gentlemen who were in the library on Tuesday evening."

The waiter ran hesitatingly through a list of names and Ormsberry checked them on the list in his hand.

"But there may have been others," Jules said finally. "You understand, sir, that during the evening I am not in the room all the time. The gentlemen order—different things—and I go to serve them."

Ormsberry caught his agonised glance at M. René, and the steward's exasperated gesture, but he affected to see nothing.

"You are certain that you remember seeing Mr. Anstruther here on Tuesday evening?"

"Yes, sir."

"What was he doing when you saw him?"

"He was standing on the hearth, sir, smoking and talking to another gentleman."

Ormsberry's heart skipped a beat, but no trace of excitement crept into his level voice.

"Who was the other gentleman?"

"I'm not sure, sir. He was sitting in that chair you asked me to sit in just now, and I couldn't see him. You see, sir, I didn't go into the room; I just looked in anything was wanted."

"Then how do you know there was any one sitting in that chair?"

"I heard him say something to Mr. Anstruther."

"Could you hear what it was?"

"Oh, yes, sir; quite clearly. He said: 'You haven't told any one else about it?'"

"Did you hear Anstruther's answer?"

"Yes, sir. He said: 'I haven't told any one yet, but I'm going to put the story in the mail to-night.' Something like that, sir."

There was a noticeable pause. Then Ormsberry said sharply:

"You said a moment ago that you could not be sure the man was to whom Anstruther was talking, that mean that you can guess who it was?"

"I think so, sir," stammered Jules.

"You recognised the voice?"

"No, sir, not at all. But a few minutes later I went back to the library and I saw Mr. Anstruther leave it in company with a gentleman. They stood in the hall a minute, talking, before they went downstairs, and I saw them plainly."

"Who was the other man?"

"Mr. Peter Jepson, sir."

Ormsberry felt at first a decided disappointment. This was no more than he knew already. But presented in this way, it had, somehow, a different aspect. Peter Jepson! Why not? After all, they had only his word that he had met Anstruther at the door of the library. Come to think of it, it was Jepson who had first introduced the mysterious unknown in the overstuffed chair. Suppose it had been Jepson himself who sat there? He had, by his own confession, left the club with Anstruther. Suppose he had followed Anstruther on to the bus? Who was the mysterious friend, who, according to Jepson, had given him a lift uptown?

Ormsberry's mind was whirling. Nonsense! He must keep his head. Jepson had no connection with either this affair or the Fortescue murder. At least, he had no connection as yet established. The detective turned to René.

"Now, if you don't mind, I'll have a word with the doorman."

He slipped the promised reward into Jules's willing hand and he and René went downstairs again.

George, the doorman, proved more loquacious.

He was a large, rubicund man with a merry blue eye that belied the dignified condescension of his manner.

Yes, he remembered very well seeing Mr. Anstruther on Tuesday evening. Mr. Anstruther came in early and conversed for a minute with George, who was not engaged at the moment. Very pleasant gentleman, opined George. Always had a friendly word for everybody. George's approval seemed, somehow, to bestow distinction on the novelist. Mr. Ormsberry agreed gravely, and went on to inquire what Anstruther had had to say.

"Well," said George, wrinkling a reflective brow, "he asked, sir, if Mr. Johns had come in yet, as he was engaged to dine with him. I said he had come in half an hour before. Then, sir, he said as how it was a nice evening but looked like a storm later. Which same it did storm, if you remember, sir."

Mr. Ormsberry remembered, somewhat impatiently.

"Then, sir, he asked if I could get him an envelope."

"An envelope?" demanded the detective, pricking up his ears.

"Yes, sir. He had a story he'd just finished—had it in his pocket, sir—and he wanted to get it into the mail that night. Said something about waiting till the last minute, sir, and couldn't wait no longer. But he hadn't an envelope to mail it in. Well, I got him an envelope from the office, sir, and put the story into it for him."

"You saw the story?"

"Yes, sir."

"What was it like?"

"Ordinary typewritten pages, sir."

"Remember the name?"

"I did notice it, sir, being something of a reading man myself, sir, and an admirer of Mr. Anstruther's stories. The name of it was *The Innocent Bystander,* sir."

"And did you mail the envelope for him?"

"No, sir. He said he might have occasion to show it to some one later in the evening. There was some legal point he wanted to make sure of, I believe, sir. 'Can't be too careful about details,' he said to me, poor gentleman."

"So he took the story with him?"

"Yes, sir. Put it in the side pocket of his coat, sir, as he went upstairs."

Ormsberry ruminated for a minute.

"You saw him again later?"

"Yes, sir; as he was going out, sir. He came downstairs with Mr. Jepson about nine o'clock, I should think, sir, and asked me if it was still raining. I told him the storm was over. Then he and Mr. Jepson got their hats from the check-room and went out together."

"Did you notice whether Mr. Anstruther still had the story with him?"

"Yes, sir. He had it in his hand."

"Who went out immediately after Mr. Anstruther and Mr. Jepson?"

"No one, sir," was the doorman's surprising reply. "No one went out for at least an hour, sir."

"But some one might have gone out without your seeing them?"

"Not then, sir. I was right by the door all the time."

For a moment the detective was stumped. Then an idea occurred to him.

"Who was the last person to go out before Mr. Anstruther left?"

"Well, sir—" George hesitated. "I'm not sure, sir. Three or four gentlemen left together fifteen or twenty minutes before Mr. Anstruther. I can give you their names, if you like, sir. But I think some one slipped out after that—just before Mr. Jepson and Mr. Anstruther. The check-room boy had asked me to look out for his coat closet while he went down the street on an errand, so when Mr. Jepson and Mr. Anstruther came downstairs, I went into the check-room to get their hats for them. It took me a minute to find the right ones, and when I came out again the front door was just swinging shut. It must have been some one going out, because there wasn't any one in the hall. My two gentlemen had gone into the side room there, to get some cigarettes, so they didn't see any one; but I'm sure some one went out, just the same."

Ormsberry frowned impatiently. The figure of this unknown had begun to loom like a sinister ghost over the whole tragic situation. And yet, come at him from what direction he would, the detective could get no more than an oblique glance at the empty spot which, a moment before, he had occupied. The sound of a voice here, a door swinging to on his passing, the empty chair where he had sat. Yet this shadow, perhaps, had been strong enough to strike a long, thin knife into a man's throat. He sighed impatiently, for he felt that, if he could only locate this unknown, Brian Channing would be free.

"Well," he said, "I'm obliged to you, George. Now take a look at this list and tell me which of these gentlemen know most about what goes on here in the club. Particularly the ones that spend a good deal of time in the library."

George frowned over the list Ormsberry gave him. Suddenly his face took on a look of inspiration.

"There's your man, sir— Mr. Salisbury Stokes, sir. He's lived here for fifteen years, sir, and if anything gets by him—well, there's little that does. Just you talk to Mr. Stokes, sir."

Once more Ormsberry thanked him, and, having ascertained that Mr. Stokes was in, sent up his name.

That gentleman received him with some curiosity in the little reception room at the end of the second-floor hall. It was clear that he was all agog with excitement at actually holding converse with the man in charge of the Anstruther murder case. He was an incredibly stout, ruddy old gentleman, magnificently garbed in garments that escaped being flashy only because they had been made—under extreme protest—by the best tailors. As he came into the room, the detective noted that he had the light, bouncing step sometimes noticeable in a very heavy man. His countenance beamed with friendly interest in the world at large and Mr. Ormsberry in particular.

"Anstruther?" cried Mr. Stokes in answer to the detective's question. "Of course I knew Anstruther. Knew him very well, you might say. Interesting fellow—very. Used to talk his work over with him. Seemed to value my opinion. Of course," he conceded, "I'm not a literary man, but I know what I like. 'Stokes,' he'd say, 'Stokes, old man, take a look at this story, will you? Something wrong with it; can't tell what it is, but you'll know.' He found my criticism helpful—very."

Again Ormsberry pricked up his ears.

"Then perhaps you discussed his last story with him— *The Innocent Bystander?*"

Mr. Stokes's face fell. Clearly it hurt his pride to confess ignorance of anything.

"The Innocent Bystander?" he ruminated. "No, can't say that I remember it. His latest story, you say? Probably he meant to show it to me. In fact, now I think of it, I met him just as he was coming out of the dining-room the night he was killed, and he said to me: 'Stokes, old man, I want to see you soon. Have something to talk over with you.' And then he was killed not two hours later. Poor chap! Poor chap!"

Mr. Ormsberry looked doubtfully at Mr. Stokes, wondering at what point that worthy gentleman's imagination began and the truth left off.

"Did you see Mr. Anstruther again that evening," he asked presently.

"Well, no," said Mr. Stokes. "At least, I did not see him to speak to. When I came up from dinner I was busy for fifteen or twenty minutes in this room with a business acquaintance of mine. When he left I went down to the door with him. On the way to the stairs, as you know, one passes the door of the library. I glanced in and saw Mr. Anstruther standing on the hearth, so I thought I'd step in and speak to him on my way up again. You see, I thought he was alone—"

"Yes," murmured the detective. "What then?"

"Well," Mr. Stokes went on, "when I came up again I met Mr. Anstruther coming downstairs with Jepson, the lawyer, whom I also know very well. They were talking earnestly together, so I only nodded and went on up. As I passed the library I glanced into it automatically—I suppose to see whether there was any one there I knew. At any rate, I did look in, and there, coming toward me down the room— Well, of course, the library was lighted only dimly, and by a single reading lamp near the fireplace at the other end, so that all the light was behind him, but I recognised him all the same. Yes, sir, there's no doubt in my mind as to who it was. I used to know him well—oh, very—although I haven't seen him for some time."

Mr. Ormsberry stared at him. The old gentleman's face was shining with excitement. He had the triumphant manner of one about to impart astonishing information.

"Well?" demanded the detective impatiently. "Who was it?"

Salisbury Stokes lowered his voice and leaned forward confidentially.

"Mr. Ormsberry," he said impressively, "for some years I have had the greatest respect for your powers, but never more so than now, as I have followed your masterly unravelling of this very intricate case. I have followed you step by step in the daily papers, and have concurred at each point with your deductions. And the speed with which you arrived at your conclusions—marvelous, my dear sir, marvelous!"

Mr. Ormsberry controlled himself with difficulty.

"You were saying?"

Mr. Stokes, however, was determined to have his say.

"Ah, my dear sir, they say only too truly that hind sight is better than foresight. Had I only had some premonition of what was about to happen, I would have stopped that young man, engaged him in conversation and so prevented this appalling tragedy. As it was, sir—imagine my subsequent feelings!—I did not even pause to greet him, but went on to the card-room to a futile game of bridge."

Mr. Ormsberry tried another means of approach.

"You say you recognised this young man?"

"Yes, sir, I did. There is no doubt in my mind on that point. And had you not sought me out, sir, I would shortly have come to you to communicate the fact. But I hoped first to complete some small deductive reasonings of my own—some logical sequences which, as you will see, I have here jotted down." And, to Ormsberry's horror, he drew from his pocket a thick sheaf of closely written pages, and prepared, apparently, to read them aloud.

At this point, however, the detective intervened determinedly.

"I'm much obliged to you, sir, but that can, I hope, wait. Meanwhile, will you be good enough—" He hesitated the barest fraction of a second as he put his question. What could it be that this crazy old man was about to tell him? Then he rushed on: "Who was the young man whom you saw in the library just after Anstruther had left it?"

Mr. Stokes looked up with surprise from his manuscript.

"Why, I thought of course you knew. Who could it have been but young Channing?"

"But—but—" stammered Mr. Ormsberry.

"Shrewd of you to guess it at once—very. And to arrest him so quickly. And it was so obviously true that Anstruther's murderer must have followed him from the club. Step by step, your logic is unimpeachable."

"But Channing wasn't here that night!" exclaimed the detective blankly. "And what would he be doing here? He isn't a member."

"Certainly he is a member," Mr. Stokes corrected him. "I put him up myself four years ago."

Ormsberry rose and paced the length of the little room and back, feverishly. Suddenly he paused in front of Salisbury Stokes.

"If you knew Channing so well, and recognised him in the library, as you say, why didn't you go in and speak to him? You say yourself you hadn't seen him for a long time."

"My dear sir," Stokes protested, "of course I haven't seen him. He's been abroad."

"Why didn't you go in and welcome him back, then?" persisted the detective.

Mr. Stokes's red face grew redder.

"I'm sure I can't imagine," he said at last. "It was stupid of me—very."

"I'll tell you why you didn't," went on Ormsberry relentlessly. "You did not go in because you did not really recognise him at all. You saw a man who looked something like young Channing, and when you read in the paper that Channing had been arrested for the murder of Mr. Anstruther, and you saw Mr. Jepson's statement about the man Anstruther was talking to in the library, then—and not till then—you decided that the man you had seen was Channing."

Salisbury Stokes looked as though he was about to have an attack of apoplexy.

"But of course it was Channing—it must have been," he stammered. "Who else could it have been?"

"Who else could it have been?" repeated Ormsberry, and his out-thrust head suggested somehow a hound on the scent. "Who else could it have been? Why, Anstruther's murderer, of course—some one who looks a good deal like Brian Channing—same build, same colouring—near enough like him to be taken for him in a dim light, at a distance."

"But—but"—it was Mr. Stokes's turn to stammer now—"but Channing is Anstruther's murderer—"

Mr. Ormsberry looked at him strangely.

"Is he?" he said softly. "I think it improbable—very. You can't think, of course, who it was you really saw in the library?"

But by this time Mr. Stokes was completely demoralised. His dignity had gone by the board. It is questionable if he could have told his own name.

"No-o. No, I don't think I could tell—really, sir."

"Good-day," said Mr. Ormsberry then, and went away.

26

Sitting over a late lunch, Mr. Ormsberry felt decidedly more cheerful than he had for some time. In spite of the apparently damning nature of the evidence presented by Mr. Stokes, he could not but feel that the case against Channing was materially weakened. It could be proved beyond any reasonable doubt, he felt sure, that Channing had not been—indeed had not had time to go—to the Fontenoy Club on the evening of Anstruther's death.

At any rate, Mr. Ormsberry felt that, in his own mind at least, the case was taking shape at last. The events of the fatal evening were falling into place. Regretfully he admitted that he had been temporarily confused by the intrigue of Johns and Tyler and Mrs. Lorimer. There was, of course, something of a serious nature needing investigation there, but that could wait; that was, he was now confident, a side issue. It was clear that neither Johns nor Tyler, nor Mrs. Lorimer nor Higgins could have been actually guilty of Anstruther's murder. If they knew who did it, well and good. It would delight him to show them to be accomplices. Meanwhile, he was on the trail of the real quarry—the shadowy figure in the library, whom Stokes had mistaken for Channing; the man who had crouched over Anstruther's desk and escaped over the garden wall, whom Joan had mistaken for Channing; the man who had

slipped out of the door of the club, after hearing Anstruther say he was going downtown on a bus, waited at the
next corner until he saw the novelist actually mount to the
top, followed him, and killed him.

For what? Why, for the story Anstruther carried in his
pocket, the story that was the exposé of the Fortescue
murder—an exposé so acute that whoever read it would
be put on the right trail—the trail of the man who killed
Fortescue, and hid behind the skirts of Fortescue's daughter. "Have you told any one yet?" this man had asked from
the cushioned seclusion of the overstuffed chair. And Anstruther had answered: "Not yet, but I'm going to put the
story in the mail to-night—" And to-night, too, Brian
Channing was to see the story—Brian Channing who had
rushed home from Europe to see it, to learn Anstruther's
theory of the Fortescue case so that he could track down
and punish the man who killed his fiancée's father. Motive?
Mr. Ormsberry surmised that there was motive enough.
He would have no trouble in proving an adequate motive, once he caught his man. And he would catch him, he
swore solemnly. He thought impatiently of Monday and
Roberts's return. Would he really be able to tell anything?

He left the restaurant at which he had lunched, sought
out a public 'phone booth, and called Hennessey. That
gentleman reported a wire from Chicago carrying the assurance that Mr. Roberts would be on the Twentieth Cen-
tury Limited that night and would arrive early Sunday
morning.

"Bully!" cried Ormsberry. "That's fine. Now what have
you been able to do about the list I gave you?"

Here the news was not so encouraging. Hennessey, it
seemed, had already interviewed four out of the six men
who Mr. Jepson had thought might possibly have been in
the library at the time Anstruther was there on Tuesday

evening, and all four had been able to account satisfactorily for their whereabouts during the evening.

Hennessey checked down the list.

"Snyder," he told his chief, "went to the theatre with
a girl; called for her at eight o'clock and was with her till
after eleven. She corroborates his statement. McKay and
Hobson were upstairs in Hobson's room all evening, and a
friend called them up there about nine-thirty. Of course,
sor, that's not what you might call an ironclad alibi; you
could upset it, I've no doubt, if you saw a good reason for
it. But I'll take me oath they had nothing to do with it.
Sommers—he's the guy that Johns ran into on his way out
Tuesday evening—"

"I remember," murmured Ormsberry.

"Yes, sor. Well, he was in the club all evening, too.
Didn't leave till midnight, or thereabouts. George, the
doorman, remembers seeing him go out."

"Well," said Ormsberry, "that's that."

"The other two men," Hennessey told him, "are out of
town for the weekend. Shall I follow them up now, sir, or
will Monday do?"

Monday, the detective decided quickly, would do.

"I had quite a talk with this Sommers chap," Hennessey
went on. "He has been following the case a bit, sor, and he's
a smart young feller. He thinks Tyler's the guilty party."

"Does he?" murmured Ormsberry.

"Yes, sor," said Hennessey. He waited hopefully but no
comment came. "They tell me at the office, sor, that Tyler's been let out." Still no sound. "I thought you mightn't
know about it, sor," concluded Hennessey apologetically.

Ormsberry took pity on him, chuckling.

"It's all right," he said. "I knew about it. Now about
Roberts." And he gave his subordinate certain instructions
about meeting the Chicago train the next morning and

conducting Roberts straight to Anstruther's apartment. Then he added, as an afterthought: "I suppose Higgins hasn't anything to say yet?" And when Hennessey said he had not, Ormsberry said cheerfully: "Never mind!" He was singularly lighthearted.

Hennessey, at the other end of the wire, grinned. The chief was on the trail all right. But he shook his head over Tyler's release. Only his blind devotion to his chief permitted him to refrain from telling himself that that was a mistake.

Meanwhile, Ormsberry stepped out into the sunlit Avenue. An old-fashioned hansom cab stood at the curb, and he hailed it and got in. All the time in the world was his. Nothing on earth to do till Roberts got in the next morning. His thoughts turned to his long-unused golf clubs. He would go home and get them. Johnson should have his car sent round, and he would drive out to the Golf Club and stay out there and dine and forget all about the detection of crime.

He gave his address to the cabby and leaned back luxuriously, before his mind's eye the cool blue shadows of trees on greensward; under his feet the yielding spring of turf.

But as his cab turned toward the green oasis of Gramercy Park, this vision vanished; for up the steps of his apartment house, two at a time, dashed Plainclothes-man Jones. Ormsberry, leaping from his cab and thrusting a bill into the cabby's hand, knew what news it was that awaited him. Only one thing in the world could account for Jones's presence there at this time of day.

The detective dashed up the steps, slipped open the door, and rang for the elevator. It was, of course, already aloft with Jones, so he had to wait for a minute while it came down again. It must be confessed that it was a very uncomfortable minute. Mr. Ormsberry's heart never quite forgave him for the stern measures dictated by his head. But when he let himself into his apartment and met Jones standing uneasily on the foyer, he was quite cool again.

"Well?" he demanded.

Jones shifted uncomfortably from one foot to the other.

"Well, sir," he said, "I'm afraid I've spilled the beans. I took every precaution, as I thought, sir, but— Well, I ask you, sir: who'd have thought he'd walk right in in broad daylight, within hearing of half a dozen cops, and pull a gun, and shoot her?"

"I sent word to you," said Ormsberry sternly, "that you could expect anything from him."

"Yes, sir; but they said not to let her know she was being protected."

"Ah," murmured Ormsberry.

"That meant we couldn't draw the ring too close, sir. I had a man on the floor below and one on the floor above, to watch the stairs. And I had a man at the servants' entrance. There ain't any fire-escapes in that building. I hung around the front door myself, and had another man stuck in a little office off the main hall, in case I wanted him. As it happened, he was the only one of us who'd never seen Johns, but I figured that didn't matter, because I'd be there to tip him off. And anyway I just had him for a reinforcement like.

"Well, about an hour ago, sir, a boy came in with a note for me from the man I'd put at the servants' entrance, saying there was a row of windows opening into the cellar, along the back of the house, and hadn't we better put some one there?"

At this point Jones looked sheepishly at the rug.

"You know, sir, it didn't never occur to me to have any doubts about that note, but I couldn't remember seeing them windows, so I thought I'd go have a look. I called the feller I had left in the office—Casey, his name is—and told him to keep his eyes open till I got back. I figgered I'd only be gone a minute, and it wasn't likely this feller'd be showing up before night, anyway, so—well, sir, I went. And no sooner had I got out the door than in sails Mr. Johns, walks into the elevator as cool as brass, rides up to Mrs. Lorimer's flat, rings the bell, holds up the butler with a gun when he tries to stop him from going in, goes into the drawing-room, and when he finds nobody there goes straight down the hall into the bedroom, finds Mrs. Lorimer, and shoots her down—all before the butler can get help. Then he goes out again. Harper, the butler, gets a nick in the arm trying to stop him. Johns makes for the stairway, but our men have heard the shot and they close in on him in the hall and disarm him before he can do any more damage."

For an instant Mr. Ormsberry considered this appalling report.

"Mrs. Lorimer dead?" he asked then.

"Yes, sir."

"Did she say anything—make any statement?"

"No, sir. She was dead by the time her maid, who was in the next room, could get to her."

"How about Johns?

"He's gone cuckoo, I think, sir. He was carrying on like a crazy man by the time I got there."

"It was he who sent you that note?"

"Must have been, sir— to get me out of the way. At any rate, my man didn't know anything about it."

Ormsberry paced the room in some exasperation. "Why the devil didn't the elevator man recognise Johns and tip your man off?"

"I'd given all the house employees strict orders to carry on as though nothing was the matter and leave everything to us."

Ormsberry nodded briefly.

"Well," he said, "there's another door shut in our face. I suppose I took a frightful risk in letting that fellow out, but I couldn't see any other way of making her talk."

Jones coughed uneasily. Ormsberry, looking at the man's miserable face, could almost find it in his heart to be sorry for him.

"I'd like to say, sir," the plainclothes-man murmured, "that I'm very sorry, sir."

At this moment the telephone rang. It was Hennessey calling from headquarters, and his message caused Mr. Ormsberry to grab for his hat, and, with a curt word of dismissal for Jones, dash out and down the stairs, never waiting for the elevator. For the message ran. "Higgins is willing to talk."

At Headquarters Mr. Ormsberry found Higgins placidly smoking a very excellent cigar in Commissioner Reagan s office. The commissioner himself, balked of a weekend in the country by the turn affairs had taken, was pacing the floor impatiently, chewing at the stub of a black stogy.

"Ah, there you are!" said Reagan with an air of relief. "Now we can get ahead with this. You wait outside," he went on to the policeman stationed inside the door. He shut the door on the officer and, returning to his desk, sat down and elevated his feet to the mahogany. "Well, Higgins?"

Ormsberry looked curiously at the ex-gunman. His air was as jaunty as ever, and his wide, humorous mouth was curved in its habitual, satirical smile, but the detective fancied, nevertheless, that Higgins's superb aplomb was a trifle shaken. He was not smoking as a man does who is entirely at his ease, but jerkily, fumbling the cigar in his mouth.

"Well, gentlemen," said the ex-convict slowly, "I reckon my sense o' humour kinda ran away with me this time. I been gettin' a lot of fun out of this, but I guess I let it

go too far. I don't like this business of Mrs. Lorimer, sir.
This has got to be more than a joke."

"So!" murmured Reagan, looking at him speculatively,
"you had the idea that this was a joke, eh? You—"

But Higgins interrupted him.

"Steady, commissioner! I ain't much used to talkin' to
the police, and if I'm gonna tell this story, you gotta let
me tell it my own way, or I guess it's all off. You can keep
your wise cracks."

Ormsberry hastened to pour oil on troubled waters.

"That's just what we want," he said soothingly. "Take
your time. Tell it any way you like."

Higgins laughed and stretched his long length in his
chair.

"That's handsome of you, Mr. Ormsberry. Well, it's
a long story. I guess"—he looked slyly from one to the
other—"I got an idea I don't need to go back to the beginnin' of it. You can piece that out for yourselves. This is
what happened, beginnin' last Tuesday:

"I was up at Mike's place on Ninth Avenue eatin' my
supper around six-thirty when a guy I used to know before
I went up came breezing in. He spotted me right away and
came over. 'Hello, Scragger,' he says. 'Been lookin' for
you. The big cheese wants ter see you.' Well, I knew who
he meant, all right, but I wasn't aimin' to do no calling till
I knew what was what. So he sits down and orders some
food, and then when the waiter had gone off he slips me
a note. I ain't got the note to show you, 'cause I burned
it up, as per directions, but what it said was: 'Come right
away to the south-east corner of Ninth Avenue and Fifty-
fifth Street. There will be a closed car standin' at the curb.
Get in. I will be waitin' for you.' And if it had been signed,
gentlemen—which it wasn't—it woulda been a name we all
know."

The Scragger paused impressively.

"You recognised the writing?" Ormsberry prodded him.

Higgins grinned at him.

"Why wouldn't I? I'd seen it often enough. Well, I fig-gered it wouldn't do no harm to hear what he had to say, so I went down to the corner and there, sure enough, was the car. I got in and he began to drive round and round, so we could talk without bein' noticed."

"Who was the man?" demanded Reagan.

Higgins rebuked him as one might rebuke an overhasty child.

"No, you don't, commissioner. I tell this my own way. Well, it seems that somebody had told this bird that Ans-truther knew about a certain little matter in his past that he was mighty anxious to keep dark and he was in a blue funk. And so was his partner, who was just as much mixed up in the mess as he was. Well, the long and short of it was, they figgered it was worth twenty-five thousand to them to get Anstruther out of the way and they put it up to me."

At this point in his narrative Higgins developed a crit-ical interest in his finger nails; he studied them carefully, holding them off and staring at them through half-closed eyes.

"Of course," he said, "I told my friend 'nothin' doin'.'"

"Of course," murmured Ormsberry.

"But then," pursued the gunman slowly, "I got to thinkin' that, after all, I'd served five years for murderin' McGuire when, as you well know, commissioner, I was miles away from the place when the murder was committed."

He grinned slyly at Reagan, but the commissioner was now his bland self again.

"Of course," he said smoothly, "we all know you were innocent."

"Well, now!" cried Higgins. "That is handsome of you, commissioner. Well, as I say, I got thinkin' that, and I

figgered the State really owed me that twenty-five thousand; five thousand a year ain't much, considering—if I
may say so—my natural gifts. So I told my friend I'd think
about it. So he says the quicker I do my thinkin' the better, and that his pal will give me a ring at Mike's around
seven-thirty and tell me where to pick up this Anstruther
bird. So then he drops me at Ninth Avenue, a couple o'
blocks from where we started, and I goes back to Mike's.

"Well, commissioner, sure enough, at seven-thirty a
guy rings up and says this feller Anstruther will be leavin'
the Fontenoy Club around nine, and goin' downtown to a
party at Mrs. Mortimer's place, and I could pick him up
there. But the more I thought about it the less I liked it,
so finally I decided to give the idea the air. Then it struck
me that, if this sort of thing was goin' on, I'd better be
seen pretty prominent for a while, in case anythin' happened, so I went round to Scipio's and got in a game with
Officer O'Hara and some of the boys, and in that game I
stayed till midnight."

The gunman paused. Reagan twisted his stodgy thoughtfully.

"So you think your friend got tired waiting for you to
make up your mind and did the thing himself?"

"No," said Higgins, "I don't—and for a damn' good
reason, too. You see, I figgered it would be bad business
to bump Anstruther off, but I did need that twenty-five
thousand pretty bad. So, when I read all about how Anstruther got his on that bus, in the papers next morning,
I argued it this way: I knew those two guys a long time
ago, you see, commissioner, and I knew 'em plenty. I knew
they was both yellow clean through, an' there wasn't a
chance they'd run a risk like that themselves as long as
they could get somebody to do it for 'em. And they didn't
know I'd changed my mind about it. So I figgered that
what they didn't know wouldn't hurt 'em. All they wanted

was to have Anstruther's mouth shut, and shut it was. They wouldn't be too particular about who did it or how. So I studied up everything there was in the papers about it, so I wouldn't give myself away, and then I went to see 'em and collected the dough."

Here Ormsberry broke in.

"In other words, you called on Mr. Tyler and Mr. Johns at a quarter to five last Wednesday afternoon."

"That's about it," assented Higgins.

"And they paid you the twenty-five?"

Higgins grinned.

"They sure did."

"Did Mrs. Lorimer have anything to do with the affair?" the detective went on.

"Not as far as I know," said the gunman.

Ormsberry considered thoughtfully.

"I imagine, since she entered the house just after Johns that afternoon, she must have overheard your conversation and used her knowledge to blackmail them afterward."

Higgins stirred uneasily.

"I never did like to have a skirt mixed up in men's affairs," he said. "That's why I've spilled the works," he went on, looking shrewdly at Ormsberry. "There's goin' to be more trouble, if you don't watch out. Mrs. Tyler knows too much about this. And when Tyler gets busy he's apt to do a nastier job than this thing Johns pulled off."

"Tyler won't have a chance," Ormsberry promised him.

27

The freshness of early morning still lingered in the air as the luxurious open car rolled down the Avenue at nine o'clock next morning. The Sunday hush lay over everything; the busy thoroughfare, deserted now, and crossed with alternate lines of sunlight and blue shadow, was caught in a net of unreality and enchantment.

But Joan, sitting silent and distrait in her corner of the car, seemed not to feel the quiet peace about her. Keyed to an almost hysterical pitch by the nervous strain of the week and the excitement of the coming interview, it was all she could do to maintain an outward semblance of composure. Mr. Speck studied her anxiously: the lovely, pale face under the shady straw hat, the tense lines of the slender figure, the fierce grip of the little hands clasped in her lap. And he hoped devoutly that the strain would soon be over.

Only the Admiral seemed to be thoroughly enjoying himself. He sat between them, radiant in his newest and bluest suit, with a collar so stiff and so high as to be at once a torment and a delight. And his small chest was expanded with an ecstatic pride, for was he not summoned to attend a conclave of the chief figures of the greatest murder mystery of the year—a conclave which he himself had made possible by his own independent investigations?

The matter had been arranged the night before in a conference between Mr. Ormsberry, Mr. Speck, and Joan Archer, in the course of which the detective had laid before them the progress of the case to date and told them of his approaching interview with Roberts the following morning.

"Of course, you'll let me be there?" Joan begged. "You surely won't keep me out of it any longer?"

Mr. Speck had regarded her doubtfully.

"I think it unwise, my dear," he began, but the girl broke in wretchedly:

"Unwise? You all think it unwise for me to do anything. Brian won't even see me—"

"My dear child," the little lawyer patted her hand gently, "he doesn't want you to be distressed by meeting him under such unhappy circumstances."

Joan cast at him a blighting look expressive of woman's innate conviction of the ineradicable stupidity of man.

"Well, unwise or not, I shall be at that meeting at Mr. Anstruther's apartment, if I have to climb in the window—shan't I, Mr. Ormsberry?"

Ormsberry had conceded the point handsomely.

"Naturally!" He smiled at her with a gentleness that few people ever saw in his face. Then he looked quizzically at Mr. Speck. "Tell you some one else we ought to have," he said: "the Admiral. He's earned it."

And so it was arranged. And so it happened that Bill was driving down the Avenue en route to join the group that was to meet Roberts on his arrival from Chicago.

Meanwhile Ormsberry paced the cool length of Anstruther's library. The case was, he realised, reaching its climax. The irrelevant branches, so to speak, had one by one been lopped off. Higgins and Tyler had been liberated;

the search had focused on one point—the identity of the man in the overstuffed chair. Curiously enough, thought the detective, he held all the other threads in his hand—motive, method, time, place; only the name eluded him. Would Roberts be able to supply the clue to that identity?

Was Roberts, perhaps, himself the man?

If he was, it was uncommonly cool of him to come back to New York. But then the man they wanted was uncommonly cool. Ormsberry investigated door and window, and saw that the men he had placed on guard were at their posts. If Roberts was the man, he would not escape him. Then he took up again his impatient pacing.

Ormsberry went rapidly over his interview with Tyler the night before. He thought they would have no further trouble with that gentleman—there would be no tragic aftermath, as there had been in the case of Reddington Johns. The detective had laid all his cards on the table. And he had given Tyler to understand that he was safe as long as he did not molest his wife. On the other hand, Ormsberry had made it quite plain that he had ample grounds for a charge of conspiracy and attempted murder and that the charge would be pressed to the limit if Miriam Tyler were not allowed to adjust her life in peace. No, they would not hear again from Mr. Tyler.

The rattle of a cab coming to a halt in the street outside took the detective to the front windows. Hennessey at last, and with him a slender, brown-haired young man with an agreeable countenance—Roberts, of course. Plainly he had come direct from the train, for the ex-secretary's bag was in front beside the driver. While he watched, Mr. Ormsberry saw a great open car turn in from the Avenue and come to a purring stop just behind the taxicab. The Admiral clambered out and gave his hand gravely to Joan. Ormsberry, stifling a smile, returned to the library.

It was a grave group that confronted Ormsberry as the great detective paused in his rapid summing up of the case half an hour later. He had been outlining the course of the investigation for Roberts's benefit, and now all eyes turned expectantly on the young man.

"Well!" the ex-secretary exclaimed. The tone was compounded with amazement, incredulity, and live, intense interest.

"I take it that you are willing to help us," the detective suggested.

"Naturally," the young man said. "I'd have been on before this, if I had had any idea that I could be of use to you."

"Perhaps you'd better begin by telling us about your break with Anstruther."

The young man stiffened. He was no fool, and he saw whither the question tended. But he answered with unhesitating frankness.

"Certainly. Mr. Anstruther was a most difficult man to work for. He had a way of leaving his work until the last possible moment and then keeping at it night and day until he got it done. At least, he kept me at it night and day, for when he'd finished his dictation—which he'd sometimes continue for nine or ten hours, almost at a stretch—I'd have to transcribe my notes and be ready to go on with him next morning. And besides the actual work involved, he would be at such times irascible and extremely difficult to get on with. I stood it as long as I could. As a matter of fact, I liked him so well that I hated to leave him. But this last time—well, I got fed up on it, and quit. And that's all there was to it."

Ormsberry nodded.

"That fits in very well with what I've heard," he said slowly. "I'm prepared to accept what you say. Now, to get on. Can you suggest any way for us to come at the plot of this last story Anstruther was writing?"

"Do I understand you to mean," asked Roberts slowly, "that the clue to the murder is to be found in the plot of this story?"

"I'm certain of it," said Ormsberry briefly.

Roberts's hands went out in a gesture of impotence.

"Then I'm very sorry, sir, but I'm afraid I can't help you. I haven't the slightest idea about Mr. Anstruther's theory of Mr. Fortescue's death. He was very jealous of his plots until after they were written. Some one stole a plot from him once, and since then he's made a practice of keeping them to himself until the story was completed. Then he'd discuss them with any one who'd listen to him."

"Then he hadn't begun this story when you left him?"

"Oh, yes, sir; he dictated fully half of it to me."

Ormsberry shot out of his chair.

"He did! And yet you still haven't any idea of his theory?"

"Not the slightest. As far as he'd gone when I left, the thing was written very much from the newspaper angle, with no indication of how it was to be concluded." Roberts looked at the disappointed faces about him almost apologetically. "I'll say this, though: I know positively that Mr. Anstruther didn't suspect Mr. Channing, for he said again and again that, with this to go on, Mr. Channing couldn't help but put his hand on the murderer."

"What I can't understand," said Mr. Speck mournfully, "is why he did not come to me—or Mr. Ormsberry—with his theories, instead of waiting for Channing to get back from Europe."

Roberts looked with some embarrassment from the little lawyer to Mr. Ormsberry and back again.

"Well, sir—if you'll pardon my frankness—he felt that—that you hadn't followed up the case with the—er—necessary firmness."

"In other words," interpolated the detective dryly, "he thought we were a pair of blockheads."

The ex-secretary smiled.

"Well, he did sometimes put it that way, sir.'

"One can't precisely blame him." For a moment Ormsberry considered. Then he shot another question: "Do you
think Anstruther actually knew the name of the man he
believed to be guilty of Fortescue's death?"

"No, sir; I'm sure he didn't, because he continually re-
ferred to the fact that it was Channing's business locate
the guilty man, not his. As far as I can make out, what
he did was to reason out that there must be some one
connected with the case in a certain way—some one who
had a certain motive for wishing Mr. Fortescue out of the
way—and that once that was pointed out, it would be easy
enough to find the man. The difficulty was that no one
had ever distantly connected the murderer with any of the
people concerned. Once attention was called to him he
couldn't escape for a day."

"Evidently Mr. Anstruther was right," murmured Ormsberry thoughtfully.

Here Mr. Speck intervened.

"I don't quite follow your reasoning."

"Clearly, when Anstruther told the man we are trying
to find—the man in the library of the Fontenoy Club—
when Anstruther told him the plot of his newest story,
this man was so impressed with the force of the novelist's
reasoning that he followed him on to the bus and killed
him. Clearly he, too, thought that he would not escape for
a day, once attention was called to him."

Joan shuddered slightly. The secretary spoke in an awed
tone:

"Then Anstruther actually told his story to—"

He hesitated and Ormsberry took up the sentence.

"To the one man in the world most interested in hearing it; the one man he had succeeded in tracking where the

police department of New York had failed—the man who killed Fortescue."

"My God!" murmured Roberts faintly.

"I imagine the way it happened," Ormsberry went on, "was, he probably said he had written a story on the Fortescue case, and this man, taking alarm, egged him on to tell the whole tale, and then—"

They sat in silence, feeling the chill upon them of that strange little scene; the murderer and the man who had, without knowing it, discovered his secret, the unknown drawing from his prospective victim every detail of plot, his plans for the story; drawing from him, too, doubtless, the fact that nobody else, as yet, knew his theory of the Fortescue case, but that he meant to tell Brian Channing, due home from Europe that very evening, and that he meant to mail the story as soon as he had checked up on a certain legal technicality; drawing from him, finally, by flattering interest in the author's craft, his methods of working, whether he set down notes for his stories, whether he kept a carbon copy and where; and then—

That scene on the bus; the swift, unsuspected stroke; the looting of the dead man's pocket for the story and his keys; the looting of the dead man's rooms for the carbon.

This was ground they had often travelled together, but it came to them again with an added sense of drama, now that they were sure that it was true—that that strange scene had actually taken place.

Ormsberry's voice broke in on the silence; it struck in their faces with the shock of ice water. Ormsberry the man was gone; only the man hunter remained.

"Now," said this strange Ormsberry, "we are going to find this man's name." He turned to Roberts. "You understand Anstruther's methods. I want you to look in the places where he kept his notes—memoranda—wherever it occurs to you that there is the slightest chance of finding a reference to this matter. And take your time about it. We will stay here till we find something."

Roberts went to work with a quiet efficiency that elicited the detective's unspoken praise and filled Mr. Speck with a desire to annex this treasure to his official staff. Joan and the Admiral followed him with excited interest. This was more like it, the boy thought. He was tired of fine-spun logical sequences. Action was what the plot required, he felt. Unwilling as he was to criticise his hero, he felt that something should be done in the way of looking for finger prints, too. Every good detective he'd ever read about looked for finger prints. He began prospecting on his own account.

No one paid any attention to him. Blissfully he crawled into corners, covering the knees of his new trousers with dust, for the rooms, at Mr. Ormsberry's express command, had not been touched since the day of the crime. He scrambled on chairs, searching the edges of the bookshelves; he explored the cavern under the novelist's desk.

Meanwhile, Roberts prosecuted his researches. But an hour's hard work, while apparently covering the ground thoroughly, brought nothing to light.

"I can't make it out, sir," said the secretary doubtfully. "There must be something, of course. I remember, for one thing, that Mr. Anstruther had a little blank book in which he occasionally made jottings and slipped newspaper clippings."

"This it?" Ormsberry drew from his pocket the little book in which he had found the clipping with the extract from the cross-examination of Estelle Fortescue.

"Yes, sir."

"Know anything about the clipping?"

"Yes, sir. Mr. Anstruther was much excited when he read it, I remember, sir. I quite got the notion that it was that clipping that gave him his idea about the case."

Ormsberry puzzled over it again.

"'Q. Why did you quarrel with your brother? A. Because of the position he was permitting Joan Archer to assume in his house.' Now, what the devil?" His eye skipped down a few lines. "'Q. Although you had lived there for many years, you left because he wanted to make his daughter the mistress of his house? A. She was not his daughter, although she disliked it very much when any one recalled the fact.' Now what did he read into that?" Ormsberry shrugged. "It's beyond me. I'm hanged if I can see it. Well, have you anything else to suggest?"

Roberts rubbed his hands on his handkerchief thoughtfully, for his progress from drawer to drawer had been a dusty one.

"Of course, sir, there are the letters. It's just possible he may have made some mention of the matter in writing to one of his friends. He was a man who kept up a very active correspondence."

But the search of the correspondence drawer elicited the information that Mr. Anstruther had either not written any letters since his secretary's departure, or had kept no carbons of them. At this point, however a new idea seemed to strike Roberts.

"We'll try the drawer of answers, sir. Some friend of his may mention the affair."

Briskly Roberts turned to this new task, choosing, evidently, the correspondents with whom the novelist kept most constantly in touch. After fifteen minutes of careful skimming, he crossed to Mr. Ormsberry, who was sitting at Anstruther's desk, and laid before him an open letter.

"What do you think, sir?" The tip of his pencil indicated a certain sentence, and Ormsberry read it aloud thoughtfully.

"I was much interested in your reference to
the Fortescue case. I remember your saying,
long ago, that you would solve it. When is the
secret to be released for publication?"

The detective turned the letter over and looked for the
signature.

"Who is Joseph Sutton?" he asked sharply.

"An old friend of Mr. Anstruther's."

"H'm!" The detective pondered the letter. "My guess is
that the most Anstruther told him was that he had solved
the case."

"Still . . ." murmured the secretary, and paused sugges-
tively.

"You're right, of course. We must have a go at Mr. Sutton. Here!" The detective got to his feet and tore the cover
from Anstruther's typewriter. "If you don't mind, I'll give
you a letter now, and we'll get it off. Where's the place?"
He glanced at the letter in his hand. "Albany. Send it spe-
cial. I don't suppose it will come to anything, but—" He
turned to Roberts. "Want to take it shorthand?"

"Won't be necessary, sir. I'll type it at your dictation."

Roberts seated himself at Anstruther's desk and got out
some sheets of blank paper. Joan watched him, rigid as a
statue and almost as pale. She had come to this meeting
with such high hopes! The Admiral withdrew his attention
from his personal researches and looked on with a bored
air. It seemed that the doings of the great were less interesting than he supposed. Mr. Speck rose and moved uneasily about. This was ghoulish—positively ghoulish. This
prowling around the rooms of a dead man, searching into
his private affairs.

Roberts took out the box of carbon paper from a drawer and found it empty. He crossed to his own desk—the

desk where he had sat as Anstruther's secretary—and rum-
maged there. Again he found an empty box.

Ormsberry, who had been following his movements
idly, while he thought out what he wanted to say, spoke
now:

"It doesn't matter. You can type off a copy."

But the Admiral also had been following Roberts's
search, and at this point he intervened helpfully.

"Here's some carbon paper, sir," he said, and he reached
into the waste basket beside Anstruther's desk, bringing
up a crumpled piece. "Wait a minute—here's a better one."
His second reach was more successful; he brought up a
scarcely used sheet, only slightly rumpled, and placed it
triumphantly before Mr. Ormsberry on the desk. After
all, he reflected with modest satisfaction, they would find
it pretty hard to get along without him. But he only said
respectfully: "This is all right, sir. It's only been used once."

He turned back to his prowling. Only Joan saw the sudden spark in the cool Ormsberry eye. But they all caught
the excitement in his voice as he said suddenly:

"By Jove!" They turned and looked at him. He was
clutching the carbon in both hands, his face white as paper, his eyes shining. Hennessey, watching from the doorway, knew that the boss was on the scent at last. Ormsberry
looked up, but he was looking at his own inspiration,
and not at the faces of his friends. When he spoke, he
was speaking to himself. "Why, of course," he said softly.
"That story was the last thing Anstruther wrote."

Suddenly he dashed into the bedroom and yanked up
the drawn shade. They followed him in a body and found
him standing at the bureau, holding the sheet of carbon
before him and staring at its reflection in the glass.

"It's the last page of Anstruther's story," he almost
shouted at them. "It's got to be. Listen!" He began to

read. Even from where they stood, they could see the clear reflection of letters in the glass, although they could not read the words.

"It begins with a broken sentence," Ormsberry went on. He began:

> "'from Europe.
>
> "'The weak point in her evidence, of course,' the detective went on, 'was the reason she gave for her quarrel with her brother. That was, on the face of it, insufficient, and consequently untrue. What then, I asked myself, was the real cause of quarrel? a cause sufficient to bring about a breach between devoted brother and sister; something, moreover, which caused the brother to adopt the curious expedient *not* of cutting his sister completely out of his will, but of leaving her an annuity: the only means of providing for her and yet, at the same time, preventing her from gaining control of a considerable fortune?'
>
> "The detective leaned back and looked triumphant from one interested face to another.
>
> "'Of course,' he finished his summing up, 'the whole thing became clear to me when I—'"

Ormsberry broke off. His eye, it was clear, had taken that last sentence at a glance. He turned the carbon from the mirror and, taking it back to the desk, laid it between two sheets of paper, rolling them carefully. His hands were unsteady with excitement.

"By Jove!" he murmured. "Of course! Naturally. Beautiful work! What an idiot—" He broke off and turned to Hennessey. "We've got him now," he said quietly, quite his imperturbable self again. "Find out what ship Estelle Fortescue came home on last year," he directed, "and get me the passenger list. Here! Wait a minute." He sat down at the desk and dashed off a note in a running hand. This note he gave to Hennessey. "Stop on your way and see that that's sent off at once to Scotland Yard. And now get a move on. I'll meet you presently at headquarters."

Hennessey rushed out and Ormsberry reached for his hat. Joan clung for a minute to his arm.

"Who is it?" she begged. "Who is it? Not Brian?"

Ormsberry pressed the clinging hand reassuringly.

"Of course it isn't Brian, my dear. I can't tell you who it is—yet—but I'm on my way to find out. Hang it! Why the devil can't I remember the fellow's name?" He was at the door when Speck's voice reached him.

"Where are you going now?" demanded the lawyer. "Aren't you going to give us a hint?"

Ormsberry turned to them his fighting face, with the strange grim smile.

"Nary hint! I'm off to spend a pleasant afternoon with the files of the New York *Sphere.*"

And then he went away and left them gasping.

28

Hennessey lost no time in obeying his chief's orders. He picked up a cab at the corner and had himself driven to the cable office. On the way he studied carefully the message Ormsberry had given him to forward to Scotland Yard. At the bottom, the detective had written:

Send in duplicate to the Paris Sûreté.

Hennessey whistled under his breath.

"Holy saints preserve us! So that's the way the wind blows," he murmured.

At the cable offices he sent his messages. Then he hurried up to headquarters. A brief scrutiny of the files of the Fortescue case gave him the name of the ship Estelle Fortescue had returned on, and he was off again, it being Sunday, he had some little difficulty in getting hold of any one at the shipping office, but he succeeded at last, and returned in triumph with the passenger list of the *Kent* on her trip from London to New York, date of February first, the year before.

Meanwhile Ormsberry went directly to the office of the *Sphere*. Gone was every doubt and question, like a mist before a March wind. Every muscle, every thought and instinct, every feeling, coordinated by a great certainty,

strained toward one end. He was on the right track now.
The fox was in view.

At the doors of the newspaper offices he almost ran
into Jim Gaynor, a tall, loose-limbed young giant who had
reported the Fortescue trial the year before. To the detective's annoyance, young Gaynor now grabbed him by the
arm and pulled him out of the human stream flowing back
and forth through the doorway.

"Say!" the youngster grinned at him. "Where's the fire?
Too proud to know your old friends?"

The detective reflected that this boy would go far in
the newspaper world. He had nerve enough for six.

"The fire, my child," he remarked pointedly, "is in your
back-number files room, and I have an engagement with it."

"Tut-tut!" young Gaynor reproved him. "Can it be that
you are annoyed with me? And I was just about to present
you with a perfectly good scoop."

"I thought there was something cocky about you," murmured the detective. "What's up now?"

"Possibly," grinned Gaynor, "you remember a certain
famous murder trial last year?"

"Possibly I do," said Ormsberry grimly.

"Well, I was taking the air past that house of worship
known as the Little Church Around the Corner, some half-
hour ago, and whom should I see popping into the edifice,
with a large and conspicuously bridal-looking bouquet on
her arm, but our old friend and playmate the sister of the
victim."

Ormsberry's absent gaze fixed suddenly on his infor-
mant.

"Not Estelle Fortescue?"

"The same. Well, there were several people in the car
with her, and I slipped along in the wake of the party
until I had a chance to get the attention of one of the
men. 'What's up?' I asked him. 'Isn't that Miss Fortescue?'

He gave me a chilly once-over, but he answered at last and admitted that it was. By this time it was perfectly certain that it was going to be a wedding and I was able to spot the groom. 'Who's the lucky man?' I asked my chilly friend. Well, he gave me a look like a fat old dowager might give a butler who's spilled ice water down her neck, and was going to quit me cold, but I grabbed his arm and said with a husk in my voice: 'You see, this is a terrible shock to me because she—I—I used to know her once—' Oh, heck, you know the stuff. I don't think the old gazabo believed me, but he loosened up enough to give me the man's name. 'Who is he?' I asked. 'I never heard of the guy before.' 'Englishman,' says my friend. 'Hasn't been over here long.' And then we were interrupted. They were ready to start, so I stuck around until the knot was tied, and then beat it over here. What do you know about that? That old lemon getting hooked up!"

Ormsberry studied him with amusement. The strain of hurry had left him. He appeared to have all day before him.

"You've saved me a trip to your files, so I'll forgive you for being a rotten newspaper man. Don't you know that Miss Fortescue's engagement was announced several days ago, and in your own inferior sheet?"

"Heck!" cried Gaynor disgustedly. "How'd I miss that?"

"Furthermore," murmured the detective, "you've left out the point of your story: what was the name of the man Estelle Fortescue married?"

"Don't you know? Thought you'd read the engagement announcement," countered Gaynor impudently. "His name is Gregory Sommers."

Ormsberry drew a long breath. Then he grabbed young Gaynor's arm.

"Are you still interested in the Fortescue case?" he demanded.

"Am I dead and buried?" countered the newspaper man. "What is it? Got something?"

"Got something? I've got everything. Where's the nearest telephone?" the detective demanded. "Come with me. You're in for the biggest scoop of your life, young man."

"This way." Gaynor led him to a nearby 'phone booth and waited impatiently while Ormsberry called headquarters.

"Reilly covering Jerry Howard?" the detective demanded of the man at the other end of the phone. "Can you pick him up? I want Howard at headquarters as soon as you can get him there." Then he gave certain other crisp, decisive directions, hung up the receiver, and joined his friend at the door.

"I've got a cab," young Gaynor told him. "Where do we go from here?"

"Headquarters," said Ormsberry briefly; "and tell him to eat it up."

An hour later Jerry Howard was facing Ormsberry in the latter's office at police headquarters: a subdued Jerry Howard, though still blustering intermittently. On the desk before the detective lay the passenger list that Hennessey had brought, and the list that had been supplied by the doorman at the Fontenoy Club. There was also Reilly's report. Reilly himself stood against the door, and Hennessey and a stenographer sat in the background, while Gaynor paced the corridor outside, impatient for his promised coup.

"So you see," Ormsberry was saying, "there's no use in your trying to put anything over on us."

"But I tell you, I don't know anything about it," protested Howard feebly.

"How do you explain the letter you received with—was it five thousand?—enclosed?"

"Poker debts," murmured Howard miserably.

"When did you play poker on Tuesday evening, Mr. Howard? You were at Mrs. Mortimer's, as I remember."

"Well, it was a private matter, anyway. It had nothing to do with this."

"What was this private matter?"

Howard said nothing.

"I'll tell you." Ormsberry leaned toward him across the desk. "You recognised the man you saw in Anstruther's library on Tuesday evening, just as you told me in Mr. Speck's office next morning. But you didn't think it was Brian Channing. You knew it wasn't Brian Channing for the simple reason that you knew it was somebody else— some one whom you have since been blackmailing."

"It's a lie," growled Howard.

"Who was that man? I want his name and I mean to have it. I may tell you, in parenthesis, that I have it already, but I want your confirmation."

"That's too easy." Howard grinned at him uncertainly. "Try something better."

"I'm not bluffing. Here!" The detective threw the two lists across the desk to him. "Look at these. See if the name isn't on both of them."

Howard reached for the papers. He realised his slip too late and drew back his hand, but the detective had seen the gesture.

"It's no good," he said. "We know that you recognised the man."

Shamefacedly Howard took up the lists and glanced down them. After a minute he nodded and threw them down.

"Yes," he said. "You're right, though how you ever got at it I can't imagine."

"You're prepared to identify him?"

"I suppose I can't help myself."

At the Grand Central Station Estelle Fortescue and her husband stood in a little group of laughing friends, saying good-bye. They were going to Canada for their honeymoon, and they were very gay. Nobody noticed that while Estelle, radiant with happiness, had eyes only for her young husband, Gregory Sommers turned often to glance at the crowd that is never absent from the great terminal.

"Well," he said presently, "let's get aboard." He nodded at the porters waiting with their luggage.

But that triumphant little passage through the gate was never made. An insignificant man had slipped beside the gate-man while they were talking, and now he tapped Sommers on the arm.

"They want to talk to you at headquarters, sir. I'm sure you'll come quietly, so as not to make a fuss."

Sommers turned ghastly white under his sunburn. His immediate impulse was flight, but he was conscious now of two or three more insignificant-looking men, all watching him covertly. He pulled himself together with a shrug. He turned to his wife.

"My dear, I'm sorry, but I shall be detained. I suggest that you go home with our friends and I'll communicate with you as soon as I can."

"What's the matter?" gasped Estelle.

The plainclothes-man looked at her pityingly. There was something in her face that touched even his sophisticated heart.

"Sorry, ma'am, but he's wanted for the murder of Anstruther and John Fortescue. You'd better come along, too, ma'am. They want to ask you some questions."

29

It was not until the following afternoon that the formalities leading to Brian's release from jail and the dismissal of the case against him were completed.

To Joan, waiting in the shadowy drawing-room of the Fortescue house, it made little difference why or how he had been liberated. It was enough for her to know that he was free, cleared of every breath of suspicion, and that she, too, was exonerated, reinstated in the eyes of the world, free to take without a qualm the happiness that was even then on its way to her.

She heard the faint disturbance in the hall that betokened his arrival, and suddenly found that her feet had carried her across the room and into his arms.

They talked very little as they sat together through that long summer twilight, and what they said had nothing to do with the murder mysteries in which their lives had been so tragically involved.

"Of course, you've given that bounder his walking papers, Joan?" was Brian's first coherent remark.

Joan made some sort of murmur against his coat, which he took for assent.

"I knew you would," he said comfortably.

"It seems to me," cried Joan with some return of her old spirit, "that you take a good deal for granted, sir!"

But he only laughed at her, covering the unruly depths of his emotion with banter.

"Little goose," he whispered, "I've known you belonged to me—ever since that day last week when you sent for me to tell me that you'd never see me again."

"Was that the bright idea you were boasting about?" cried Joan, laughing and crying at once.

"That was it," he assented. "The best one I ever had, too!"

Mr. Speck, dining that Monday night in Mona Adams's pleasant apartment, would also have willingly postponed until the morrow any discussion of the hows and whys of the solution of the mystery. But the Admiral did not see eye to eye with him in this matter. His face was fairly shining with excitement, and his small body wriggled with impatience while his elders discussed plans for their approaching marriage. That was all right, too, as far as the Admiral was concerned. He had been graciously pleased to express his approval when the matter had been put up to him. But he didn't see why they had to talk about it so much, now it was settled.

"Gee!" he murmured hopefully, "wisht I could go an' see Mr. Ormsberry t'night."

This elicited no response and he tried again.

"Gee! Guess it was lucky you took me along yesterday. Guess it was a lucky thing I found that carbon paper in the waste basket!" This drew their attention at last. He went on to the subject nearest his heart. "Guess I've showed you now what I can do," he remarked, his chest swollen with complacence. "I guess nobody'll have much to say about me being a detective now—after I've just solved two murder mysteries."

Mr. Speck choked slightly over his coffee.

"I guess they won't, son." But he was not really thinking of the Admiral. His thoughts reverted, by a logic comprehensible to lovers, to Brian and his happiness. "Brian will be with Joan now," he said, and smiled at Mona Adams.

Bill looked from one to the other in disgust. Then he slid from his chair and slipped, unnoticed, from the room. An hour later Johnson, somewhat startled, was admitting to Ormsberry's apartment a freckled-faced youngster who stated calmly that, if the detective was out, he would just as soon step into the drawing-room and wait.

Meanwhile, in his office at police headquarters Ormsberry was still pursuing his long-drawn-out examination of Gregory Sommers and Estelle Fortescue, which had begun early in the afternoon, and now, with the late summer dark closing in, was still at a deadlock. The two persisted in their denial of any guilty knowledge of the crime. They gave straightforward accounts of their whereabouts at the time of both murders, and stuck to them during hours of cross-examination.

Sommers had demanded, and had immediately been granted, the right to legal advice; but William Strang, senior partner of Strang and Strang, who had sat with them through the grueling hours of that blazing hot afternoon, had been more ornamental than useful. It appeared that Mr. Sommers was quite capable of handling the matter himself. Despite his disarming air of ingenuous youthfulness, it was clear that he had a very shrewd perception of the strength of his position. He was, it is true, unable to produce a very strong alibi; but he quickly perceived that the State, in the person of the redoubtable Mr. Ormsberry, was unable to prove a motive. So he stuck to his story and his injured innocence, and could not be stirred. He very quickly saw that the detective shrank from the painful

duty of availing himself of the hysterical state of Estelle
Fortescue.

Ormsberry sat back in his swivel chair and studied the
man thoughtfully. Here was an opponent worthy of his steel.

"So you still persist," he said slowly, "in your statement
that you remained at the Fontenoy Club until midnight on
Tuesday evening?"

Mr. Sommers smiled imperturbably.

"Certainly. George, the doorman, will vouch the hour
at which I left the club."

"Yes; you called his attention to it, I believe," said
Ormsberry dryly.

"I believe I did," assented Sommers.

"We have this morning," went on the detective, "examined the rear of the club house, and we find that it would
have been quite possible for you to get into the yard at
the back by means of an alley from the next street, enter
the club through a rear window of the steward's office, go
upstairs by the back stairway, and leave the club again at
your convenience by the front door."

Sommers raised interested eyebrows.

"Yes? And have you also proved that I did these things
you speak of?"

"Do you deny that you did?"

"Certainly."

"In spite of the fact that Mr. Howard recognised you in
the library of Anstruther's apartment shortly before ten?"

Sommers shrugged.

"In view of the fact that Mr. Howard first identified
Brian Channing in the role of the burglar, and that Miss
Archer, too, saw him there, I can't say that I think his
statement of much value."

"You deny that he attempted to blackmail you with his
knowledge, and that you paid him five thousand to hold
his tongue?"

"Certainly I deny it!" Sommers added a polite query of his own. "Why should I allow myself to be blackmailed for being in Mr. Anstruther's apartment when I've never been there in my life, and knew nothing about his death until the next day?"

"Do you deny that you talked to Mr. Anstruther at the club on the night he was killed?"

Mr. Strang leaned forward.

"You are not obliged to answer that, Mr. Sommers," he said. "I should advise—"

Sommers shrugged aside the suggestion.

"I see no reason to make a mystery of it," he said.

"Certainly I talked with Mr. Anstruther at the club. So, I imagine, did a number of others. Why not? I often saw him there, although we never met elsewhere."

"Do you deny that he told you the plot of his latest story?"

Sommers considered.

"He didn't tell me the plot of it," he said; "he simply told me he had just finished a mystery story that had rather sensational possibilities, and that he meant to send it off that evening."

"And you didn't ask him, I suppose," said Ormsberry dryly, "what it was about?"

"As a matter of fact, I did," countered Sommers with disarming candour, "but he refused to tell me. Said he'd rather promised to keep it to himself until he'd given his ideas to—the man most interested." And the accused affected a profound concern with the mirrorlike perfection of his immaculate boots. "It's unfortunate for the cause of justice that he didn't tell me the theory back of his story—if, indeed, as you suppose, that was the motive for his murder—for then I could give you a leg up, as it were, in tracking your man. You're sure, I fancy, that he didn't leave any notes—any jottings of the general idea?"

"Quite sure," said Ormsberry dryly.

Here Mr. Strang took a hand.

"I would be glad to know, Mr. Ormsberry," he said, "what reasonable grounds you have for holding my client. You say that he killed Mr. Anstruther for the purpose of suppressing the novelist's theory of the Fortescue murder mystery, but you have not shown that Mr. Sommers had any connection whatever with hat case, or any motive in wishing to suppress anything in relation to it."

Ormsberry glanced at Estelle Fortescue.

"In view of yesterday's event, I think it possible to indicate that Mr. Sommers had a motive for wishing to prevent the disinheritance of Miss Fortescue by her brother."

"My dear sir!" Clearly Sommers was shocked. "At the time of Mr. Fortescue's death it would have been in the highest degree presumptuous for me to have any plans whatever in regard to Miss Fortescue."

"You returned from Europe on the same ship."

"Mere shipboard acquaintances!" protested Sommers.

"You escorted her to her brother's house."

"Again the courtesy of a mere acquaintance. If, at that time, I hoped already that the acquaintance might ripen into something more, it was a hope founded only upon my ardent wish. There was no understanding of any sort between us."

"This is true?" Mr. Ormsberry addressed Miss Fortescue, now Mrs. Sommers, almost for the first time.

When she answered it was in a tone broken by fatigue and strain.

"Quite true."

The detective looked from one to the other. Then he drew open the top drawer of his desk, took out a cable blank, and spread it out before him.

"Then how do you account for this?" he asked softly. "I have here a cable from the Paris Sûreté, received this afternoon, which reads as follows:

"Marriage recorded at Fontainebleau, January
20, 1925. Estelle Fortescue to Gregory Sommers."

"Now," said Mr. Ormsberry briskly, "I think we will
have the whole story."

Mr. Strang intervened at once.

"I shall advise my client to say nothing further at this
time, until we have had opportunity to consult as to the
proper means of defence against this charge."

"Very well," Ormsberry agreed.

"No, no!" cried Estelle Fortescue. "Tell him the truth,
Greg—the whole truth. It's the only way."

The only way!" Sommers turned on her, and lor an instant the smiling mask was torn aside. "The less you say
the better," he said shortly; "and the less you forget that
you are—after all—my wife."

"I'm beginning to remember that I'm John Fortescue's
sister," she moaned wretchedly. She turned beseechingly
to Ormsberry. "I can't stand this any longer," she said.
"Please believe me that I didn't know! Sometimes I've had
suspicions, but I fooled myself along because—because I
was in love with this man. I'd married him—"

"Estelle!" It was Sommers who spoke, and his voice was
as sharp as a knife.

"I think," said Ormsberry to Hennessey, "that I shall
not require Mr. Sommers's presence any longer to-night."
He turned to Strang. "You are, of course, quite free to go
with him," he said politely.

"I must object," countered the lawyer, "to this most
irregular examination of my client's wife."

"You may file your objections in the morning," said the
detective quietly.

Hennessey tapped Sommers on the shoulder.

"Step along," he said briskly.

For an instant Sommers seemed about to attack his wife. Then he pulled himself together and shrugged philosophically.

"We shall, no doubt, meet again," he said to her politely.

She looked at him like a woman beyond despair. Her breath came quick and hot between her parted lips. She tried to speak and could not. He bowed to her and Ormsberry, and left the room with Hennessey and Strang.

Ormsberry motioned the plainclothes-men to follow, nodding only to the stenographer to remain.

"Now," he said gently to Estelle, "I want you to tell me the whole story from the beginning. It's a bad business, but you won't make it any better by holding back."

She seemed to collect herself and nodded miserably.

"That's what I've been thinking this whole wretched afternoon—ever since you convinced me that Jerry Howard really had recognised Greg in Mr. Anstruther's rooms. I've known, of course, recently, that something was wrong."

"Tell it right from the beginning," urged Ormsberry.

She tried to speak, but he saw she was near collapsing. He poured her a stiff whisky and soda. The drink seemed to steady her. Presently she began, faltering at first, her recital gathering coherence as she went on. This is her confession, as taken from the stenographer's notes of this strange interview:

MRS. SOMMERS: I met Gregory Sommers here in New York in the winter of 1924. He was engaged in some stock deals in which my brother was interested, and he came to the house occasionally. We fell in love with each other and he asked me to marry him. I consented, but before we told any one of our plans, my brother thought he discovered some irregularities in Gregory's business dealing, and quarreled with him.

When I attempted to defend him, my brother got so angry—he was always irascible, you know—that I gave it up, trusting that something would happen to clear up the misunderstanding. Gregory went back to England, saying that he could obtain proof that he was innocent of my brother's charges. I think now that he was afraid to stay in this country, but at the time I believed everything he told me.

Early in the summer I followed him across. I saw him at intervals, during the months I was abroad, and at last we met in Paris in mid-winter. He begged me to marry him at once, and return with him to America. He assured me that he now had means of making his peace and proving his innocence.

So at last I consented and we were married, as you have discovered—though how I cannot imagine—on January 20, 1925. I wanted to cable Mr. Fortescue at once, but my husband convinced me that it would be better not to tell him of our marriage until he had reinstated himself. So we told no one. We returned to this country on the same ship, it is true, but in the role of chance acquaintances. When we landed he drove me to my brother's house, and I told Mr. Fortescue, as we had arranged, that we were engaged, and that Gregory was prepared to refute the charges against him.

Well, Mr. Ormsberry, the long and the short of it is that my brother flew into an ungovernable rage, said that he now had definite proof that Mr. Sommers had perpetrated fraud against him, and that he would see me dead before he would permit me to marry such a man. I have some share of the Fortescue temper myself, Mr. Ormsberry, and when my brother said that, I flared out and told him he was too late to prevent it. That we were already married and that he could, if he dared, make such an accusation against his sister's husband.

He was, of course, furious, and it was then that he said he would alter his will and leave me an annuity which "that man"—meaning my husband—could not touch.

MR. ORMSBERRY: Do I understand that Mr. Sommers was present at this interview?

MRS. SOMMERS: Yes, he was present. And afterward he drove me to the station to get the train to Philadelphia. I know nothing more about it.

MR. ORMSBERRY: When you heard of your brother's death, did you have no suspicions?

MRS. SOMMERS: No, frankly, not at first. It never occurred to me. I had always disliked Joan Archer, and it was easy for me to believe her guilty. It was only when Gregory Sommers refused to allow me to publish the fact of our marriage that I began to have a dread. At first he simply suggested postponing the announcement, and then, when I urged it—almost insisted on it—forbade it and gave as his excuse that, now that my fortune was gone, it was necessary for him to reinstate himself with his own family in England before telling them that he had married without their knowledge and consent.

Well, I allowed myself to be persuaded. You see, I was very anxious to be convinced. All this, you understand, happened after Joan Archer's trial. If it had been before, I might—well, I can't say what I might have done. He had me pretty well under his thumb.

Things became very difficult. By the time Joan made me that present of the money my brother had originally intended to leave me, and so took away Gregory's last excuse for refusing to acknowledge our marriage, it had become impossible to do so without starting all sorts of nasty speculation and gossip, so he suggested that we should simply start all over again; that he should pay me marked attentions—be seen everywhere with me, and so on—and that after a reasonable time we should announce our engagement and be married all over again. It would be quite simple and nobody need ever know about that first, ill-advised marriage in France. It seemed on the whole the best thing to do, and I agreed. We had planned to have the regular fashionable wedding, but last week—last Wednesday night, to be exact—he began to urge haste. He—he put it on flattering grounds, and I—well, I allowed him to make a fool of me. I knew nothing about the police theory of the Anstruther case. I didn't know that there was the remotest connection between that and my brother's death. And on Thursday I agreed to an immediate marriage.

MR. ORMSBERRY: I suppose he got panicky when he found that Jerry Howard knew his secret, and wanted to get out of the country.

MRS. SOMMERS: What I can't understand, Mr. Ormsberry, is how you found out that we had already been married abroad.

MR. ORMSBERRY: By cabling the Paris Sûreté, madame.

MRS. SOMMERS: But what put it into your head? How did you think of doing that?

MR. ORMSBERRY: We found the last page of Mr. Anstruther's story, the page containing the detective's summing up of the evidence. The last lines on that page read: "Of course, the whole thing became clear to me when I realised that the quarrel between brother and sister, the curious change in the will, and the brother's subsequent death could all be explained by a secret and undesirable marriage abroad. Who was the man the sister had married? Find him and we find the brother's murderer."

MRS. SOMMERS: But—but I don't see yet. You arrested Gregory before you got that cable from Paris. How did you know who it was?

MR. ORMSBERRY: When Mr. Channing was arrested, he said that, if we had one suspect actually in jail, the murderer would feel himself safe and would do something to betray himself. Mr. Channing was right. Mr. Sommers permitted you to announce your engagement to him in the *Sphere*. I knew, under the circumstances, that you would hardly be planning to commit bigamy.

At midnight Mr. Ormsberry and the Admiral, sitting on either side of the table in Johnson's immaculate pantry, faced each other over the remnants of an enormous raspberry shortcake. The detective had just finished recounting the final episode of the Fortescue mystery, for his young confrère's benefit. The Admiral regarded him with glowing admiration, yet also, it must be admitted, with the easy poise of an equal and a brother.

"Well," he said, drawing a long breath, "I guess we cleared up that mystery pretty quick."

Ormsberry cut another slice of shortcake and grinned.

"Rather!" he said emphatically. "I'm going to remind Mr. Speck to order that dinner at Louis's to-morrow. I'll get him to ask you, too, old chap."

The Admiral's eyes glistened.

"Honest?" he gasped. "Gee!" He drew another •deep breath, "Yup, we cleared this thing up fine. There's one other question you oughter have asked her, though."

"Huh!" queried Ormsberry, his mouth inelegantly full of shortcake.

"You shoulda asked her," pursued the young Sherlock Holmes, "where

Mr. Sommers got the key."

"The key? What key?"

"Why, the key to get into Mr. Fortescue's house. 'Member? That butler fellow said the windows was all locked when he went in and found Mr. Fortescue. I been in that room and all round that house. I went there with Mr. Speck and I went there afterward to see Miss Joan, and there couldn't anybody get in that place unless he had a key. It's got those burglar things all over it."

"Well, by George!" murmured the detective helplessly.

"So you see Mr. Sommers would have had to have a key. You shoulda asked her if she gave it to him."

Ormsberry considered this with the seriousness it deserved.

"But that would make her an accessory," he demurred.

"Yes, sir."

"Well," said Ormsberry comfortably, putting another slice on the Admiral's plate. "I don't really think she knew anything about it. And anyway, if I'd asked her, she'd have said he stole it out of her bag or something. I don't think we can prove anything against her."

"No," admitted the Admiral, adding oracularly: "It's pretty hard to prove anything against women." He leaned back comfortably, patting a patently enlarged tummy with a tentative hand. "I expect I've had enough, sir." Bliss was his. Had he not proved his worth in the eyes of the man whom most in all the world he admired? He looked across at his friend with eyes gone suddenly blurred with sleep, and found the great detective regarding him with a gaze oddly at variance with his usual stern expression. As a matter of fact, Ormsberry was seeing in that bright, eager face the ghost of his own childhood, the shining skirts of his own vanished illusion. He understood suddenly what it was the boy wanted. He said handsomely:

"I'm certainly grateful to you for helping me out, old fellow. Hope you'll lend me a hand again some time."

"You bet, sir!" cried the Admiral heartily, as man to man, and on these terms they parted for the night.

BLAIR'S ATTIC

Joseph C. Lincoln
Freeman Lincoln

CLUES OF THE CARIBBEES

Being certain criminal investigations of Henry Poggioli, Ph.D.

T. S. Stribling

GOLD BULLETS

CHARLES G. BOOTH

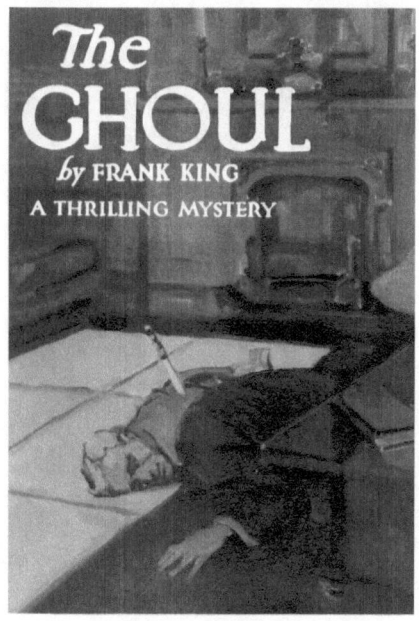

The GHOUL
by FRANK KING
A THRILLING MYSTERY

Coachwhip Publications
CoachwhipBooks.com

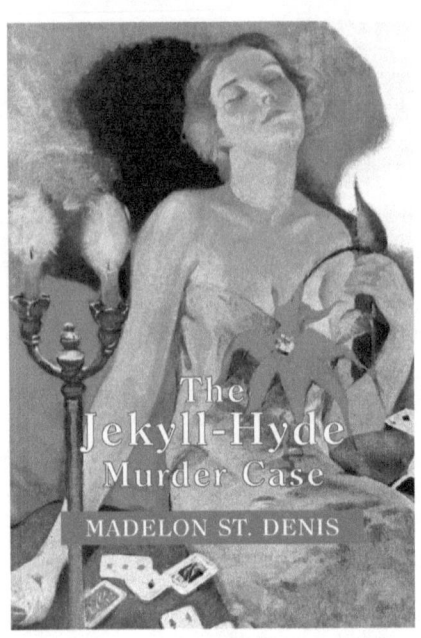

Coachwhip Publications

CoachwhipBooks.com

I'll Hate Myself in the Morning

Murder on the Left Bank

Elliot Paul

THE BAND PLAYED
MURDER

EDITH HOWIE

CRY MURDER

EDITH HOWIE

NO FACE TO
MURDER

EDITH HOWIE

Coachwhip Publications
CoachwhipBooks.com

FULL CRASH DIVE
ALLAN R. BOSWORTH

GRIMM DEATH
DOROTHY FOSTER BROWN

LADY IN LILAC
SUSANNAH SHANE

MURDER IN THE WPA
ALEXANDER WILLIAMS

Coachwhip Publications
CoachwhipBooks.com

Coachwhip Publications
CoachwhipBooks.com

Coachwhip Publications

CoachwhipBooks.com

MURDER
À LA RICHELIEU
THE ADELAIDE ADAMS MYSTERIES
ANITA BLACKMON

MARIAN
GALLAGHER
SCOTT

TALL MAN WALKING

THE ATTIC ROOM

DEATH
IN THE
DUSK

Virgil Markham

CRIME IN
CORN-WEATHER

MARY MEIGS ATWATER

Coachwhip Publications
CoachwhipBooks.com

Jack Dolph

MURDER MAKES THE MARE GO

THE CASEBOOK OF
MR. CARRINGTON
SIMON
CARRINGTON'S CASES
J. STORER CLOUSTON

THE THING IN THE BROOK

PETER STORME

HIDE AND GO SEEK
with, GOING TO ST. IVES

HOTEL

COLVER HARRIS

Coachwhip Publications
CoachwhipBooks.com

The
Hollow Tree
Mystery
MADELON ST. DENIS

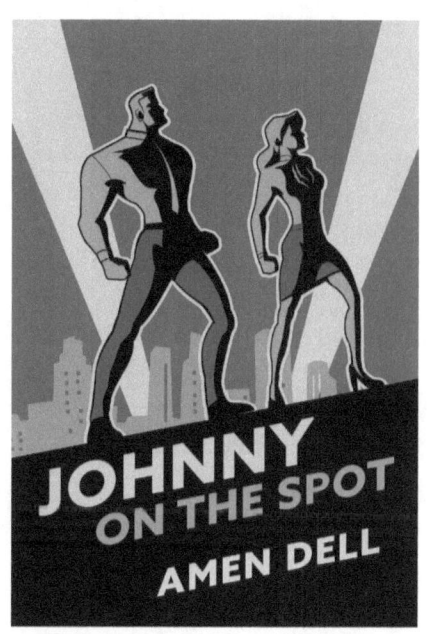

JOHNNY
ON THE SPOT
AMEN DELL

VULTURES
IN THE SKY
A HUGH RENNERT MYSTERY

TODD DOWNING

SAMUEL ROGERS

YOU'LL BE
SORRY!

YOU LEAVE
ME COLD!

Coachwhip Publications
CoachwhipBooks.com